AFTER WE FALL

Melanie Harlow

USA TODAY BESTSELLING AUTHOR

Cover Design: Letitia Hasser, Romantic Book Affairs
http://designs.romanticbookaffairs.com/

Cover Model: Joseph Cannata
https://www.instagram.com/josephcannats/

Editing: Tamara Mataya
http://tamaramataya.blogspot.com/

Publicity: Social Butterfly PR
http://www.socialbutterflypr.net/

Paperback Formatting: Shanoff Formats
http://www.shanoffformats.com

TABLE OF CONTENTS

For J & C

Your love and courage inspired me.

Second chances are not given to make things right, but are given to prove that we could be even better after we fall.

Unknown

CHAPTER ONE
MARGOT

I didn't throw the pie.

And really, I think that's what everyone should be focused on: the supreme restraint, the Buddhist-like control, the fucking *regal* nature with which I glanced at the award-winning Cheery Cherry Delight and decided against it. (Just so you know, that was only because of the shirt he wore. Furious as I was, even I could not bring myself to desecrate a snowy white, crisply starched Brooks Brothers button-down. I'm not a monster.)

Not that hurling a tray full of scones—one at a time, with admittedly poor aim—at your ex-boyfriend is behavior to be commended. I completely understand that. And anyone who knows me will tell you it was *utterly* out of character. I, Margot Thurber Lewiston, pride myself on my ability to control my emotions. Maintain grace under pressure. Keep calm and carry the fuck on. My composure rarely slips, and it certainly doesn't slip in a room full of donors to my father's Senatorial campaign.

Honestly, I've never thrown food in my life. I've never thrown much of anything, which is probably why I had a bit of trouble hitting the target (I have apologized profusely to Mrs. Biltmore about the singed linen. Also the Belleek vase), and I certainly don't throw things indoors.

Because I was raised with manners. Good old-fashioned, old-money manners. We believe in modesty, courtesy, and—above all—discretion.

No matter what, we do not Cause a Scene.

According to my mother, Margaret Whitney Thurber Lewiston (known to all as Muffy), nothing says *poor taste*—or worse, *new money*—like Causing a Scene.

She tells me I have caused one that people will be talking about for years to come.

This is probably true.

I can explain.

It was a text no one wants from an ex-boyfriend at one in the morning on a Tuesday night. Or any night, really.

Tripp: I need to see you. I'm outside.

Me: It's so late. Can we talk tomorrow?

Tripp: No, it has to be tonight. Please. I need you.

Frowning at my phone in the dark, I wondered what this could be about. We'd broken up well over a year ago, and though we'd maintained a cordial if stiff relationship since then, we hadn't had a private, in-person conversation since the night we split. While I was considering how to politely handle this request, he texted again.

Tripp: Please, Gogo. It's important.

I softened slightly at the nickname, not because I liked it that much, but because it reminded me of better days. We'd known each other a long time, our families were close, and once upon a time, I'd thought we'd spend the rest of our lives together. I could be gracious.

Me: OK. Give me a minute. Front door.

I used the minute to yank out my ponytail, put on a bra under the Vassar t-shirt I'd been sleeping in, and slip into a pair of pink silk pajama pants. A heavy summer rain drummed against the roof of my townhouse, so I hurried down the stairs to open the front door, but of course, Tripp was perfectly dry.

"Hey," I said, standing back as he closed his dripping umbrella and entered the foyer. Hot, humid air followed him in, and I quickly shut the door against the heat, then snapped on the light.

"Hey." He set the umbrella in the stand near the door and ran a hand through his neatly trimmed dark blond hair. He wore a pink button-down shirt with the sleeves rolled up, and it was tucked in to a pair of white shorts with kelly green whales embroidered on them. He had pants with little embroidered whales on them too, in multiple colors. My eyes lingered on his familiar Sperry deck shoes. No socks.

"Thanks for letting me in," he said.

"What's going on?" I twisted my long hair over one shoulder and crossed my arms over my chest.

"Can we sit down? I need to talk to you." On his breath, I detected a whiff of scotch, and upon closer inspection of his face, I noticed his eyes were bloodshot.

"Can't we talk right here?"

He fidgeted. "Look, I know the way things happened

with us wasn't cool."

"That was last year. I'm over it, Tripp." It was mostly true. Sometimes I still felt a tug of sadness when I thought about the three years we'd spent together and the hopes I'd had we'd be engaged or even married by now, but my therapist had me mostly convinced it wasn't so much about the loss of *him* as it was the loss of the dream life I'd envisioned for us. Secretly, I still wasn't sure what the difference was.

"Well—what if I'm not?"

I shook my head, taken aback. "What?"

"What if I'm not over it, or over us?"

"What do you mean? That makes no sense, Tripp. You were over us before I was. It was *you* who said you didn't want to marry me. I was ready."

"I never said that. It wasn't personal like that." His thick slab of a chin jutted forward. "I just said I wasn't sure I wanted to get married."

"Well, I was sure. And I wasn't going to wait around for you to decide once and for all. I moved on, Tripp. And so did you." *Moving on* was a bit of a stretch for me, since I hadn't dated anyone seriously since the split. But he'd been seen around town with a whole slew of sorority girls. Lately he'd been dating someone my friends called Margot 2.0, since she was basically a younger, blonder, bigger-breasted version of me. (But according to Muffy, none of that mattered because she was *new money*; i.e., completely unsuitable in the eyes of Tripp's parents, Mimi and Deuce.) "What about your girlfriend? Does she know you're here?"

"Amber?" He frowned. "No, she doesn't. She thinks I'm

with my father, and I *was* with him earlier. He…" The frown deepened, and Tripp swallowed hard.

"He what?" For the first time, I started to get a little worried. Deuce was over seventy, with high blood pressure and a penchant for thick steaks and stiff drinks. He'd had his third heart attack at the end of last year. "Is your father OK?"

"Yes. He's fine. But—" He shifted his weight from one foot to the other, his wet shoes squeaking on the wood floor. It occurred to me I had never seen Tripp this nervous or uncomfortable. On any other day, he was Mr. Confident, especially after some good scotch—brimming with all the entitled self-assurance of a handsome, wealthy, Ivy League-educated white man.

"Spit it out, Tripp," I said, stifling a yawn. "Otherwise we can talk about this tomorrow. I'm tired, and I have to work in the morning. I'll call you a car if you can't drive home, because it smells a little like you've been—"

"Marry me, Margot!" He threw himself down on his knees in front of me. "I want to get married. To you."

"What?" My heart was thundering in my chest. Was this for real?

"Marry me. Please. I'm so sorry for everything." Wrapping his arms around my legs, he buried his face in my knees.

I thumped on his shoulders. "For God's sake, Tripp. You're drunk. Get up."

"I'm not drunk. I know what I'm saying. I have to marry you."

I stopped hitting him and stared down at the top of his

head. "What do you mean, you have to marry me? Why?"

He froze for a moment, then recovered. "I have to marry you because I've realized you're the only one for me. We're perfect for each other. You've always been the one, Margot. Always."

OK, it was a fairly pathetic display, what with the squeaky deck shoes and the bloodshot eyes and the whale shorts, but I sort of felt for him. Tripp had never been great at declaring his feelings. I wasn't particularly a champ at it, either. "Tripp, please. Stand up. Let's talk about this."

"First say you'll marry me. Look, I have a ring," he said, as if he'd just remembered he'd brought one. From his pocket he pulled out a small black box, his fingers fumbling a bit as he opened it.

I gasped and covered my mouth with my hands. The huge, brilliant cut stone winked at me from its slender diamond band. It had to be at least two carats, with gorgeous color and clarity.

"Put it on," he urged, taking it from its velvet cushion.

I wanted to. God, I wanted to. But I didn't want to marry Tripp. It would be wrong to put the ring on when I knew I was going to turn him down, right?

Because I had to turn him down. Despite what he said, we weren't right for each other anymore, were we? I didn't love him anymore.

Maybe I should try it on just to be sure, I told myself. I mean, what if I put it on and suddenly the hall was filled with music and rainbows and sunshine? What if I still loved him and just didn't know it? Biting my lip, I held out my left hand and let him slide the ring onto my finger. Perfect fit. I shivered as he got to his feet.

But there was no music. No rainbows. No sunshine. Just the rain outside, the sound of those squeaky deck shoes, the puddle they were leaving on my nice wood floor, and those infernal whale shorts.

Sighing, I looked at it on my hand one last time before starting to pull it off. "It's beautiful, Tripp, but I can't—"

He covered my hands with his, preventing me from removing the ring. "Don't say that. Please don't say that. You have to marry me."

Annoyed, I yanked my hands away and slipped the ring from my finger. "I don't have to do anything."

"I'm begging you, Margot. Please." His voice cracked, and in his eyes I saw real desperation. I hadn't seen that in him since—

"Tripp," I said slowly. "Is something going on with you?" Years ago, Tripp had struggled with a gambling addiction, racking up hundreds of thousands of dollars in debt his father eventually had to pay off. But as far as I knew, he'd stopped the compulsive betting by the time we were together. And why would that prompt him to propose to me, anyway?

He swallowed hard, his Adam's apple bobbing. "No. Honestly, Margot. It's just that I've been so miserable and lonely since we broke up."

"You didn't look miserable or lonely."

"I was. Really, I was. And I was a total asshole to you."

"Well, we can agree on that, at least."

"I'm sorry." He pulled me into an awkward hug, but I kept my arms at my sides, the ring caught in one fist. "We're so right for each other, you know we are. We make sense together. And we're both going to be thirty soon, so we should stop dicking around."

Pushing him away, I stood back and crossed my arms again. "That is not romantic. At all. And you're the only one who's been dicking around."

"I'm sorry. I'm bad at this stuff, you know I am. But… but…" He looked inspired for a second. "You complete me, Margot."

Battling the urge to call him out on his blatant pilfering of Jerry Maguire, I grabbed the ring box and (somewhat reluctantly) tucked the ring back inside. "Listen, this is crazy. We've been broken up for over a year. You can't just show up out of the blue and propose."

"But I want to marry you," he whined, his eyes darting to the left.

"Then maybe you should take me to dinner first." I held out the ring box, feeling a surge of pleasure at how well I was handling this situation. A year ago, I'd have been texting Jaime and Claire pictures of my engagement ring already.

He nodded glumly as he stuck the box back in his pocket. "Sure. OK."

At the door, I handed him his umbrella and gave him an impulsive hug. I could appreciate how hard this had been for him—it wasn't easy for a guy like Tripp to admit he was wrong and ask forgiveness. It showed maturity and growth, didn't it? "Let's talk again in a day or so, OK? I need to think."

I opened the door and he left without saying anything else, opening his umbrella against the punishing rain. After snapping off the light, I moved into the living room and watched him get into his car from the big picture window. Rain cascaded in sheets down the pane, blurring his form. When I saw the headlights come on and then disappear into the rainy dark, I went back upstairs to bed.

Holy shit, I thought, sliding beneath the covers again. What a crazy turn of events. Never in a million years had I thought Tripp would come to my doorstep in the middle of the night, with a diamond ring, begging me to marry him. It was such a complete reversal of his mindset a year ago.

Part of me was mad that *now* he'd decided we were right for each other, but another part wondered if he'd just needed more time all along. Had I been wrong to pressure him when he wasn't ready? Had I been too hasty to issue a "now or never" ultimatum? Had I been too insistent that we do things according to my timeline?

But dammit, we'd talked about everything! For three years, we'd fantasized together about the country club wedding, the center-entrance Colonial, the two kids, the sailboat, the King Charles Spaniel…it wasn't just me who'd wanted all that. He had too.

And didn't I still want it? Should I consider his offer? Annoying as it had been when he brought up my thirtieth birthday, he sort of had a point. My social circle was small, and I hadn't met anyone I was even attracted to in a year—

how much longer did I want to wait to start the next phase of my life? As Muffy was fond of telling me, *Thurber women marry and have children by thirty, Gogo. Even the lesbians.*

It wasn't that I was unhappy. I had great friends, close family, a new job I loved, a beautiful place to live. So why did I feel like something was missing?

I was tired, but I lay awake for a while, playing with the fourth finger of my left hand.

CHAPTER TWO
MARGOT

"You're kidding me." Jaime paused with her dirty martini halfway to her mouth. Claire seemed just as shocked, but took an extra gulp of her cocktail.

"Not kidding." I shook my head and smiled.

"Why didn't you say something earlier?" Jaime demanded. "I saw you this morning at the office and you didn't say anything about it!"

Jaime and I worked together at Shine PR, the marketing and public relations company we'd started together last year. Her degrees in psychology and marketing and her experience in advertising paired well with my experience in PR and social connections, and our little startup was a big success so far. We'd already hired an assistant to manage social media for several clients and planned to hire another by next year.

"Because we were busy this morning, and you were with clients all afternoon. I figured I'd tell you both here tonight."

"Well, I'm glad you waited," Claire said from the other side of Jaime. It was our weekly Wednesday Girls Night Out, and we were at the Buhl Bar, a little earlier than usual since I had to attend a fundraiser for my father later on.

"Now that you guys work together and see each other every day," Claire went on, "I fear I'm missing half the life gossip. So he actually *proposed*?"

I nodded. "On bended knee, with an exquisite diamond ring."

"What a surprise!" squealed Claire.

"What a dipshit," said Jaime. "I hope you told him to stick that ring where the sun don't shine."

I sipped my gin martini and replied with careful consideration. "I did nothing of the sort. I was kind and understanding, and I let him down easy."

"Why?" Jaime continued to gape at me with wide blue eyes. "He was such an asshole in the end."

"Because I have manners. Yes, he was an asshole," I admitted, "but he copped to it. Said he was sorry and basically begged to have me back. He said a lot of nice things, actually."

Jaime's stare made me uncomfortable, and I focused on my drink. She knew me too well. That's the problem when you've been best friends with someone since the ninth grade —even for someone like me, usually an expert at concealing how I feel, that friend sees through you.

"Well, it's nice that he finally realized what he had," offered Claire, eternal optimist. "Even if it is a little too late."

"Is it too late?" I braved, giving voice to the question that had been on my mind all day.

It was silent as they both registered what I'd said. "What do you mean?" Jaime's tone said *I know what you mean but you can't actually mean that.*

"I mean, do you think it's too late for us?"

"Fuck yes, I do." She banged a fist on the bar, and the surface of my drink rippled.

"Well, hold on. Maybe not," Claire said wistfully. "I love a good second chance romance."

"This isn't a movie," Jaime insisted, turning to Claire. "This is real life, and he was a real dick to her."

"But people can change," Claire countered. "Look at you and Quinn. You swore you'd never have a boyfriend, least of all him, but you gave Quinn a chance."

"That's different," Jaime said testily. "Plus Quinn is insanely good in bed. Tripp was a disaster, wasn't he Margot?"

I winced. "I don't know if I'd say *disaster*. The sex was just a bit…uninspired. Maybe that's not the most important thing, though. Maybe there are more important elements in a relationship than good sex."

Jaime looked at me incredulously. Blinked. "Like what?"

"Like common interests," I said, sitting up a little taller. "And family ties. And a shared history. Shared values."

Jaime rolled her eyes. "So your families both sailed here on the Mayflower or whatever. Big fucking deal. If you didn't want to tear his clothes off when he walked into your house last night, you don't have any chemistry."

I thought about that for a minute. Then I started to laugh at the idea of tearing off those whale shorts and the pink shirt. "We're just not like that," I said. "We've never been like that. We're both more...reserved. Conservative, maybe. Would I like better sex? Sure." I shrugged. "But I'm almost thirty. And maybe I need to worry less about that kind of thing."

"Thirty isn't old," Jaime scoffed. "And I don't want to see you go backward, Margot. A year ago you were so unhappy. You've made so much progress."

"I agree," I said. "But underneath it all, I'm still the same person. I still want the things I wanted then. I'm traditional, OK? I want a traditional life, the life I grew up with. Husband, house, family."

"And that's OK," Claire soothed, reaching over Jaime's lap to pat my hand. "We're not judging you for wanting those things."

"And Tripp *gets* me," I said, annoyed because it was true. "The ring he picked out was perfect. He knows my style, my taste. He's got a good education, a good job, a good family. Those things matter to me more than sex."

Jaime refused to give up. "But what about passion? What about that mind-blowing physical connection? Don't you want those butterflies in your stomach when he walks in the room? That racing pulse when he gets close?"

"But what if I'm not cut out for that?" I asked, voicing a fear that usually lurked silently in the back of my mind. "What if I'm just not that passionate a person? What if I'm not the type to blow anyone's mind? Does that mean I have to be alone?"

"No," Claire said firmly, shooting Jaime a look. "And if you want to give Tripp another chance, that is completely your choice. We stand by you no matter what."

I looked at Jaime. "Will you?"

"Of course I will." Her face softened, and she tipped her head onto my shoulder. "I'm sorry. You know I love you, Gogo. I just want you to be happy. If you think Tripp is the one, then go for it. I'll always be here for you."

"Thanks. I'm still thinking it over." I checked my phone and noticed the time. "Oh, shoot. I better get over to that thing for my father."

"A dinner thing?" Jaime picked up her drink.

"No, just drinks and dessert with some donors who've written fat checks to the campaign."

"How's the campaign going?" Claire asked.

"Fine, I think. I haven't been involved much since my politics are a bit different than my father's, but we don't talk about that."

Jaime shook her head. "God, I love your family. Have fun tonight. Will Tripp be there?"

I put a twenty on the bar and finished off my drink. "Not sure. But I know Deuce is a major donor, so it's possible. How do I look?"

They glanced at my sleeveless navy blue sheath, which I wore with nude heels and my favorite pearl necklace. My blowout was smooth, my nails were manicured, my legs were shaved. My lipstick would be reapplied in the car, since my grandmother had taught me never to apply cosmetics in public.

"Perfect," said Claire. "Very Grace Kelly."

Jaime nodded. "Classic Margot."

"Thanks. I'll see you tomorrow." After giving them each a kiss on the cheek, I walked out the back to the parking lot.

As I drove to the large private home on a gated street in Grosse Pointe where the fundraiser was being held, I had a strange feeling in my stomach. I can't say it was butterflies exactly, more like a gut instinct that something in my life was about to change. I get a similar feeling when I cut more than an inch off my hair at the salon, like I'm sort of scared but also sort of exhilarated.

After pulling into the drive and handing my keys to the valet—who gazed longingly at the pristine, powder blue 1972 Mercedes my grandmother had given me last year when she finally decided to stop driving—I entered the house.

The strange feeling intensified when I saw Tripp standing to my right in the cavernous living room. It was so large, even the nine foot Steinway in one corner didn't seem out of place. Sofas, chaises, and love seats were arranged in several conversational groupings, and the furniture, drapery, and even the rug had that faded, slightly shabby look that old money homes have. The look that says, *We're terribly wealthy but we don't get rid of anything with a day's use left in it, and we don't like things that are shiny and new.*

I saw my father shaking hands with someone near the fireplace and my mother nursing a G & T, probably her third, on one of the sofas, but I headed toward Tripp, doing my best to will that edgy feeling into butterflies. He was chatting with a group of women near the window, and they were clearly enthralled by whatever he was saying. As I got closer, he took a step back, and I saw that he wasn't alone. Amber was there too, wearing a dress that nearly fit, and she was holding out her left hand toward the little group, as if she were showing off a—

Oh no.

Oh no, he didn't.

He couldn't have.

He wouldn't even.

But he had.

And the ring on her finger was the exact same one Tripp had proposed to me with *last night*.

"It was, like, *so* romantic," she was gushing. "He came over in the middle of the night. Said he just couldn't wait any longer because he knew for sure I was the one."

I nearly gagged. Backing away unseen and shaking with rage, I found the bar and ordered a martini. (One good thing about people with old money, there's never a shortage of good gin.)

In a daze, I took my drink out onto the terrace, where my older brother, Buck, spotted me and roped me into schmoozing with a bunch of men in suits whose names I forgot immediately. All I could think of as I stood there, drinking and half-listening to them banter about politics and boats, was what an asshole Tripp was. *He must have gone right from me to her last night*. What the fuck was wrong with him?

Eventually the men wandered off to refill their scotch glasses, and Buck turned to me. "What's with you? You were totally mute during that conversation, and your expression makes Muffy's Resting Bitch Face look downright pleasant."

"Sorry. I was thinking about something."

He grinned cockily before tipping back his whiskey on the rocks. "Let me guess. Tripp's engagement? Don't let it bother you."

"Why not? It sort of makes a fool of me, doesn't it? Everyone knew we broke up because I wanted to get married and he didn't." I wasn't sure if I wanted to tell him about last night yet.

He took another swallow and shook his head. "He still doesn't. But Deuce changed the conditions of his inheritance because he's such a fuck-up with the gambling. He owes like three hundred grand or something. And if he wants the money, Deuce said he has to quit dicking around, get married and settle down."

My jaw dropped. Quit dicking around and get married? That sounded way too familiar. "You're kidding me."

"Nope. I heard it today from some guy who works for Deuce and heard *him* talking to the lawyers about it." He laughed. "What an asshole. You dodged a bullet, as far as I'm concerned." He clinked his glass to mine. "Cheers."

Fuming, I tipped back the rest of my drink. "Excuse me."

I set the empty martini glass on a passing server's tray and went directly to the bar to order another. Locking myself inside the first floor powder room, I took a gulp of my drink, set it down, and leaned on the marble vanity. I breathed heavily, staring at my reflection in the mirror. Scolding myself. Hating myself.

You fucking idiot! Of course he didn't want you! He told

you last year he didn't! He just wanted his money and you were the ticket. You ridiculous, stupid, gullible woman, thinking of giving him another chance.

But I hadn't. Thank God I hadn't. Except now I was filled with gin and frustration and rage—with Tripp, with myself, and even with Amber, for being so blind to his deceit. For once, I wished I was the kind of person to unleash my feelings in public, to go out there and publicly shame him for what he'd done, call him out on his slimy desperation and his lies, expose him for what he was. I wished it so hard I was shaking.

But I couldn't.

That is, I couldn't until I discovered Tripp and Amber holding court in the dining room, regaling yet another crowd of bystanders with the romantic story of their surprise engagement.

"He didn't even want to get married before me," she bragged. "Did you, honey?"

"I sure didn't, baby doll."

Baby doll. What an asshole. I set my third empty glass down on the floor—at least, I think it was the floor. Levels of things were a bit hazy at this point.

"I guess it just took finding the perfect woman to make me change my mind." He gazed at Amber with wretchedly fake adoration. "And when you find her, you know."

Perfect woman. I think I snorted at that, because a few people turned around and looked at me. But I ignored them, looking over the desserts laid out on the table and sideboards, pretending to search for the perfect after-dinner treat.

"The ring's gorgeous," someone said.

"Isn't it?" Amber said delightedly. "He had it custom made for me."

Custom made for her. My hands started to shake as my eyes alighted on a silver tray of scones. I wrapped my fingers around one and eyeballed the possible trajectory.

"That's right." Tripp kissed the back of her hand. "Just for you."

A second later, I hurled the first scone, which missed its target—his smug face—and hit him in the chest.

Startled, he looked up just about the time the second scone pinged off the chandelier and landed at his feet. "What the hell?"

People started looking around, some getting out of the way. Good thing, because the third scone knocked a vase off the table, and it crashed to the floor at Tripp's feet.

He finally made eye contact with me. "Margot, what the hell are you doing?"

I wound up and launched another. "Three years!" I exploded as it beaned him on the forehead. *Finally!* I tried again, but that one curved toward Amber, who ducked out of the way. "*Three years* I put up with your boring golf stories and your pants with the little whales on them and your tiny clueless dick!"

A titter went through the crowd. Tripp was stunned motionless, and I took the opportunity to pelt his chest with another scone.

"Ouch!" he said, which I found hilarious. "Stop throwing things! And my dick isn't tiny! Or clueless!"

"Yes, it is!" I flung another one at him, but he was moving now, so I missed him completely and it bounced off the wall. "You don't know the first thing about a woman's orgasm! I used to have to get myself off after you took me home, asshole!"

I heard muffled laughter as I threw the next scone, which tipped over a skinny pillar candle that, unfortunately, happened to be lit. It burned a hole in the white tablecloth before someone nearby blew it out.

"Margot, have you lost your fucking mind?" Tripp yelled from across the table, hands in front of his face like I was throwing grenades, not scones.

"Maybe," I seethed, reaching for another one but feeling nothing but an empty tray. "Maybe I have, because I was going to tell you tonight that I'd decided to think about your shitty proposal."

Tripp's face went white.

"What proposal?" Amber asked, looking from him to me.

I opened my mouth. Watched him squirm. It felt fantastic.

"Margot, please. Don't do this." His eyes begged me for mercy. "You'll embarrass us both. Let's talk in private. I have a good reason for everything."

I had no desire to talk to him in private ever again, and I already knew about his fucked-up "good reason". But he was right—if I told the truth about last night, I'd be embarrassed too. I'd just announced that I'd come here willing to consider his proposal, which had been a sham anyway.

Glancing down, I spied the cherry pie, slipped my palm beneath it, and briefly considered one final, humiliating heave. Someone in the crowd gasped.

But I looked at Tripp again and felt a surge of power, which prompted a return of my self-control. My dignity. My manners.

I was Margot fucking Thurber Lewiston, and I had class. No one could take that away from me.

Gathering my tipsy wits, I assumed a cool expression and stood tall. "Actually, I never want to talk to you again. Enjoy your evening, everyone. Lewiston for Senate."

As I walked out, I heard him say. "Jesus. Crazy bitch."

I know what you're thinking.

I should have fucking thrown the pie.

CHAPTER THREE
JACK

I couldn't sleep.

Not like it was a surprise. I didn't sleep well in general, but August was always the worst. I was lucky to get a couple hours a night.

"It's the heat," my sister-in-law Georgia had said last week. "Why don't you come sleep at our place for a few nights?"

"Better yet, put air conditioning in that old cabin," my younger brother Pete had put in. "Wouldn't cost much to get a window unit."

It wasn't the heat.

"Maybe it's the light," Georgia had said last year. "Maybe if you tried going to sleep with the light off, you'd relax more."

But I needed the light. Sometimes I felt like I couldn't even breathe until the sun came up.

I tried not to get mad when my family members told me what to do or tried to solve my problems with simple solutions when the real issue was something so complicated, they'd never understand. But I wasn't always good at thinking before speaking or controlling my temper.

Just yesterday I'd let loose on Pete for sneaking up on me from behind while I was repairing a fence along the property line in the woods. In hindsight, throwing him to the ground while screaming at him for being a "cocksucking motherfucking asshole with shit for brains" was probably a little out of line, but damn it—he knows better than to tap me on the shoulder when I don't know he's there. The whole reason I don't listen to music while I work is so that I can stay aware of my surroundings. I don't like to be taken by surprise.

The only person who ever understood that about me was Steph. A few years ago, my family planned a surprise party for my thirtieth birthday, probably because they knew I'd say fuck no to any kind of social event that required talking to people, and Steph made sure to tell me every detail ahead of time. She'd tried and tried to convince my brothers and parents it was a terrible idea, but they'd insisted that "getting out of the house" and "celebrating my life" would be good for me.

I only went because Steph begged me to. At first, I'd been furious and refused to consider it, but then she told me how my mother and aunt had flown up from Florida, and my sister-in-law had made cassata cake, and my niece Olivia had learned how to play "Happy Birthday" on the piano just for me. It was hard to resist Steph when she really had her heart set on something, plus she'd given me this really amazing blowjob in bed that morning.

She knew all my weaknesses.

Lying there in the dark, I twisted my wedding ring around my finger.

Three years.

It seemed impossible it had been that long. Her glasses were still on her nightstand, her clothes still in the closet, and I still expected her to be there when I rolled over in our squeaky-springed old bed wanting to tuck her little frame against mine.

And then, in other ways, it seemed like forever since I'd heard her singing in the shower, or watched her get ready for bed, or lost myself inside her body. She'd always made me go slow at first, claiming she was worried about my size, even after we'd been together for years. Probably she said that just to flatter me (it worked every time), although she'd been a tiny little thing, with curves in all the right places. I'd never minded the fifteen extra pounds she insisted she had to lose—in fact, I loved them, loved the way her body was soft and mine was hard, the way those curves felt beneath my hands and lips and tongue, the way she'd wrapped herself around me. It had felt so good to take care of her.

Fuck, I missed sex. I missed everything.

"You need to get out there again," said my oldest brother, Brad, because he knew everything. "Let me introduce you to April, the new realtor at the agency. She's hot, and I think you'd have a good time. Or at least get laid."

I told him to piss off.

"Come on, man," he'd said again last week as we jogged together down one of the dirt roads that bordered our forty-six acre farm. "It's been three years. You're not even trying to move on. When are you going to get over her?"

"Fuck you, Brad," I'd replied, taking off with long, fast strides that left him in the dust. Not trying to move on? Every fucking day I got through meant I was moving on. Every morning I got out of bed meant I was moving on. Every goddamn time I took another breath meant I was moving on.

And as for getting over her, it would never happen, so he could parade an endless supply of hot women in front of me, but it would just be a waste of time.

I'd already met the love of my life; I'd known her since we were kids.

I'd married her, and I'd lost her.

There was no reprieve from that. There was no redemption. There was no second chance.

I didn't even want one.

CHAPTER FOUR
MARGOT

"Are you sure you want to take this on right now?" Jaime reached across my desk and handed me the client file, her expression doubtful. I'd just volunteered to take over a new account that involved a few days of travel, a lot of research, and not much money. The client was a small family farm focused on sustainable agriculture. The perfect place to get the hell out of town and not bump into anyone I knew. "A farm doesn't really seem like your thing."

"Why not?" I asked, stuffing the file into my bag. "I used to ride horses, remember? I think I even have a pair of boots laying around."

"You kept your horse at a hunt club. This is a *farm*."

"How different can it be?" I flipped a hand in the air. "I'm sure I can handle a farm. And like I told you, Muffy says it's best if I leave town for a while anyway, at least until the gossip dies down."

"Until the gossip dies down?" Jaime grinned as she crossed her arms. "That's going to take a while, Sconewall Jackson."

She wasn't kidding. It had been almost a week, but

Sconehenge was still a wildly popular tale among the country club set, who hadn't witnessed a good Scene in months. ("All this good behavior is so tiresome," my grandmother had complained at dinner last week.) The story had been embellished to include Tripp taking a scone right in the nuts (a change I liked) and Amber throwing a plate of beignets at my head (one I didn't). Scones were selling out at local bakeries, the shop that made the ones I threw started calling them Jilted Heiresses (I turned down the endorsement deal), and people were fond of quipping, "Revenge is just a scone's throw away" at cocktail parties all over town.

My mother was beside herself ("Really, Margot, who on earth is going to want to be seen with you now?") although my grandmother had cackled with glee when she heard the story. My father seemed rather confused by the whole affair, and Buck was only sorry he'd missed it.

But we'd agreed that after a sincere apology to Mrs. Biltmore (made the following day when I'd had to go back and pick up my Mercedes since I'd been too drunk to drive it home), I should probably make myself scarce for the rest of the summer. "Or at least until someone else behaves badly," Gran whispered. "I'll keep an eye out. Nobody pays any attention to old ladies, and we see everything."

"So tell me what you know about this client," I said to Jaime, packing up the rest of what I'd need from my office over the next two weeks. Valentini Brothers Farm was in the thumb area of Michigan, about two hours north of Detroit. I'd rented a little cottage on Lake Huron that was less than a mile from it, and I figured I'd use the time I wasn't working to relax in a beach chair, read a book, rethink a few things about the direction of my life.

"Not much," admitted Jaime, perching on my desk. "It's owned by three brothers. Quinn met one of the brothers, Pete, and his wife, Georgia, at a local farmers market and they got to talking. You know how Quinn is, he makes friends with everybody." She rolled her eyes, but I saw the blush in her cheeks, which always appeared when she talked about him. Jaime didn't like to believe she was a romantic, but she was head over heels for Quinn. "Anyway, the guy mentioned that they were struggling to grow their brand awareness and increase customer engagement—although he didn't put it like that—and Quinn, of course, was like, 'Oh, my girlfriend can help you. That's exactly what she does!' He gave them my card, and Georgia called me last week."

"But they know it's me coming and not you, right?" I stuck some pens and highlighters into my bag along with a stack of post-it notes.

"Yes. They were fine with that. I think they're just anxious to get some advice."

"Are they farmers too?" In my head I imagined a couple that looked like Auntie Em and Uncle Henry from the Wizard of Oz.

"No. I mean, I think Pete *does* work on the farm but there's another brother who runs things. Georgia and Pete are both chefs, actually." She cocked her head. "Or they were. But a lot of this I'm getting second-hand through Quinn, so you'll definitely want to read the New Client form they filled out, which I just emailed to you this afternoon.

That has more info."

"Will do." I closed up my laptop and tucked it into the case, then switched off the lamp behind me. "I'll keep in touch with you while I'm there, and I'll definitely be calling to consult with you."

"Sounds good." She stood up, a mischievous grin on her face. "I'll be trying to picture you on a farm. Milking a cow. Riding a tractor. Maybe a cowboy."

Rolling my eyes, I breezed past her. "The only thing I'm interested in riding is maybe a horse. I have zero interest in tractors or cowboys."

"You never know," Jaime said following me out of my office. "Maybe a roll in the hay with a strapping young cowboy, all big burly muscles and country drawl, is just what you need to get out of that dry spell."

Halfway down the hall, I turned around and parked my hands on my hips. "I'm going up there to get a job done, Jaime. Then I'm going to hide out and just breathe for a while, and I don't need any man, muscled or otherwise, to help me do it."

She clucked her tongue, a glint in her eye. "You're a scone cold bitch, you know that?"

I turned for the door so she couldn't see the smile on my face.

I made it to Lexington shortly after seven that night, having made only one wrong turn on my way there, which I saw as a victory. Like all Thurber women before me, I have zero sense of direction. I seriously don't know how any of them got around before GPS. "It was called a chauffeur," says my grandmother.

The property manager had said to call her when I arrived and she'd come over with the key. While I waited for her, I wandered around the side of the quaint shingled cottage down to the beach. It was warm and windy, waves rolling in briskly over the rocky shoreline. Holding my hair off my face, I slipped off my sandals and wandered to the water's edge. The water felt icy cold on my bare feet.

I breathed in the damp air, smelling lake and seaweed and something being grilled nearby. My stomach growled. Had I eaten lunch? I couldn't even remember. But whatever that was smelled delicious.

"Hello?" called a voice behind me. "Ms. Lewiston?"

I turned and saw a stocky, middle-aged woman wearing a hat and sunglasses waving at me, keys dangling from her hand. Heading up the beach toward her, I decided I'd ask if there was a grill at the cottage. I'd never actually used one, but I was sure I could figure it out with a little help from Google. It was time to step out of my comfort zone, anyway.

Without throwing things.

The manager, Ann, gave me the key and showed me around the cottage—not that there was much to show. Bedroom and bathroom at the back, one big living room with a kitchen over to one side, and windows along the front with a view of the lake. But it was clean and bright, newly decorated with a beach theme, and almost had a little Cape Cod vibe to it. I felt at home there.

After settling in, I went to the little market I'd seen passing through town and picked up some groceries. There was indeed a small grill on the cottage's patio, but Ann said she had no idea if there were instructions anywhere. "But it's just a standard charcoal grill," she remarked, as if that made any sense to me. "There might even be some charcoal and lighter fluid in the utility closet."

Lighter fluid? Good God, for cooking? Sounds dangerous. I thanked her and said I'd look around, but figured I'd better stick to what I knew how to do in the kitchen, which was basically hit buttons on the microwave, boil water, and spread peanut butter and jelly on bread.

I ended up eating the prepared chicken salad I'd bought, but I did manage to cook some green beans, which I'd picked up on a whim because the sign said they were local, and they were delicious. Same with the peach I ate for dessert with some vanilla ice cream. I wondered if the vegetables or fruit—or even the chicken—had come from Valentini Brothers Farm, and thought how strange it was that I'd never, not once in my life, considered where the food on my plate had been grown.

But then, that would be part of my challenge, wouldn't it? To make people like myself more aware of where the foods I ate came from? Convince them it matters?

I thought about it as I ate, and then later I went through the file and learned as much as I could about the farm and the family that owned it. I read the New Client info sheet Jaime had forwarded, researched terms like "certified organic" and "sustainable agriculture," and googled Valentini

Brothers Farm.

Right away, I saw problems.

They had no social media accounts, and the website definitely needed to be updated, if not completely redone. It was cluttered and outdated, difficult to navigate, and had minimal engaging content. Zero personality whatsoever.

But there *was* a family photo.

Zooming in, I studied each person and wondered who was who. The oldest brother was already losing some hair, but he was tall and handsome, in decent shape with only the beginnings of paunch around the middle. He had his hand on the shoulder of a gap-toothed girl who looked to be about seven or eight. Next to them was the couple I assumed Quinn had met at the farm stand, Pete and Georgia. He was definitely the shortest of the three brothers, but had an adorable smile and thick dark hair. His fair-skinned wife, the only blond in the picture, was pretty and slightly taller than he was. Both her hands rested on her huge, pregnant belly, and I wondered how old the baby was now. On the end was the third brother, the only member of the family who wasn't smiling. I zoomed in a little closer.

Well, damn. Maybe I would ride a cowboy.

He was tall, thick through the chest and trim at the waist. His jeans were tight, and because of the way he angled his body in the picture, almost like he was trying to back away from the camera, I could see the roundness of his butt. The sleeves of his plaid button-down were rolled up, revealing muscular forearms, and he had the same thick dark hair as the short brother, although he wore it slightly longer. His full mouth was framed by a good amount of stubble, and the set of his jaw was stubborn. Two vertical little frowny lines appeared between his brows. (Muffy would say he needed a "beauty treatment," which was code for any number of expensive things her dermatologist injected into her face every few months.)

Was he as sullen as he looked, or had the camera just caught him at a bad moment? Maybe the sun had been in his eyes or something.

Still thinking about his ass, I fell asleep to the sound of the waves and dreamt about picking lush, ripe peaches off a tree, biting into them with ravenous delight.

CHAPTER FIVE
JACK

"Wait a minute. Stop right there." My brothers and I were sitting at Pete and Georgia's kitchen table going over expenses, when Pete said something about a marketing budget. "Why the hell do we need a marketing budget?"

"Well, for one thing, the PR consultant is coming tomorrow, and I'm pretty sure she expects to be paid for her time," Brad said.

I stared at both of them. "What PR consultant?"

"The one we hired last week to help us promote what we're doing," said Pete. "And can you please keep your voice down? Cooper is finally quiet."

"I have no idea what you're talking about," I snapped, although I tried to lower my voice. My one-year-old nephew, Cooper, had a hard time falling asleep on the nights when Georgia worked. I adored him—and I sympathized. "I never agreed to any fucking consultant."

"That's correct, you didn't." Brad was maddeningly calm. "But we outvoted you. The three of us own this business together, and we each have an equal say in how it's run."

"So you didn't even tell me you went ahead with it?" I was yelling again, but I couldn't fucking help it. I hated it when they sprung shit on me.

"Hey, it was *you* that stormed out after you didn't get your way," Pete said. "We sat here and discussed it for a while. And we decided that it would be worth the added expense to hire someone to help us promote."

I crossed my arms. "We can't afford it."

"We can't afford to do nothing, either," Brad said. "Dad was a good farmer with ideas ahead of his time, but he was a terrible businessman, so we inherited a huge amount of debt when we took over. Then we had to buy Mom out when she moved to Florida."

"I'm not a fucking idiot," I snapped. "I know all this."

"We also have families and our own bills to pay."

They had families. I didn't, and the reminder didn't help. "Hey, it's not my problem you've got an ex-wife who sued for alimony. Maybe you should have thought of that before you fucked around."

"Hey." A warning note from Pete. "Don't be a dick about this. We're doing good things here, Jack, but organic farming isn't cheap. And what good will our principles and hard work do us if we can't keep the lights on?"

"And competition is stronger now," said Brad. "The market is getting saturated. We need to do what we can to stand out."

I sank deeper into my chair, a scowl on my face. I didn't need any reminders about competition or market saturation or debt or mortgages or anything else on the list of Reasons

Why Farmers Have the Highest Suicide Rate of Any Profession.

Pete put a hand on his chest. "Listen. I'm a chef, not a businessman, Jack. You're an ex-Army Sergeant with farming in your blood and a commitment to doing it responsibly. But if we want to keep this place going, we've got to start thinking of it as a business too." His voice softened. "I know it was always a dream of yours and Steph's. But it's more than a dream now, Jack. It's reality. For *all* of us. And if you want to keep it, we have to invest in it."

"Look, we know you," Brad said. "We are well aware that you prefer to keep to yourself and do things on your own, your way. And we've let you make every major decision so far, supported your vision even though we knew how expensive it was going to be. Fuck, I was ready to sell this entire place when that soybean guy expressed interest. I never wanted to be a farmer."

"Me neither," said Pete. "I saw the ups and downs Mom and Dad dealt with year after year and wanted something more stable for my family. But you had a vision, a good one. It was enough to convince me to move back and help out. And we have history here. We want this place to thrive. That won't happen unless people know about it."

From the monitor on the counter came the sound of Cooper crying, and Pete sighed. "Dammit." He started to get up, but I stood faster.

"It's my fault. Let me." Grateful for a break from the discussion, I switched off the monitor on the kitchen counter and headed up to Cooper's bedroom. My bad mood lifted as soon as I saw him, and I scooped him up from his crib. "Hey, buddy."

He continued to cry as I reached into the crib for the soft little blanket I'd given to him when he was born. It was about six inches square, pale blue, and it had a bunny head on one corner. "Bunny" was one of the only words Cooper said, and he was rarely without it in his little grasp.

I spread Bunny over my shoulder and cuddled Cooper close, and he rested his cheek on the blanket, stuck his thumb in his mouth, and quieted down. Lowering myself into the rocker in his room, I held his warm little body against mine, rubbed his back, and hummed softly. He was a little restless at first, but after a few minutes, I felt his body relax as his breathing became slower and deeper. I kissed his soft brown curls and inhaled the sweet scent of baby shampoo, torn between feeling lucky to be an uncle and heartbroken I'd never be a father.

I'd been close to my own, and his death had been tough.

It had happened suddenly, not even six months after I'd left the Army. I'd been a fucking mess at the time, still struggling to process the things I'd seen and done after deployments to Iraq and Afghanistan. Still trying to fit in again at home when all I wanted to do was isolate myself. Still feeling so on edge that every time I saw so much as a plastic bag in the road, I panicked. I was drinking too much, lost my temper too easily, battled nightmares and constant anxiety. Then in the middle of that, my father had a heart attack.

I'd felt powerless. And I'd wanted to give up.

It was Steph who pulled me back from the edge. God knows why, since I was an emotional fuck-up, and I'd never treated her right when we were young. She'd always been there for me, though, claimed she'd loved me since she was six years old and wasn't about to stop now just because I was going through something. "I'm not letting you wreck yourself, Jack Valentini," she'd said in her toughest voice, all five foot two inches of her. "You promised me you'd come back, and you did. I promised you I'd be here, and I am." Her voice had softened. "Stay with me."

With her support, I saw a doctor about my sleeping problems, a therapist for my PTSD, and stopped abusing alcohol. I thought more about what I was putting in my body and read up on the benefits of organic foods—both eating them and growing them. I remembered my father's beliefs about responsible farming, and researched modern approaches to small-scale, sustainable agriculture. It gave me a purpose. It felt like a way to honor my dad, and I felt a connection to nature that I didn't feel with people.

It took a while, but I got better. Not cured, but better. And Steph was there for me the whole way.

We got married the following year and worked our asses off on the farm, with a plan in place to buy out my brothers within five years.

Less than two years later, she was gone.

God, I fucking miss you, Steph. You should be here with me. I always felt better with you by my side.

Now I'd be stuck with some stranger here telling me what to do, butting in, wanting to make changes so we could *stand out*. She'd probably cook up some bullshit publicity stunt and expect me to participate. Well, I didn't want to stand out. I just wanted to do what I did and lead a quiet life. And it wasn't like we were poor. We weren't rich, but we were doing OK. Certainly better than our parents had done. Frowning, I rose to my feet and carefully laid Cooper on his belly in his crib. Kissing my fingertips, I touched his forehead one last time and slipped out of the room.

"He asleep?" Pete looked at me hopefully when I entered the kitchen.

"Yes." I switched the monitor back on.

"Thanks. You're so good with him."

I shrugged, although secretly it pleased me I was good with Cooper. I was crap with the adults in my family. What did that say about me?

"Did you have a chance to think about what we said?" Brad asked.

I remained standing, hands shoved in my pockets. "I just don't think it's necessary, and I bet it's expensive. What the hell will some city girl know about how to help us here anyway?"

"Maybe nothing," Pete admitted. "But we're going to find out. She'll be here tomorrow at one for a lunch meeting. You coming?"

I scowled. I didn't want to go to their damn meeting, because that would imply giving in, but if I skipped it, I might end up with no say whatsoever, and no clue what they agreed to do or how much they offered to pay her. Which was worse?

I'd decide tomorrow, but I didn't want to show any chinks in the armor. "Whatever. You guys can deal with her. I want nothing to do with this." I strode angrily through the kitchen and out the back door, but I was careful not to let it slam so that it wouldn't wake Cooper.

The sun was setting behind the trees as I walked across the yard. I lived in an old hunting cabin tucked into the woods, which suited me perfectly. It had been on the property when my grandparents bought the land, and my parents had lived in it when they first got married; after that they'd used it as a guest house. When I'd moved back, its privacy and simplicity appealed to me, and I'd asked if I could live there and pay rent.

I'd made some structural improvements, and when Steph moved in, she spent every spare moment making it beautiful—paint and pillows and pictures in frames. Our little hideaway from the world, she called it. Not that she ever wanted to hide away, social butterfly that she was, but she knew I sometimes needed to, and that was OK with her. She never tried to make me into someone I wasn't, unlike the rest of my family.

As soon as I let myself into the cabin, Steph's cat leaped down from the windowsill and twined around my feet. "Hi, Bridget. You happy to see me?" The moment I knelt down and pet her, I felt my anger abate somewhat. I'd always been a dog person, but Steph had been allergic to them. When she came home with a kitten a few months after we were married, I'd groaned, but damn if that cat hadn't grown on me. Whenever I had nightmares, she'd jump up on the bed and crawl over me, purring softly. It reminded me of the way Steph used to whisper to me during those long, arduous, sweat-soaked nights, her hands rubbing slow, soothing circles on my back.

When Bridget had gotten enough attention, she wandered into the kitchen, and I looked around, hoping to see something left undone, some task to distract me from going to bed.

But there was nothing. I always did the dishes right after I ate, and I never let laundry pile up. I'd just cleaned the bathroom two days ago, and I'd washed the kitchen floor over the weekend. The shelves were organized, the furniture dusted, the windowpanes clear. Georgia was always amazed at how clean I kept the cabin. "Your brother could take some lessons from you," she'd say. "He's such a slob."

There was only one chore I refused to do, and that was cleaning Steph's clothing out of the closet. Georgia had offered to do it. Steph's sister Suzanne had offered to do it. Even my mother had said she'd be glad to fly up if I wanted someone else to take care of her things.

But I always said no. What would be the point? To make it easier on myself to live there without her? I didn't want it to be easier. And if my family couldn't understand that, well fuck them.

It was *my* pain. I'd earned it.

I guarded it closely.

CHAPTER SIX
MARGOT

I knocked on the wooden screen door of Pete and Georgia Valentini's picturesque white farmhouse at one in the afternoon for our business lunch. While I waited on the porch, I looked around. The house sat about a hundred feet back from the highway, on the west side but facing east toward the lake, and although I'd driven, I could easily have walked. The house itself appeared old but well-maintained—fresh white paint on the exterior, hanging baskets of flowers on the porch, comfy chairs on both sides of the center entrance.

To the left of the house were some birch trees, a baby swing, and some other toys scattered on the lawn. A giant red barn sat just beyond the trees, and another white one behind that. To the right of the house was a garage, and on the other side of that were smaller trees planted in neat rows. Apple, maybe? Beyond those was a dirt road, and just across it sat a massive old Victorian, abandoned by the looks of the peeling paint and overgrown gardens.

I was about to knock again when the blond woman I'd seen in the picture answered the door, a pudgy little boy on her hip. Her hair was much shorter, about chin-length, and her body much slimmer. “Hi. Georgia?”

She greeted me with a smile. “You must be Margot. Come on in.”

I entered the front hall and held out my hand. “Margot Lewiston.”

After giving it a firm shake, she shut the door and switched her son to her other hip. “Georgia Valentini. And this is Cooper. I’m just about to put him down for a nap.”

I smiled at the chubby-cheeked boy. “Sweet dreams, Cooper.”

“Go on back to the kitchen,” Georgia said, gesturing down the hall. “Pete’s just making us some lunch. Have you eaten?”

“No, actually. Not even breakfast.”

“Perfect. I’ll join you in five minutes.” She headed up the creaky stairs behind her and I walked back to the kitchen, where Pete stood at the counter, wearing an apron and slicing tomatoes at an alarming speed.

“Hi there.” I smiled when he looked up. “I’m Margot. Your wife said to come on back.”

“Of course. Welcome.” He set down the knife, wiped his hands on a towel, and came around the counter to shake my hand. “Pete Valentini, nice to meet you. Have a seat.”

“Thanks.” I slid onto one of the stools at the counter and looked around. “Nice big kitchen. Was this original to the house?”

Pete shook his head and returned to his vegetable platter. “No, my parents added this part about twenty years ago. And as you can see, it hasn’t been touched since.”

I laughed. "It's not so bad." The decor was a little dated, but I was used to houses where nothing changed for long periods of time. "When was the house built?"

"It's about a hundred years old. How was your drive up?"

"Not bad at all. Less than two hours."

"And you're staying nearby?"

"Right across the street and down a couple blocks toward the lake. I got lucky. Someone had booked the cottage for the entire month of August and ended up canceling at the last minute."

"That *is* lucky. This is our high season up here."

I admired the confident way he moved around the kitchen. "Did I hear that both you and Georgia were chefs?"

"We were when we met in New York, but right now Georgia is managing a restaurant in town and I'm only cooking there two days a week because of the work here at the farm, plus taking care of Cooper. When we moved here three years ago, we were hoping to start a farm-to-table restaurant, but…" He sighed as Georgia came into the kitchen. "We haven't gotten there yet."

"We'll get there, babe," she said. "One thing at a time."

I liked the way she smiled at him, which seemed to communicate more than just words.

While Georgia set the kitchen table, we chatted a little about the area, what shops and restaurants they recommended, and how they'd met Quinn. We were joined shortly by the oldest Valentini brother, Brad, who greeted me kindly but seemed more businesslike than his younger brother and sister-in-law. He wore a suit whereas they were both dressed in jeans and t-shirts. I kept glancing at the back door, wondering when the third brother was going to make an appearance, but he still hadn't shown up when Pete suggested we sit down to eat.

"Should we wait for Jack?" Georgia asked, glancing out the window toward the backyard.

Pete and Brad exchanged a look, and neither of them spoke right away. "I'm not sure he's coming," Pete finally said.

"And I have showings this afternoon, so it's better for me if we don't wait around." Brad took off his jacket and hung it on the back of a chair before sitting down.

"Oh. OK." Looking slightly defeated for a second, Georgia indicated a chair for me and filled four plates with slices of quiche and bacon and fresh vegetables. "Everything on the plate in front of you is from this farm," she said proudly. "Eggs from our chickens, bacon from our pigs, veggies from the gardens."

"Wow." I smiled as I unfolded my napkin and laid it across my lap. "That's really—"

Bang!

The sound of the kitchen door slamming shut made me jump. I glanced up, and there he was. Jack Valentini. He appeared even taller and more imposing than he had in the photograph online. Maybe it was because I was sitting. Maybe it was the sweaty t-shirt that said ARMY (was he a Veteran?), which hugged his narrow waist, broad chest, and bulging biceps. Or maybe it was his stance—feet apart, chest out, fists clenched at his sides. If I didn't know better, I'd have sworn he came here looking for a fight.

And from the way he was eyeballing me, I had a pretty good idea who the opponent might be. (Had I known, I'd have brought a tray of scones.)

"Jack, glad you could make it," said Georgia brightly. "Come sit down, I'll get you a plate."

"I'm not staying."

"At least say hello to Margot Lewiston." Pete tried hard to sound casual, but I could sense the tension. "She's the woman we talked about last night."

"I figured." Jack stared at me, crossed his arms over his bulky chest, but offered no hello. His expression was shadowed by the brim of a black cap, but the clenched jaw was plainly visible.

Was he an asshole or was he just having a bad day? *Either way, he's a client.* Rising to my feet, I turned on the charm, flipped my hand in a little wave. "It's nice to meet you. I'm looking forward to working with your family. You've got a beautiful place."

"I was just telling Margot that everything on her plate was grown or raised right here," Georgia said, obviously trying to engage him.

I smiled at him. "That's so impressive. I was thinking as I ate dinner last night that it's never even occurred to me at a restaurant or in the grocery store to wonder about where or how my food was grown."

"You're not alone in that," said Pete, pouring four glasses of wine. "But I think if more people knew about the hazards of large-scale industrial agriculture—to humans, to animals, to the environment—they'd definitely care more about where their food comes from."

"And the food they feed their children," added Georgia as she seated herself next to me. "Jack's taught me so much about the harmful effects of things like pesticides, antibiotics, food additives."

A plaintive cry from the monitor on the counter made everyone look in that direction. Georgia sighed and stood up again. "I knew it was too good to be true when he barely fussed. I'll be right back."

"I'll do it." Jack flipped a switch on the monitor and took off toward the now-distant sound of the crying child. As he passed me, our eyes met. He immediately looked away, but not before I saw up close how handsome he was—or would be if he took the scowl off his face. It left me a little breathless, and I needed a moment to regain my composure.

"Works for me." Georgia sat down and picked up her fork. "Jack's so good with Cooper, especially when it comes to getting him to sleep."

"We have no idea what he does up there." Pete laughed. "I think he drugs him."

"Oh, hush," Georgia said. "He's just gentle and patient. He sings to him."

He sings to him? I couldn't picture it. "Does Jack have kids?" I glanced in the direction of the stairs, curious about the handsome, broody farmer who appeared to have a soft side.

"No." Something in Georgia's voice made me pause. It

was a one-word answer, but I felt like there was a story there somehow.

"Come on, let's eat," Brad said impatiently.

We dug in, and a few minutes later, Jack returned, heading through the kitchen toward the back door without stopping. I didn't miss the glance he sent in my direction, though. It made my heart beat a tiny bit faster.

Georgia spoke up. "Why don't you sit with us for just a minute?"

"Because I'm busy," he snapped, his hand on the door handle. "I'm the only one working out there today."

"We're working in here, too, Jack," Brad said.

Jack made a noise, something between a snort and a grunt. "I told you last night I don't want anything to do with this." And by *this*, it was clear he meant *me*, since he looked at me right as he said it. I felt it like a slap in the face, and my cheeks burned.

"Then go on back out." Brad's tone was sharp.

"Gladly." Jack was through the door without another word, and as soon as it slammed behind him, Pete sighed.

"Sorry about that. Jack has…some issues."

I was still reeling, but I tried to find my balance. "I think I can guess what one of them is. He doesn't want to hire me?"

"It's not you," Georgia said quickly. "Jack's just really protective of the farm. He gets prickly when he thinks people are going to tell him what to do."

"Especially if those people are not from around here, I bet." I understood his reluctance to take advice from an outsider, but it didn't excuse his rudeness. *What a waste of a handsome face.*

"Jack doesn't understand that we're not just running a farm, we're running a business," said Brad with more than a trace of annoyance. "And a business needs marketing."

"We don't have a lot of extra money." Pete met my eyes with genuine concern. "But if you think you can help us, we'll find a way to pay for it. Jack would be content to work in the dirt, tend to the animals, and never talk to anyone, but Georgia and I have dreams of our own."

"The farm-to-table restaurant." I smiled at him, vowing to put Jack out of my head. This was my favorite part about what I did—helping people grow their businesses and achieve their goals. And I could help this family, I was sure of it. *Or at least those members who want my help.* "I want to hear about it. And I'm positive we can work something out that fits your budget. Although before we get to that, I'd like to learn more about you, your family, the history here, what your hopes are for the future. That will help me a lot."

I savored every bite of lunch as the three of them told me about how they'd come to own the farm. It was clear that Brad was the least enthusiastic about it but willing to give his brothers a chance to succeed. He mentioned that he hoped they'd be able to buy him out eventually.

"The plan was five years, but after Steph died, no one wanted to hound Jack about it."

For the first time, there was an awkward silence at the table.

"Who was Steph?" I asked.

"Jack's wife." Georgia's voice was so hushed I could hear the tick of a clock on the wall behind me. "She died three years ago."

My breath caught. "How?"

"She was hit by a car. Drunk driver."

"Oh my God. That's awful." Some of my antipathy for him let up.

Brad cleared his throat. "We've been patient with him. And as you'll see, he needs it. Don't take it to heart if he's short with you, or silent altogether at first. But Jack's not dumb. He knows if he wants to keep his farm, he's going to have to take some advice. He just doesn't like it."

I nodded, hoping I was up to this challenge, wanting to prove myself. "Well, I'm going to do my best. Let me ask you some questions and jot some things down."

As I reached into my bag for my notebook, Georgia stood and began stacking plates. "I'll get this stuff out of the way, and then I'll join you."

"Sounds good. Thank you so much for lunch. It was delicious, and I loved hearing about this place. I'm excited to get started." I uncapped my pen. "Let's talk about your brand."

"What brand?" Pete blinked at me.

I smiled. "Exactly."

Later, Georgia walked me out to my car. "Thanks for coming up here," she said. "We really appreciate it."

"My pleasure. You have a gorgeous setting, and I'm looking forward to seeing more of it. Learning more about it.

Think I could maybe get a tour of the entire place?"

"Of course. Pete could show you around tomorrow." She frowned. "Jack would be even better, but…" A sigh escaped her. "He can be so difficult."

"That's OK." I didn't want to stir up any more trouble where the middle Valentini brother was concerned. He wasn't happy about my being here to begin with—he certainly wouldn't want to take time out of his work day to show me around.

Georgia shook her head. "It's not. I'm sorry he was rude today. He's such a sweet guy underneath, but he hides it. The last few years have been so rough on him."

Since it was just us women and I was curious, I decided to ask more about him. "I noticed he wore an Army shirt. Is he in the military?"

"He was," she said, tucking her blond bob behind her ears. "He's been out about six years. But he served in Iraq and Afghanistan, and when he got back, he—" She grappled for words. "Well, it was hard for him to adjust."

"Hard how?"

"He had a lot of anxiety. My dad was in the Army too, served in Vietnam when he was really young. It affected him his whole life. Sometimes Jack reminds me of my dad." Her voice was wistful. "Moody, sullen, defensive. It's hard for them to connect with people. And they keep their feelings locked up inside. My dad had my mom, at least, but Jack has no one, and his brothers can be hard on him. They don't understand. So I try really hard to be someone he can turn to."

Something squeezed my heart. "How sad that he lost his wife."

"Devastating. They were so in love. But anyway." She waved a hand in the air. "That doesn't give him the right to be mean to you."

"No, but at least I can better understand where he's coming from. Thanks for telling me. I'll keep it confidential."

She smiled. "Thanks."

We said goodbye, and I told her I'd be in touch tomorrow.

As I drove the short distance back to the cottage, I thought about what she'd said. *They were so in love.* What was that like? Tripp and I had been together for three years, but never once had I felt "so in love" with him, nor could I imagine him thinking that way about me. "So in love" sounded so passionate. And it must have been visible to other people. *Maybe they couldn't keep their hands off each other.*

For a moment, I let myself wonder what Jack was like in bed. Rough or sweet? Selfish or generous? Fast or slow? That hard, muscular body...what would it look like naked? What would it be like to feel his weight on me? Was he a good kisser? Did he use his hands? Did he have a big dick?

My stomach whooshed, and suddenly I realized I'd gone from imagining Jack with his wife to picturing him with *me*. What the hell was wrong with me? The man hadn't even offered me a smile today! In fact, he'd been downright rude! Muscles were nice, but manners were better, and Jack's were sorely lacking.

Still, what Georgia had told me about him made me think there was more to him than boorish bluster.

Someone who'd loved like that had to have a big heart, even if it was buried beneath prickly layers of grief and bitterness.

I'd give him another chance.

CHAPTER SEVEN
JACK

I stayed away from the house all afternoon, even though it drove me crazy to think that they were in there talking about *my* farm, making plans that would affect its well-being. Plans that would affect me. Sure, I technically owned only one third of it, but neither of my brothers had invested their heart and soul here like I had. Pete just cared about his restaurant idea, and Brad would be happy to chop the land into bits and sell it.

So go in there and stand up for yourself. Put your boot down. Say no.

But I couldn't do that. It was two against one, and I wouldn't win.

And now they had that fucking Barbie on their side too. How the hell could they think that woman knew anything about farming? She looked like she wouldn't know the difference between a cock and a hen. Maybe I'd ask her.

The thought actually made me crack a smile as I left the barn after checking on one of the older horses who seemed to be struggling with the heat more than the others. *You ever seen a cock before, Barbie?*

I chuckled as I imagined the expression on her face. Her cheeks going pink. Her eyes going wide. She had pretty eyes, I'd give her that. Huge and bright blue. A pretty smile, too.

But she wasn't my type. I liked natural. Down to earth. No makeup. Steph had lived in jeans and boots, her nose freckled in the sun, and I don't even think she owned a hair dryer. She always let her dark, curly hair dry on its own.

Barbie had been wearing some kind of business suit, probably with high heels. Her skin looked like she never left the house, and her lips had been artificially pink. Her hair was nice, though, smooth and gold and shiny. What would it feel like slipping through my fingers? Wrapped around my fist? Brushing over my bare chest?

When my dick answered the question by twitching in my pants, I forced myself to quit thinking about her and move on to the next task.

She was nothing to me.

Around five, Pete came out to the little greenhouse I'd built with our dad and found me prepping some kale seedlings for planting. I needed to rotate some beds this weekend.

"Hey. Want help?"

"I'm about done in here. But I could use help repairing some fence along the western property line if you have time."

"I do."

We took a four-wheeler and drove in silence, me dying to know what had been discussed at the meeting but too stubborn to ask, Pete probably trying to figure out how to broach the subject without my taking his head off. I caved first.

"How'd it go with Marketing Barbie?"

Pete sighed. "She's very nice, Jack. And she's smart too. I think she's going to help us a lot."

"For how much? Did you see what she drives? A classic Mercedes in mint condition. Do you have any idea what those cost?"

"No."

"Me neither. But I bet it's a fuck ton of money."

"You know, you don't have to be such an asshole about this. No one is conspiring against you or wants to take anything away from you."

"What the fuck would they take, anyway? Like you said, I don't own this farm, I don't own my house, I don't even have a family." I threw his words back at him as I pulled up at the fence that needed work and parked.

Pete stared at me for a few seconds, then shook his head. "I refuse to argue with you anymore. And I'm done trying to bring you in on this. You want to know what her ideas are, you can ask her."

"I don't," I lied.

"Fine." He jumped to the ground. "Let's just get this done."

I finished working for the day, cleaned up, and made myself some dinner. But I felt so tense sitting around the cabin by myself that I decided to go into town and grab a beer. I chose a little pub called The Anchor, sat at the end of the bar, and hoped I wouldn't see anybody I knew. Nothing worse than wanting to nurse a beer and some self-loathing and being constantly interrupted by people who wanted to chat. They'd ask how I was doing with that sympathetic look in their eye, but they didn't want the truth. They wanted to hear I was doing fine and then move on to small-town gossip, or better yet, get some to spread.

It was Friday night and the place was busy, but thankfully the last couple seats at the end of the bar were free, and the baseball game was on the TV right above them. I sipped my beer and tried to appear like I was really into the Tigers so no one would take the stool next to me and try to talk. My plan worked for about ten minutes.

"Excuse me. Jack Valentini, right?"

I looked over my shoulder, and there she was. Up close, she was even prettier than she'd looked across the kitchen, which did nothing to help my mood. "Yeah?"

She smiled, revealing perfectly straight white teeth between those painted lips. "I thought that was you." She held out a hand. "I'm Margot Lewiston. From Shine PR? We met today at Pete and Georgia's?"

I didn't want to touch her, but I saw no way to get out of it. I slipped my hand into hers. Her fingers were pale and slender, and mine wrapped around them easily. Our eyes met, and something strange happened in my chest—a hitch. I pulled my hand away. *What the hell?* Directing my attention back to the screen, I hoped she'd take the hint and leave me alone.

Nope.

"Is this seat taken? I'm dying for a cold drink." Without waiting for me to answer, she slid onto it.

Out of the corner of my eye, I saw those legs extending from short shorts and ending at sandals with straps that twined up her legs like vines. I shifted nervously in my seat as the bartender approached her with a smile.

"Hi, what kind of gin do you have?" she asked. He rattled off some names, which she apparently did not find up to her standards. "Hm. How about a wine list?" He handed her one, and she looked it over briefly before sliding it toward me. "Any recommendations? I see they have some local wine. Should I try one?"

"Get whatever you want." I tried not to look at her as she leaned toward me. Jesus, I could smell her perfume—something floral and summery and sexy and probably hundreds of dollars a fucking ounce. I held my breath.

She looked up at me a moment and then settled back on her stool. I exhaled.

"I can make a recommendation if you like," offered the bartender, fucking college-age sap who probably thought he could get in her pants tonight if he poured her the right Riesling.

"That would be lovely," she said, handing the menu back to him.

A few minutes later, she was sipping on a glass of local Pinot Noir, and I quickly finished my beer, feeling like I should get out of her presence sooner rather than later. Something about her made me uncomfortable. Well, not *her* exactly, but my body's reaction to her.

"You don't want me here, do you, Jack?" she said after I'd put a twenty on the bar.

"It's not that. I'm just done with my beer. I'm ready to go." I braved a glance at her.

"I don't mean here in this bar, I mean here in this town. At the farm. Working for your family." She smiled tightly. "It's pretty obvious. No use denying it."

I frowned as I pocketed the change and left a tip. "Look, it's not personal. I just don't think we need to spend money on publicity. There's plenty of real things we need."

"But publicity *is* a real need." She shook her head. "What good will all your investment do if you don't get the word out about your farm? The food you grow? The animals you raise? The benefits of eating and buying local from small, sustainable farms like yours? I spent the entire afternoon researching your practices, the costs and the benefits, the hazards of industrial farming. People don't know about this stuff, Jack. You can help teach them."

I opened my mouth to speak, but she cut me off, a hand in the air.

"Don't tell me. You don't want to be a teacher. OK, fine. So you let me do it." She touched her chest right below the pearl necklace she wore. (My mind immediately took an unauthorized detour.) "Or you let me map out the strategies for you, and family members can do it. Bottom line is, your brothers are right. Just from the initial research I've done so far, competition is only getting tougher and you need to set yourself apart."

"And do what?" I crossed my arms over my chest, which seemed to distract her for a moment. She stared at it for a solid five seconds, her cheeks coloring slightly, before she answered, looking me in the eye again.

"What about agritourism? Have you ever considered that?"

"You mean whoring out my farm so people can traipse all over it and complain about the high price of my funny-looking tomatoes when the ones at Meijer are a lot cheaper and prettier? *No*."

"It's one of the fastest-growing segments of the travel industry!" she went on, as if I hadn't spoken at all. She was tenacious, I'd give her that. "An opportunity not only to educate and increase profits but also to offer an *experience*. There's an entire generation of young people—which, by the way, is the most likely to be concerned about their food and more willing to pay more to get healthier options—who value *experiences* over things."

"What do you mean?" I asked, confused.

"I mean they prize *doing* things—and showing off pictures of themselves doing things—more than cars or jewelry or electronics. And they're willing to pay to do them. So they come to the farm, have whatever amazing and authentic and delicious experiences we come up with, and then they post pictures of themselves on social media with a bunch of fun hashtags that make all their friends and followers go, 'Hey! I want to do that or make that or eat that or buy that' or whatever. Then they're doing the PR work for you. For free!" Her smile lit up her face. "Doesn't that sound good?"

Good? The last thing on earth I wanted was a bunch of people at my farm looking for me to provide them with entertainment. Fuck that. Not that I'd have a choice—I could just see Brad and Pete and Georgia getting all turned on by this idea. It was enough to make me pissed and resentful again, plus I could still smell her, I couldn't stop looking at that pearl necklace at her throat, and every time our eyes met, my stomach tightened. I needed to leave.

"No. It sounds like a fucking nightmare. I gotta go." Ignoring the twinge in my gut when I saw the way her face fell, I strode down the bar and out the door.

I wanted her out of my sight.

CHAPTER EIGHT
MARGOT

"So how's it going?" Jaime asked. I'd called her on the walk home.

"It's going well, I think. I met the clients today and they were very nice—well, most of them were."

"Uh oh. Someone's not nice?"

"Not to me, anyway. It's the middle brother, Jack." I pictured him sitting next to me at the bar and my heart pumped a little faster. He filled out a t-shirt like nobody's business. Had he noticed the way I'd stared at his chest? I liked his eyes, too. They were dark but had flecks of gold in them. And I hadn't missed the way he'd looked at my legs, the care he took not to get too close, the spark when he took my hand. *Something* was there. Why'd he have to be such a jerk?

"Is that the hot one? I saw the family picture."

I bit my lip. "You think he's hot?"

"Yeah. Don't you?"

"I guess so," I said cautiously, then quickly followed it up with, "but he's not my type at all."

"Why not?"

"Uh, besides the fact that he's a scruffy, sweaty farmer who needs a haircut, he's stubborn, grouchy, and ill-mannered." Truthfully, I hadn't minded his hair, his scruff, or his sweat earlier in the day. And tonight, he'd been cleaned up, combed and trimmed and smelling faintly like a beach bonfire. I kept wanting to lean over and sniff him.

Jaime laughed. "What's he grouchy about?"

As I walked, I described my meeting with the family and what they'd told me about Jack. When I got to the part about his wife, she gasped.

"Oh my God, how?"

"Drunk driving accident."

"That's so sad!"

"Isn't it? He still wears his wedding ring." I'd noticed it right away tonight. "Georgia said they were so in love."

"God, that sucks. Poor guy. This is why people shouldn't get married. Bad things happen."

I had to smile. "Is Quinn hinting around about proposing again?"

"Yes. God, if he really does it, I'll fucking kill him."

"Don't be ridiculous. You guys are madly in love, you've been together for a year and a half, and you've lived together for months. Why not get married?"

"Because we're happy!" she exploded, as if that explained it all. "Why fuck with that?"

Sighing, I glanced around. Had the walk to the bar taken me this long? "OK, whatever. Don't get married. I think I'm lost."

"Lost where?"

I stopped walking and turned a full circle, positive I hadn't seen that park on the corner before. Nothing creepier than a playground in the dark. "Lost walking from town back to my cottage. What the heck, there weren't even that many turns."

Jaime laughed. "Hang up with me and use Google Maps or something. Then text me when you get there so I don't worry about you wandering alone in the dark somewhere."

"OK."

"And then call me tomorrow so we can talk more about what you're thinking for strategy."

"I will. I want to do some more research and brainstorming, but I have a few thoughts. Their budget isn't much."

She sighed. "I figured."

"But that's OK. You know what? I really want to help them. I'd do it for free."

"You need to stop doing things for free," Jaime scolded. "You're not working for Daddy anymore. You're a grown woman with her own company."

"And her own trust fund." I laughed a little. "I don't mind doing things for a good cause, and I like their cause. Plus it's not only for them, it's for the community and the economy and the common good! Did you know there's such a thing as food insecurity?"

"What the hell is that? Tomatoes with trust issues?"

"Lack of access to adequate, nutritious, affordable food. And it's not only in urban areas, it's in rural areas too. People who live surrounded by farms might never eat what's grown and harvested right in their backyard! We export what we grow and import what we eat. It's crazy!"

She laughed. "*You're* starting to sound a little crazy."

"Sorry. I got sidetracked today by poverty statistics when I was researching sustainable agriculture and food justice."

"Food justice?"

"The right of communities to grow, sell, and eat healthy food. It's a huge movement I had no idea existed, but now I'm really inspired. I want to get involved."

"Gah. You're such a softie. Let me know when you're home."

"I will. Night." I ended the call, and punched the address of the cottage into Google Maps. While jabbering away to Jaime, I'd kept walking when I should have turned, and missed my street by about three blocks. I backtracked, found my way home, and texted her that I made it.

Fifteen minutes later, I turned off the lights and got in bed, curling up on one side. As soon as I shut my eyes, Jack Valentini popped into my head and stubbornly refused to leave. *How predictable of him.*

I flopped onto my back. He was so aggravating. Was he going to shoot down every idea I had? I wondered if he'd always been so crotchety. Did he ever laugh? Had he been different before his wife's death? Before the Army? Was it any one thing that made him so different than his brothers, or was it everything?

On a whim, I turned the lamp on again and got up to grab my laptop. I brought it back to the bed and sat cross-legged in front of it, trying not to feel creepy as I Googled

Stephanie Valentini.

The first search didn't turn up anything enlightening, so I added Michigan and drunk driving death to the search words, feeling even worse about what I was doing. But it worked. Eventually I found a local news article about the accident, and I clicked on the link.

Two photos appeared at the top of the page, and I covered my mouth with one hand. On the left was a close-up of a pretty, dark-haired woman with huge brown eyes and dimples. On the right was a wedding picture of Jack and Steph, and it stunned me to see him smiling and happy, breathtakingly handsome.

The headline was chilling: **Man with 2 previous drunk driving convictions kills local woman in hit and run.** The details were sickening. She'd worked a shift waitressing at a bar just up the highway, and her car had conked out on the ride home. Her cell phone was dead, so she'd been walking the half-mile toward the farm when a drunk driver with previous convictions and an open container of alcohol in the car struck her. He drove away but drove into a ditch not two miles down the road. Another driver saw the accident, and called 911. Steph had been airlifted to the hospital but died several hours later of her injuries. The driver had been taken to jail and held on a $1 million bond.

I read the article once more and stared at the wedding photo for a long time. Finally, I closed the computer, plugged it back in to the charger, and slipped beneath the covers again.

No wonder, I thought. No wonder he was the way he

was. That kind of loss, plus the loss of his father and whatever he'd experienced in the Army, could harden anybody.

I felt bad that my being here was causing him more distress. *I pushed too hard tonight. That was my fault.* I needed to convince him that I honestly cared about what he was doing and really did want to help, but I needed a less direct approach. What would it take to make him look at me differently? See me as a friend?

Or something more…

No. Just stop that train right there and get off, Margot. For God's sake, he's a client! And he's still wearing a wedding band! You're a little attracted to him, yes. You feel sorry for him, fine. You want to help his farm, sure. But leave it at that.

Sighing, I rolled onto my stomach and tried to stop thinking about him.

But I tossed and turned all night.

At five thirty, I gave up on sleep and tugged on running shorts, a tank top, and running shoes. If I couldn't sleep, I might as well try to get a little exercise. I figured I'd make my way up to the highway, then head across and up the dirt road next to the Valentini farm. Scout it out a bit.

I put my hair up, locked the door, and tucked the cottage key into the little hidden pocket on my shorts before setting off at a light jog. Behind me, the sun was just peeking up over the lake, turning the sky a gorgeous orange-pink. The punishing heat of the day was hours away, and the air felt cool and refreshing against my arms and legs. I smiled at an early dog walker and an old couple out for a hand-in-hand sunrise stroll, but my spirits flagged when I reached the highway and realized I should have gone to the bathroom before I left.

Oh, well. I'd be OK for a quick jog, wouldn't I? I'd just loop around their property and head back. How big could a "small farm" be?

As it turns out, pretty fucking big.

I headed west on the dirt road—past the orchard, big plots planted with vegetables, a pasture, and finally thick woods. By the time I turned left at the far edge of their property, I had to go, and the pressure in my bladder quickly escalated from bad to worse.

Biting my lip, I eyed the woods behind the Valentini fence on my left and the open pasture of someone else's farm on the right before glancing back the way I'd come. I hadn't seen a single soul back here. But…but I was *outside.* Could I really?

I don't think I need to tell you I'm not a terribly out-doorsy type of girl. My idea of "roughing it" is a three-star hotel, I certainly don't camp, and the one time I had to use a port-o-potty at a concert Jaime dragged me to I thought I was going to die of disgust. Or a bacterial infection.

Would peeing outside like an animal be worse than the port-o-potty? What would I use to wipe myself? I'd heard stories about girls having to do this before, but clearly I'd never paid close enough attention! Did you drip dry like a boy? Use a leaf? But I had sensitive skin! And what if I used poison ivy by mistake? Or some other harmful plant? Wasn't there something called poison oak? I didn't know what those things looked like! Why hadn't I brought my phone? Throwing scones was one thing, but *this* was something I still found dreadfully unpalatable.

I hopped from foot to foot, desperately wishing for another solution to magically present itself so I would not have to relinquish my dignity or give my vagina a poisonous rash. But none appeared, so I climbed over the Valentinis' fence and ducked into the trees, cursing myself for being so out of it before I left the cottage.

Hurrying across the forest floor of dirt and pine needles and dry leaves, I moved away from the road until I couldn't see it anymore. I was about to squat (good grief, what an inelegant word) when I heard a splash nearby. Gasping, I straightened up and looked around, frantically yanking my shorts back into place. When I heard another splash, I cautiously made my way in that direction.

Oh my God!

Not far from where I'd been about to relieve myself was a clearing in the trees, and beyond it was a small lake. Jutting into the lake was a short wooden dock, on which stood Jack Valentini, dripping wet and *buck fucking naked.*

It was as if an electrical switch had been flipped inside me. Suddenly I was driven by one gut instinct: *I need a better view.* There was a weeping willow about twenty feet closer to the lake, and without giving it a second thought, I darted toward it and then scrambled up onto a low branch.

Yes, I actually *climbed a tree*.

Hanging onto a branch above my head, I carefully side-stepped out a little bit and peered through the leaves. Tongue caught between my teeth, I watched him push his wet hair back from his face and stretch a little, arms over his head. *Hmm, a farmer's tan is actually a thing.*

My eyes automatically went low, and my jaw dropped when I saw the size of his dick. If it was that big when it wasn't even hard, how big would it get when it was? Suddenly I felt like a kid who'd been told she could look at her birthday cake but not taste it. A hundred irrational—and frankly perverted—thoughts assaulted my brain.

I want to see him get hard. I want to touch him. I want my mouth on him. I want to watch him touch himself. Damn, he's huge. I want to be fucked with a cock like that. I bet it could tear me apart. Christ, he could probably fuck me from clear over there.

No! No, he should find me here. He should discover me in the woods and get angry. Then he'd have to punish me for spying on him. He'd be ruthless.

I realized I was panting.

What the hell was the matter with me? I'd never had these kinds of thoughts about anyone, let alone a veritable stranger. Was I having a midlife crisis at age twenty-nine?

He turned away from me, giving me a chance to appreciate the nice round butt I'd noticed in the photo, but also the muscular back and shoulders, the tattoos that snaked around to his ribs on his right side. What were they? I'd never known a man with tattoos before, not personally. And I'd definitely never seen one naked.

I hadn't seen that many men naked at all, really. Maybe

that was my problem—fascination, sort of like he was a museum exhibit or exotic animal or circus sideshow. The male bodies I'd seen in the flesh were pale and thin—*nothing* like the beautiful work of art in front of me now, which had bulges and ridges and lines, the morning sun burnishing his skin to bronze. I wanted to—

CRACK!

The branch I was standing on snapped, and I hit the ground in an ungraceful belly flop.

(Also, I may have peed myself. Just slightly.)

I picked up my head and looked at Jack, shocked to see he'd quite literally hit the deck, his body flattened against the wood. A second later he looked up and saw me. *Not* the discovery fantasy I'd concocted by a long shot.

Oh, Jesus. This is worse than Sconehenge.

How the hell was I going to explain myself?

CHAPTER NINE
JACK

First, terror. Adrenaline-fueled, heart-pounding, blood-pumping, gut-wrenching terror.

Then, anger. That I hadn't been vigilant enough. That I'd missed some sign of danger. That I'd failed.

Finally, awareness. That I was OK. That everyone was safe. That nothing had happened.

Well, nothing dangerous.

My heart rate and breathing slowed as I took in the scene—Margot Lewiston, flat on her belly—and realized the noise that had startled me had been the snapping of a tree branch, which had apparently given out under her weight. "Fuck," I muttered, feeling foolish, like I always did when this happened.

And that's when I *wasn't* naked.

I jumped up and yanked on my sweaty running shorts, which were lying on the dock next to my socks and shoes. Since Pete was checking on the animals this morning, I'd decided to take a quick swim after my run. I hadn't counted on an audience.

Once I had the shorts on, I stood up straight, fists

clenched, ready to rip into her for trespassing, for spying, for scaring me. *For refusing to get out of my head.* But one look at the way she hopped to her feet and started running toward me—on her toes, knees pressed together, hands over her crotch—and I was momentarily stunned.

"Oh hey, Jack," she said casually, like she just happened to be in the neighborhood, "I know you're probably wondering what I'm doing here. And I'm sure I can explain. But first, can I please, *please* use your bathroom?"

"Uh, OK." Annoyed as I was at the invasion of privacy, I nearly laughed out loud at her awkward rush for the cabin's back door. I jogged ahead of her and let her in, gesturing toward the bathroom.

"Thank you," she mouthed as she raced by me.

While she was in the bathroom, I stayed out on the back porch, uncomfortable with the thought of being in the cabin alone with her. What the hell was she doing here? Bad enough I'd spent an entire sleepless night trying not to think about her legs and her eyes and that fucking pearl necklace. She had to show up first thing this morning in those tiny shorts and a tight shirt? My dick started perking up, and I did my best to crush its hopes, thinking about crop rotations and drip irrigation systems and long range weather forecasts.

Thankfully, I had myself under control by the time she came out, a relieved smile on her face.

"Wow," she said, shutting the screen door behind her. "That was close. Thank you so much."

"You're welcome." I crossed my arms, wishing I'd thought to grab a shirt. "Want to tell me what you were doing out there?"

Her cheeks colored. "Um, I was taking a run."

"Up a tree?"

She laughed nervously. "No. Well, I didn't start out in a tree. That happened later."

I cocked my head, unable to resist giving her a hard time. *Not so sure of yourself now, are you, Barbie?* "Oh yeah?"

"Yes. See, I left the cottage I'm renting without using the bathroom by mistake," she began, twisting her fingers together, "and I was planning on running a loop around the farm, but it's bigger than I thought."

"Ah. So you were looking for a bathroom in the woods?"

"Well, yes." She swallowed. "Sort of. But then I heard a splash and saw you..." Her cheeks were practically purple now.

I played dumb. "Saw me what?"

"Saw you naked, OK?" she blurted, throwing her hands up. "I admit it—I saw you naked."

I had no hang-ups about nudity, but I was damn serious about my privacy, *and* about people sneaking up on me.

But her embarrassment was funny. The two times I'd seen her before, she'd been so polished and poised. It felt good to put her in her place a little. "So you climbed a tree for a better view, is that it?"

Bowing her head, she dragged the toe of one shoe across the wood planks of the porch floor. "Something like that." Then she looked up at me. Took a breath. "I'm really sorry. I shouldn't have done that. I was—I mean, I got—I couldn't —" She sighed, briefly closing her eyes. "I have no excuse. Will you accept my apology?"

She was prettier without makeup, I decided. And the way she wore her hair off her face emphasized the wideness of her eyes, the angle of her cheekbones, the arch of her brows. Her lips didn't need all that glossy crap, either. They were a perfect rosy pink, and I wondered if they'd feel as soft as they looked.

Fuck. I hadn't kissed anyone in three years.

Clearing my throat, I took a step back. "Yeah. It's fine." *Now get out of here.*

She didn't move. "So you're not going to fire me?"

"I never hired you."

"I know. But I really want this job. I think I can help, Jack. I know I can."

"Suit yourself." My name on her lips was trouble. Needing some distance from her, I started walking toward the dock to get my shoes and socks, but she followed me. God, she was a pest. It reminded me of the way Steph used to tag along after the boys when we were kids, wanting to get in our games.

"Are you going to be like this the entire time I'm here?" she asked.

"Like what?"

"Moody and uncooperative?"

"Probably."

"Why? Do you hate me that much?"

"I don't hate anybody. I just don't see why we should

pay some city girl who's never set foot on a farm to advise us." We reached the dock, and I leaned down to get my stuff.

"I'm not even asking to be paid, so piss off!" she shouted, her voice carrying on the water.

I straightened. "Oh, you're working for free?"

"Yes!"

"Then you're an idiot. Or so rich you don't need the money."

"I'm not an idiot," she said through clenched teeth.

"So you're rich, then." I don't know why I was being such an asshole. But for some reason, I did not want to let her see another side of me, or see another side to her. "I should have guessed."

She crossed her arms. "And what's that supposed to mean?"

"It means you look like you've led a charmed life. Like you've had everything you've ever wanted handed to you. Like you've never gotten your hands dirty."

"So get them dirty."

I almost fell off the dock. "What?"

"Get them dirty. Teach me about working this farm. I want to learn."

Was she serious? The last thing I needed was to drag her ass around all day, explaining things. *Or stare at her ass all day, imagining things.* But one glance at her defiant face and I shook my head. "Why do I feel like if I say no, you'll just keep bothering me?"

She smiled and clasped her hands behind her back, rocking forward on her toes. "Because I will. I don't like being told no."

"Of course you don't." Jesus, she was trouble. A bad apple—smooth and shiny on the outside, spoiled rotten on the inside. But for no good reason, I found myself giving in. "Fine. Go change your clothes."

She grinned. "Where should I meet you? It will take me about a half hour to run home, change, and get back here."

"No idea where I'll be then. You'll have to find me."

"Fair enough." She glanced over her shoulder at the trees. "What's the quickest route back? Through there?"

"No. Take the path toward the house to get back to the highway."

She turned in a circle. "Which way is the house? I'm not very good with directions."

"Jesus. It's that way." Jabbing a thumb into the air over one shoulder, I decided I'd better get her going the right way or I'd be waiting around for her forever. "You can cut through the cabin. Come on."

We walked back to the cabin and she followed me from the kitchen into the front room. "Hey, I like your place. It's cozy. And so clean."

"Thanks."

The cat jumped down from the front windowsill and crossed in front of us, checking out the situation.

Margot knelt down to pet her. "How sweet. What's her name?"

I grimaced. "Bridget Jones."

She burst out laughing. "You have a cat named Bridget Jones?"

"Yeah. What's so funny about it?" I snapped.

"I don't know. Take it easy. You just seem more like a dog person, I guess."

"I am," I admitted, some of the tension leaving my voice. "The cat was my wife's." I opened the front door, hoping Margot would take the hint, but not surprised when she didn't.

"Have you always lived here?"

"Since I got out of the Army."

"When was that?"

"Six years ago."

She nodded, rose to her feet, and glanced around the room. Her eyes lingered on the framed wedding photos hanging on the wall. "Oh, how beautiful. Can I look at them?"

"I guess." I let the screen door swing shut as she went over to examine them. God, how long had it been since someone other than me had looked at those pictures? I felt nervous about it, but also pleased she'd noticed them.

There were three—one family photo; one of us during the ceremony, holding hands beneath a floral arch; and one taken in the barn where Steph stood on a bale of hay so her head would be level with mine when I kissed her. When Margot got to that one, she laughed. "That's adorable! Look how tiny she is—and she's wearing cowboy boots with her big wedding dress, I love it!" She pointed at the way Steph was holding up the bottom of her dress to show off her feet.

"Yeah. She loved her boots. She said she wasn't a heels type of girl in real life and didn't need to be one on her wedding day." I could still hear her proclaiming it with no apology in her voice.

Margot nodded. "I'm a heels type of girl."

"You don't say."

"But everybody should be free to be who they are on their wedding day. I love that she wasn't afraid to be herself."

"She wasn't afraid of anything." In general, I wasn't the kind of guy who opened up to people I didn't know. Or to people I did. But it felt good to talk about Steph in front of Margot. It felt safe.

"You don't look too bad yourself here. You wore boots too, I see."

"Yeah, I'm not much for fancy shoes. Or clothes. But Steph said I had to wear the suit."

"You wore it well."

"Thanks."

A beat went by. "I was sorry to hear about what happened." She kept staring at the picture. "You must miss her."

"Yeah. I do."

She sighed and turned around. "Well, I guess I better go get changed."

Nodding, I opened the door again, and as she went by me, her shoulder brushed my bare chest. Gooseflesh rippled down my arms, and my nipples puckered. Quickly, I shut the screen door in front of me before giving her directions. "Head for those trees straight ahead and stay on the path that runs through them. You'll see the house on the other side."

"Got it." She started down the steps.

"And be careful crossing the highway."

At the bottom of the steps, she stopped and looked back at me. "I will. Promise."

She took off running at a decent pace, and I tried not to look at her butt.

I had a feeling I'd be fighting that battle all damn day.

CHAPTER TEN
MARGOT

I hurried back to the cottage, more excited than I should have been about the day ahead. For heaven's sake—Jack and I could hardly spend five minutes together without getting on each other's nerves. But something about this felt like a victory to me.

I'd blown up at him by mistake—my plan had been to kill him with kindness, but instead I'd spied on him before calling him moody and uncooperative. But he was so frustrating! I was trying to help him!

The strange thing was, he hadn't seemed that angry about the whole tree incident. In fact, he'd seemed almost amused by the whole thing—I could've sworn I *almost* saw him smile at one point.

Why that had me grinning I had no idea.

Inside the cottage, I peeled off my damp running clothes and decided, in the interest of saving time, not to shower. I didn't want Jack to use tardiness as an excuse not to show me around today, and it's not like I had to worry about him getting close. I'd never met a man so uncomfortable being next to me. He was always backing up or moving away, crossing his arms over his chest.

I pulled on fresh underwear and socks, my skinny jeans and a plaid button-down, and tugged the elastic from my ponytail. In the bathroom, I brushed my teeth, braided my hair and unzipped my makeup bag.

Then I caught myself.

What are you doing, Margot? This isn't a date. You don't need mascara in a barn.

I zipped it back up, but I did put on my pearl necklace… and a spritz of perfume.

A girl's got to have a *hint* of pretty, right?

Right before I left, I yanked on my old riding boots, thankful I hadn't given them away. They were beautiful brown leather, and still had plenty of wear left.

I raced out the door just fifteen minutes after I rushed in, and headed out to the car, pleased with myself. Not only would I learn more about the farm, which would help me do my job, but I'd get the chance to prove to Jack that I wasn't the enemy. I respected his work and honestly wanted to help. And if it made him look at me in a more favorable light, well…so much the better.

I was determined to make him smile for real.

CHAPTER ELEVEN
JACK

"Are you sure about this?" Margot peeked into the first nesting box, where three eggs sat in the hay.

"Yes. You just reach in, take the eggs, and put them in your basket." I'd thought gathering eggs might be an easy place for her to start, but Christ Almighty, I was beginning to wonder if even that was too much for her. She was *such* a city girl—although she did look cute in her tight jeans and little plaid shirt, and I liked the way she wore her hair in one long braid down her back. Her boots were hilarious, though—some sort of equestrian riding boots that looked like they belonged in a movie about a rich girl who has her own show pony. At least she hadn't put makeup on.

But believe it or not, she *had* put on the pearl necklace.

It was killing me.

"Come on," I prodded, annoyed more with myself than her. "Get the eggs, we have work to do."

"Won't they get mad?" She looked around the coop, nervously eyeing the hens about our feet.

"No. They're used to it."

"OK." She reached in and took out two eggs, then laid

them gently in the basket. "I did it!" she said, smiling proudly.

I nearly smiled back before I caught myself. "Good job. Now keep going. Or we're going to be here all day."

She took the third one out, gingerly placed it next to the others and studied them. "So do the brown chickens lay the brown eggs and the white ones the white eggs?"

"No. You can tell what color eggs a chicken will lay by the color of her ears."

Her eyes bugged. "No way!"

"Yes. Now come on, work faster. Like this." I reached into the next box, quickly pulled three eggs out with one hand, put them in the basket, and moved on to another.

"Wow, you're really good at this."

"I've had a lot of practice. Now you do the next one."

She moved in front of me, bent over, and looked into the box. "There's somebody in there."

"So reach beneath her and take the eggs." I struggled to keep my eyes off her ass.

"I don't think I should. She's giving me the evil eye."

"Jesus Christ. Move, I'll do the rest." I took her by the waist and swung her to the side to get her out of my way, but once I had my hands on her, I didn't want to let go.

And I'm a fucking weak-willed asshole, so I didn't.

I left them there a couple seconds too long.

"Jack?" She looked at me over her shoulder, her expression confused.

I dropped my hands.

What the fuck are you doing?

"Just give me the basket," I ordered roughly, yanking it from her hand.

She turned around. "Did I do something wrong?"

"No." I angled away from her and started grabbing the remaining eggs, angry with myself.

This was a bad idea.

It was a long day.

As I'd suspected, Margot was clueless about everything and had a thousand ridiculous questions.

"So you don't milk a male cow?"

"Why do you need an electric fence?"

"How big is an acre?"

"Are those goats?"

"What's a CSA?"

"Why do you have to rotate crops?"

"Isn't it weird to butcher an animal you spent all that time raising? Do you ever want to keep the cute ones?"

"So chickens lay eggs from their butts?"

I did my best to answer her questions, figuring the more she realized she didn't know, the more likely it would be that she might decide she couldn't help. But she learned fast, and by late afternoon, her questions grew more thoughtful, her hands steadier, her pace quicker. I found myself admiring her curiosity about the farm, her willingness to tackle any job I gave her, and the fact that she never once complained about the sun or the heat or the smell or the dirt lodged under her fingernails and caked on her fancy boots.

But the worst thing was the way I kept wanting to *touch*

her. I couldn't stop thinking about what I'd done in the chicken coop, and I stopped myself a dozen times from doing it again. What the hell was my problem?

Finally, I had to admit that for the first time since Steph died, I was seriously attracted to a woman.

It was almost a relief.

I wasn't happy about it, but logically, I knew it was just a biological urge and I shouldn't be too hard on myself, especially since her presence here was temporary. And who wouldn't be attracted to Margot? She was beautiful, smart, and kind. And aside from her ignorance about life outside the bubble she lived in, she was nice to be around. She could laugh at herself, tried again if she failed at something the first time, and was actually really good with the horses. I wondered if she'd had experience with them.

"Do you ride?" I asked her when we were in the barn at the end of the day.

"I had a horse growing up," she said, stroking the neck of the mare I'd been concerned about yesterday.

"Of course you did. Rich girl." I couldn't resist giving that braid a tug. What I really wanted to do was wrap it around my fist. Yank her head back. Kiss her neck.

Fuck. Stop it.

"Hey," she said, pouting. "None of that. I did everything you asked today, didn't I?" She looked so hopeful, a smudge of dirt on her sweaty forehead, I didn't have the heart to shoot her down.

"You did fine," I told her, giving the horse's nose a little rub, trying to keep my hands busy. But my dick was swelling in my pants, as if owning up to my attraction for her had woken a sleeping beast. And the voice in my head would not stay quiet. *I'd like to give you a little rub—right between the legs with my tongue.*

"Thank you. And thank you for taking me around today. I really appreciate it."

"You're welcome." *How'd you like to appreciate my big hard cock in your pussy?*

"And look!" She laughed. "I got my hands dirty!"

"Oh yeah? Let's see." I grabbed her wrists and turned up her palms between us, examining them. "Well, look at that. They're filthy."

She giggled. "All of me is filthy. I can't wait to take a hot..." Her voice trailed off as she stared at my fingers circling her wrists. Then she looked up at me. Those blue eyes wide. Those pink lips open. That pale white throat beckoning.

I knew what I was going to do before I did it.

I knew it was a bad idea. I knew I'd regret it.

And I still did it.

Heart pounding in my chest, I pulled her forward by the wrists until her mouth was so close I felt her breath on my lips.

And I kissed her—lightly at first, my lips barely resting on hers, and then harder, my mouth opening, my hands sliding around her back, over her ass. I pulled her in tight against my hips, my erection trapped between us.

She looped her arms around my waist and rose up on tiptoe, pressing her chest to mine. Our tongues met and I tasted her hungrily, like I'd never get enough. It actually reminded me of the time Pete and I ate all the vanilla ice cream our mom had bought for Brad's tenth birthday the day before his party. We knew we shouldn't and we were bound to get caught and punished, but damn if it didn't taste so good we couldn't stop. Margot tasted like that—sweet and forbidden at the same time.

Just let me have this, I thought as my conscience pricked. *Just this once.*

I wound her braid around one hand and pulled her head back, moving my mouth down her throat. I inhaled the scent of her skin, reveled in the velvety feel of it beneath my lips, the salty sweet taste. Slipping one thigh between her legs, I ran my tongue along the pearls resting against her neck. Her fingers dug into my back.

"Jack," she whispered.

My name—whispered by another woman.

The wrong woman.

This isn't right.

Get away from her.

CHAPTER TWELVE
MARGOT

He was kissing me like I'd never been kissed before.

Like he was going to war. Like he didn't care about breathing. Like something in him needed something in me so desperately, he had to find it or die trying.

Not that I wasn't willing to give it up. At that moment, I'd have flung my panties across the barn like a scone at a political fundraiser.

He was so *different* from any man I'd ever kissed—everything about him exuded strength and raw masculinity. His chest was so broad, his arms so muscular, his cock so hard, his mouth so commanding as it moved down my throat. It was *intoxicating*. I'd have let him do anything he wanted to me, just to experience being at the mercy of such power.

Jesus Christ, where did this come from?

I'd sensed him warming toward me throughout the day, and there had been that electric moment in the chicken coop when he'd put his hands on me, but this… *This.*

He shifted my body so I straddled his thigh, pulled my head back and ran his tongue along the strand of pearls at the base of my neck. My clit pulsed. My hands flexed on his back.

Oh my God.

Oh my God, I'm going to have an orgasm. In a barn. With a farmer. Who I met yesterday.

And it's going to be SO. GOOD.

I whispered his name…and he pushed me away.

As if hearing his name had signaled the end of a scene we were filming, he put his hands on my shoulders and stepped back, separating us.

We stared at each other in silence, both of our chests rising and falling with rapid breaths. His eyes were clouded with something I couldn't read—I saw desire there, but pain too.

He dropped his hands. "You should go."

"Jack, please, can't we—"

"Go!" He roared, putting his hands on his head. "Just get the fuck out of here, Margot! Now!"

Hurt and confused, I turned and ran from the barn across the yard, tears burning my eyes. I cut a wide berth around the house, hoping Pete and Georgia wouldn't see me, and darted out to the road where I'd parked. When I reached the safety of my car without being seen, I pulled the door shut and collapsed against the steering wheel.

A few tears spilled over, and I wiped at them with my filthy hands, angry I was this upset over a stupid kiss. "Fuck you, Jack Valentini. I was right about you to begin with. You're nothing but a foul-mannered jerk."

So what if he was handsome underneath that scruff and

dirt? So what if he had a big, broken heart somewhere inside that massive chest? So what if he had a big dick and probably knew how to use it?

He was an asshole.

And he was a *client*.

But that kiss…*that kiss*.

Why did the best kiss I'd ever had have to be with *him*?

"Dammit!" I banged my head against the steering wheel a few times, then pulled myself together.

In my purse, I found a handkerchief and dabbed at my eyes and nose, dismayed by the amount of dirt that came off my face. I stared at it, noticing how the embroidered navy blue M of my monogram was beginning to fray. Tossing the soiled linen aside, I started the car and drove back to the cottage, berating myself the whole way.

What the hell had I been thinking? It didn't matter what he looked like naked or how he kissed or why he'd pushed me away. I worked for him, and that was a boundary that shouldn't be crossed.

He probably realized that too. You should be glad he came to his senses before you started flinging your panties around.

Back at the cottage, I took a long, punishingly hot shower, vowing to put Jack out of my mind and concentrate on the work that needed to be done. I had a meeting with Pete and Brad and Georgia tomorrow, and I wanted to go in prepared. More than prepared—if Jack said anything to them about my less-than-professional behavior, I had to counter that with proof I was good at my job.

When I was finally clean, I put on my pajamas, pulled from the freezer a pitiful frozen lasagna that probably came off an assembly line six years ago, and opened a bottle of wine. While I waited for the lasagna to heat up in the microwave, I called Jaime.

"Hey," she said. "How's it going?"

"Great." I forced myself to be cheerful. "I'm fired up. I've got lots of ideas."

"Awesome. Hit me."

I told her about some of the ideas I had—beyond the obvious ones like creating a logo, revamping the website, and using social media, I described agritourism and why I thought it would work for them. "I've done the research and there aren't that many places around here offering unique experiences…I'm going to talk with Pete and Georgia tomorrow about the possibilities of a small restaurant on site with a chef's table, cooking classes, weddings and other special events. I think their place could be a real destination."

"Sounds great. What about the grouch? He gonna go for all that?"

I sighed as I pulled the lasagna from the microwave. It was still frozen in the center but bubbling at the edges. "Nope. Probably none of it."

"Ugh, what a pain. Can you work around him?"

"Who knows? He basically told me earlier he doesn't care what I do as long as I don't involve him. Of course, he might have been mad because I saw him naked."

"Excuse me?"

While I nuked the lasagna some more, I told her what had happened this morning, and she laughed.

"What's going on with you, anyway? For thirty years, you've lived this perfect, well-mannered life and now you're throwing scones and climbing trees to spy on naked men."

Pulling the entree out again, I stabbed at the lasagna, now burnt at the edges. "Maybe I'm tired of behaving properly all the time. I'm experimenting with letting my gut take over."

"I heartily applaud this experiment. You've always been way too well-behaved. Have some fun. Throw scones. Spy on naked men. Do more than that if you want."

As I chewed a bite of tasteless, rubbery lasagna, I considered confiding in Jaime about what had happened in the barn. I wasn't usually a kiss-and-tell kind of person, but maybe if I talked it out with Jaime, I could make more sense of it.

"Actually, I did a little more than that today." I filled her in, and she was silent the whole time.

"Wow," she said once I'd gotten to the part where he yelled at me to leave. "That is messed up."

"I know." Giving up on the lasagna for the moment, I took a bag of baby carrots out of the fridge and munched on them instead. They reminded me of the meal we'd had at Pete and Georgia's house today at lunchtime—a delicious beet salad, everything from their own garden except the goat cheese (but that was made at a Michigan creamery) and some grilled pork tenderloin in barbecue sauce made with local peaches. I eyed the carrots in the bag, perfectly uniform and lacking in any personality whatsoever. Perfect could be so boring.

"And he's a client," Jaime reminded me.

"I know. I keep telling myself that. It's just…I'm drawn to him for some reason, not that I could tell you what it is," I said irritably. "I can list *ten* reasons I *shouldn't* be."

She laughed. "I'll tell you what the reason is. He's fucking hot. Here's two more—he's got a big dick, and you haven't been laid since Tripp the Drip."

I groaned. "Thanks for the reminder." The memory of Jack's dick pressing into my pelvic bone made my insides tighten.

"Sorry, Gogo. I shouldn't tease. So what are you going to do?"

"Forget about him. What else is there to do?"

She sighed. "That's probably for the best. I fully support getting outside your comfort zone, but a widowed Vet farmer who's also a client might be *too* far out."

"Way too far." *So far it shouldn't matter this much.*

"You OK? You need me to come up there for the meeting tomorrow?"

"No. I'm fine." I tried to sound confident. "I promise this thing will not affect my work."

"I know it won't. You're a perfectionist. That will never change." She paused. "But did you really feed pigs today?"

That made me smile. "I sure did. And cows and horses and goats. And gathered eggs from chickens. Did you know they lay them from their butts?"

"No. And I really didn't need to."

I clucked my tongue. "Jaime Owens, you should really pay more attention to where your food comes from."

"In this case, I think ignorance is bliss. Call me tomorrow?"

"Will do. Night."

"Night."

I spent the rest of the evening preparing for the meeting and trying to keep thoughts of Jack from distracting me.

But it was impossible.

I relived that kiss a thousand times. I felt his hands around my wrists. His tongue on my neck. His thigh between my legs.

Closing my eyes, I pictured him in his little house. What was he doing right now? Was he thinking about me? Did he still miss his wife at night? Did he ever try to ease the loneliness with other women? I felt a vicious stab of envy for any woman who'd been with him, and a pang of longing so fierce it shocked me.

Yes, his mood swings made me dizzy, but he was masculine and strong and real. He was a soldier. A survivor. And he'd worked for what he had—worked long and hard with his own two hands. He wasn't afraid to get dirty.

That was sexy.

I'd never been so attracted to a man in my life.

But there was nothing I could do about it.

CHAPTER THIRTEEN
JACK

What the hell had I done?

You know what you did. You let your guard down. You lost control. You fucked up.

I had fucked up. Badly.

I'd been a complete asshole to Margot, who didn't deserve it. I'd messed around with a woman who was working for me. And I'd betrayed Steph's memory.

I felt guilty about everything. I needed to talk to someone…someone who knew me, someone who would understand.

It wasn't that I sought forgiveness—I'd never have that—but more a need to remind myself who I was. So after I finished up in the barn, I went home, cleaned up, picked some of the wildflowers growing in front of the cabin, and drove out to the cemetery.

We'd buried Steph according to her family's wishes. She and I had never even talked about what we wanted in terms of burial—who thinks of death when they're young and newly married? And afterward I'd been in such a fog of grief and regret, I'd let her parents and sister make the decisions, everything from where she would be buried to what clothing she'd be buried in.

The only thing I'd asked was that they let her wear her boots.

"Hey, babe." I lowered myself to the grass in front of her stone and hung my arms over my knees. "Brought you these." Laying the wildflowers in front of the pink granite marker, I took a minute to pull some weeds that had sprouted around it since last week. *I bet Margot likes hothouse roses, not wildflowers.*

Tossing the weeds aside, I frowned and put Margot from my mind. Concentrated on imagining Steph here beside me, on all the familiar things I loved and missed about her until my heart ached. "I'm having kind of a rough time. August is always hard for me."

If I closed my eyes, I could hear her voice, and I always knew what she'd say.

Are you sleeping OK?

"Not much at all."

What about the meds?

"I don't take them."

She'd get exasperated. *Jack. You have to! They were helping! You were finally getting a full night's sleep on them.*

"Fuck sleep."

Did you come here to argue with me? We've been over this a thousand times.

"It's my fault. Everything is my fault."

You weren't driving the car that hit me.

I closed my eyes and saw her walking along the

highway, headlights careening toward her in the dark, felt the guilt slam into me with the force of five thousand pounds of metal and glass.

You weren't driving the car that hit me, Jack.

I shook my head, tears in my eyes. "Doesn't matter how many times you say it. I'm to blame."

Why do you think that?

In my mind, another car moved through the dark—toward me this time. "You know why. You're the only one who knows why."

Stop it.

"'Just as he has done, so it shall be done to him.'"

Jack! I'll never believe that. Never. You did what you had to do.

My throat constricted. I tried clearing it, but my voice still cracked. "The price was too high."

She was silent. Of course she was.

She only ever saw the good in me. And yet what I'd done had cost her life—I was sure of it.

Even on my good days, I carried the burden with me.

The truth was, I didn't deserve to sleep peacefully. I didn't deserve the love and sympathy of my family. And I certainly didn't deserve to give in to my desire for another woman.

No matter how much I wanted to.

Later that night, I was sitting on my back porch watching the sun set with a beer in my hand when Georgia appeared around the side of the cabin. In her hands was a plate covered with foil.

"Hey," she said. "I brought you some dinner."

"Thanks."

She came up onto the porch. "I knocked in front but you didn't answer."

"Sorry. I didn't hear."

"Everything OK?"

"Fine." I kept my eyes on a family of ducks in the pond.

Georgia was silent a minute. "You go to the cemetery today?"

How the hell she knew, I had no clue. But I didn't have it in me to deny it. "Yeah."

She nodded slowly, and for a second I hoped she'd ask me about being there, or say something about Steph, or just acknowledge her existence—or even her memory—in some way. People rarely did. All they ever wanted to know was how *I* was doing, how *I* was feeling. Did they think by avoiding the subject, I wouldn't feel the pain?

Sure enough, Georgia moved on.

"Have you eaten, or should I throw this in the fridge?" She held up the plate and grinned. "It's fried chicken. Yum yum good."

"I ate. Fridge is fine." I hadn't eaten, but I wasn't hungry. I felt sick about what I'd done, but worse, I couldn't stop thinking about that kiss with Margot as I sat here. How much I'd liked the feel of her body against mine, her hair in my hands, her skin under my lips. How much I'd wanted to wrap myself up in her perfect, perfumed, pearl-necklace sweetness and forget for a while. How badly I wished I could.

You can't. So stop fucking thinking about it.

Georgia sighed, but she went into the cabin and I heard the fridge door open and shut. Then a bottle being opened. "Mind if I have a beer with you?"

"No." Actually, I wanted to be alone in my misery, but didn't want to be a dick to Georgia. She was always good to me. Maybe she could distract me from thinking about Margot.

She came back out and dropped into the chair next to me. "How was the rest of your day with Margot?"

So much for that idea. "Fine."

"She drive you crazy?"

Fuck yeah she did. She still is. "Yep."

Georgia took a long drink of her beer, then laughed. "I know it's not nice, but I keep picturing her doing chores in her little outfit with the fancy boots and jewelry."

A smile threatened. "Farmer Barbie."

Georgia slapped her leg. "Right? She's so sweet, though. And it was nice of her to be so interested and offer to help. Don't you think?"

"She wasn't that much help," I muttered wryly.

"I wasn't either when I first got here. You guys used to laugh your asses off at me trying to get on a horse. Remember?"

"Ha. Yes." But the memory of us laughing together actually made me a little sad. Steph had been there, too. "We thought you were hopeless."

She reached over and poked my arm. "But I learned."

"You learned." I tipped up my beer, thinking about

Margot riding a horse. "Actually, I think Margot knows how to ride a horse."

"Oh?"

"Yeah, she said she owned one growing up. She was pretty comfortable with ours today."

She looked at me, her head cocked. "What do you know, you two have something in common. You should let her ride you while she's here."

I almost choked. "What?"

"I said, you should let her ride with you while she's here. Maybe one day this week."

"Oh." Jesus, now the thought of Margot riding me was stuck in my head. I couldn't get a moment's fucking peace! "Maybe."

"She'll be over tomorrow morning to go over some ideas." A not-so-subtle suggestion.

"Hmph."

Georgia sighed and sat back, evidently giving up for now. We drank in companionable silence as the sun went down, slapping at the occasional mosquito and listening to the crickets. When our bottles were empty, she stood.

"Well, I should get back. Thanks for the beer."

"Anytime. Thanks for bringing dinner." I rose too. "It's dark. I'll walk you back."

"You don't have to."

"Yes, I do."

She knew better than to argue. If it was dark, I never let a woman walk anywhere alone.

When we reached the house, she gave me a quick hug.

"Think about coming tomorrow, OK? Nine o'clock. I'm making the French toast casserole you like."

I moaned. "With the brown sugar and banana? Now you're just being mean."

She laughed and patted my cheek. "Not mean, just smart. Maybe I'll see you in the morning."

"Maybe."

"Night."

I watched her go inside the house and shut the door before turning around to head back. As I walked through the trees, I remembered Margot falling out of the willow this morning, and shook my head. Now that I knew her a little better, I was amazed she'd even managed to climb it. *She must have really wanted that better view.* I smiled briefly, wondering what she'd thought once she got an eyeful. Had she liked what she'd seen? Then I wondered what she'd thought of the way I'd dropped to the ground when the branch snapped.

She probably thought you were a fucking lunatic, but what does it matter? What she thinks about anything—you, this farm, that kiss—doesn't mean shit.

But I couldn't stop thinking about her. About kissing her. About touching her. About getting to know her better. Was she just a spoiled rich girl intent on getting her way or was there more to her? Was she actually attracted to me or was she just messing around with the stable boy, so to speak? Did she think I was an asshole for grabbing her that way? Did she think I was a dick for pushing her away? What would have happened if I hadn't?

It doesn't matter. She doesn't matter. In a few days she'll leave town and go back to Detroit where she belongs and you'll never see her again.

Something tightened in my gut.

I'd never see her again…unless I went to that meeting tomorrow.

Don't. Seeing her again will only cause trouble.

Maybe. Or maybe by seeing her again and remaining in control of my temper and my desire, I could prove to myself —and to her—that yesterday was a fluke. I'd sit right across the table from her, look her dead in the eye, and force myself to feel nothing.

I was still a soldier, wasn't I?

I could do it. I had to.

CHAPTER FOURTEEN
MARGOT

The first thing that threw me off was that Jack was *there* when I arrived at Pete and Georgia's house the next morning. Sitting at the kitchen table with a cup of coffee, looking a little tired but rugged and handsome and sexy as hell. His t-shirt hugged the muscles of his arms so tight, I went dry in the mouth and wet in the panties. All I could think of were those arms around me yesterday in the barn. Our eyes met—and both of us immediately looked away.

Frantic, I glanced around at everyone. Was it obvious there was awkwardness between us?

"Good morning, Margot," Georgia chirped, setting a giant glass pan of something that looked and smelled delectable on the table. "Hope you're hungry."

"Um, yes. That looks amazing." My heart was racing, and I turned away from the table to set my bag down in one corner of the room, telling myself to stay calm. This was a work meeting, and I was a professional. I had to act like it. *Come on, Margot. You're good at this. Grace under pressure.* A few deep breaths later, I went back to the table.

"Why don't you sit there, Margot?" Georgia said, indicating the chair across from Jack.

Great.

I lowered myself into the chair and smoothed my skirt. Patted my hair. Touched my necklace.

My necklace, where his tongue had been not even twenty-four hours ago. I risked a glance and caught him staring at my fingertips on the pearls. My stomach fluttered.

What the fuck? *Now* the butterflies made an appearance? I couldn't handle butterflies right now!

So stop looking at him.

But I couldn't help it. And when I looked again, I found him looking right back. Eyes hard. Jaw locked. Neck muscles tense. Almost as if he were angry with me. He swallowed. Sat up taller and squared his shoulders.

What the hell? What had I ever done to him?

Unexpectedly, my eyes filled and I furiously blinked the tears away. And something happened—his eyes softened for a second, his lips parting slightly before pressing together again. God, he was all over the place! Did he want to kiss me or punch me?

Just pretend he isn't here.

It wasn't easy. Although he said nothing, I felt his angry eyes on me constantly. I was so aware of his presence I might as well have been sitting on his lap. But I kept a mask of cheerful nonchalance on my face, praising the meal, sipping coffee with cream, and chatting with Pete and Georgia about New York. Beneath that mask, though, I was a nervous wreck.

"This is delicious! Is it French toast?" *Please don't let*

my cheeks be too pink.

"Could you pass the cream, please?" *Oh God, I said that too loud, didn't I?*

"I love that restaurant! They have an amazing brunch." *Look at his forearms. Christ, they're huge.*

After breakfast was over and the table was cleared, I concentrated on pulling my notes from my bag and preparing to talk. *Don't look at him. Who cares if he's staring at you like he can't decide whether to tear your clothes off or tear you to shreds? He doesn't care about this anyway. Focus on the issues and strategies. You got this.* When everyone was seated again, I began.

I'd outlined a three-pronged strategy for building brand awareness as well as increasing revenue. The first involved the basics: they needed a logo, they needed a new website, they needed social media accounts and someone to run them. "I've listed contact information for a few graphic designers I know, but I encourage you to shop around for someone local as well," I said. Brad threw a few names out, Pete asked a couple questions and took notes, and Georgia smiled at me as she bounced Cooper on her lap. Jack, however, sat with his arms crossed and continued to give me the evil eye.

Ignore him. Keep going.

The second prong involved creating content—they had to be prepared to put a lot of work into engaging potential customers and getting people talking. "And I don't mean ads saying how great you are. I mean pictures and stories about what you're doing here—the messes *and* the successes. Show off those funny-looking vegetables! Talk about the time you failed at beekeeping or whatever! Admit your first attempt at homemade pie crust was a disaster! People relate to that. Make them *feel* something, make them laugh, make them wonder. This isn't about you—it's about them."

Jack snorted.

"I love that," Georgia said, shooting Jack a look over Cooper's head. "And I like to write, too."

"Perfect." I smiled at her with grateful relief. "Let them get to know you all. Be real, be fun, be visible. They'll associate your brand with you as people, make that human connection."

"Do we all have to be visible?" Brad frowned.

I shrugged. "Not if you don't want to be. But I think the whole concept of the family-owned and operated farm is stronger if the whole family is involved. Plus, the name is Valentini Brothers Farm." I didn't miss the way they glanced at Jack, but I kept my eyes off him.

"I like photography," Brad said. "My daughter Olivia does too. Maybe we could take pictures for the site?"

I snapped my fingers. "There you go. That's perfect. Maybe your daughter could even have her own little corner on the website, a blog where she talks about things for kids. Teaches them about eating local and organic."

"And easy recipes," Georgia added. "She likes to cook too. This is great, Margot."

Jack cracked his knuckles.

"Moving on," I said, this time giving him a pointed stare, "let's talk about agritourism. A lot of smaller farms are using it to supplement their income." I explained the concept, and everyone but Jack was excited about it.

"We can't do weddings here. We don't have the space." Even though what he said was argumentative, it was almost a relief to have him say something and not just sit there bristling.

"We had *your* wedding here," Pete reminded him.

"That was a one-time thing."

"He's right to be concerned about space, though," Georgia said. "For his wedding, they rented a tent. Would the client have to do that every time?"

Jack groaned. "Then we have people trampling everywhere to set up a tent every weekend? Catering trucks? Port-o-johns? No."

I tried to help. God knows I didn't like port-o-johns either. "What about a semi-permanent structure or space dedicated to that purpose? What if you invested in a huge tent that stayed up the whole summer?"

"We could do that," Pete enthused, earning a dirty look from Jack. "And we wouldn't need catering trucks." He sat up taller in his chair. "*We'd* want to cater it. But we'd need to get a license."

Georgia nodded grimly. "Kitchen inspection. And generally, a home kitchen won't cut it."

I thought for a moment. "When you imagine your farm-to-table restaurant, where is it? Somewhere on the premises?"

Pete and Georgia looked at each other. "We had this idea at one point," Pete began cautiously, "about buying the old house across the street. It's vacant, has been for years. And the property has enough space for a tent, maybe even a barn, for events."

"The Oliver place?" Jack sounded shocked. "The roof will cave in on your heads! That place is falling apart."

"Old houses have good bones, though," Brad put in. "That house is solid. I didn't know you guys were interested in it. My office has the listing."

"It's really just an idea we're kicking around at this point," Georgia said. "We can't afford it right now anyway."

"But I can see how it would work," I said, my mind filling with images of intimate dining tables in high-ceilinged rooms. "You'd have to put in a brand new kitchen, I'm sure, and—"

"This is ridiculous. Do you know what a new commercial kitchen costs? And that's on top of the price of the house!" Jack grumped. "And there's no guarantee people will even want to get married here."

"*You* did," I pointed out.

The look he gave me could have cut steel. "That's because I belong here. It *means* something to me. Other people want fancy halls with marble and glass, not some tent right next to a barn."

"Calm down. It's worth considering, Jack," Pete said. "That's all we're doing. Considering ideas."

"I know what you're doing. You're trying to change things around here, make this farm into something it was never intended to be, and you don't care what I say about it." He stood, his chair scraping the wood. "So go ahead and make your website and take your pictures or whatever if she's got you convinced that crap will make a difference, but she knows fuck-all about this farm and this family. She's been here, what—two days? You can't just show up some-where and start messing with people's lives like that." He glared at me across the table, and suddenly I knew what this was about.

"Hey!" Pete stood up too. "Apologize to her, right now. She's a guest in this house and you have no right to treat her that way."

Jack's face went even darker, and his fists clenched at his sides. His expression was a mixture of anger and shame, but his posture was pure Fuck-You-I-Won't-Back-Down. No way would he apologize. Instead, he turned around and stomped out, slamming the back door behind him.

My own temper flared—and I didn't need a tray of scones to hurl at him, I had plenty of words to use.

"Excuse me," I said to everyone at the table. Then I raced out after him.

"Hey!" I yelled, my heels poking into the grass as I chased him across the lawn. "I want to talk to you!"

He didn't even turn around.

I broke into a run. "I said stop!" Catching up with him as he reached the path through the woods, I yanked on his arm.

He turned on me angrily, shook off my hand. "I don't want to talk to you, Margot. Get away from me."

"What the hell is your problem?" I demanded.

His eyes were dark and tortured. "My problem is you, OK? You come in here with your fancy ideas and expensive clothes and shiny hair and big blue eyes and everyone loves you and it's fucking with me. Everything about you is fucking with me. Just leave me alone." He turned and took off again.

"Get back here!" I yelled. "We're not finished!"

He didn't even glance back, just kept marching through the woods toward his cabin.

Dammit. *Dammit!* I stifled a scream that threatened to claw its way out of my throat and fisted my hands in my hair. He was so frustrating! So stubborn! So irrational! Why couldn't he see that his family wasn't trying to ruin his dream, they were trying to make it better? And I wasn't trying to fuck with him, I was doing my job. It's not like coming here had been my idea—they'd hired me!

And what the hell was that about my eyes and my hair? What did he want me to do, put a bag over my head? I couldn't help it if he was attracted to me! Did he think I enjoyed being attracted to him any better? Because I didn't! I wished to God I'd never laid eyes on him! Fuming, I watched him disappear around a bend in the woods.

Calm down, Margot. Pull yourself together.

After a few deep breaths, I walked slowly back toward the house, trying to think of a way to explain what I'd just done. Jesus, I was a disaster these days.

What was going on with me?

As it turned out, the family members left at the table were twice as mortified as I was, and bent over backward apologizing for Jack's behavior, assuring me they loved my ideas, and begging me not to take his words to heart.

I said I was sorry for running out, promised I was OK, and asked them to contact me in a few days, after they'd had a chance to go over everything I'd proposed. "I have some vacation time coming, so I'll just be parked in a beach chair," I said, hoping my smile looked genuine.

Georgia walked me out and insisted on giving me left-overs. "Please, take it," she said, holding out the plastic container. "I'll feel better."

"You've got nothing to feel bad about, Georgia."

"I do, though." She shrugged helplessly. "I went to see Jack last night and pleaded with him to come today. I thought he'd listen with an open mind."

"Really?" *I could have told you he wouldn't.*

"Yeah. He's not always this bad, it's just…" She sighed, closing her eyes briefly. "I don't know what it is. Something is going on with him, but he won't talk about it."

"He's a tough nut to crack, I agree." And I wasn't going to waste my time trying. He might look like a grown man on the outside, but he had the temperament of a stubborn brat. "Thanks for the leftovers. Breakfast was delicious."

I went back to the cottage with every intention of changing into my bathing suit, grabbing some sunscreen, a towel, and my book, and sitting in the sand for hours. I'd earned it, hadn't I? I'd read, I'd swim, I'd relax—what I would *not* do was waste one more second thinking about Jack Valentini.

At least, I *tried* not to think about him.

I put on the suit, rubbed in the sunscreen, and sat on the towel with my book, but all I did was stare at the same page, cursing his name and letting my anger fester.

I mean, what an asshole! How dare he treat me that way! How dare he make those shitty remarks after I'd tried so hard to please him yesterday! And after that kiss—which *he'd* initiated! I'd been doing a good job keeping my hands to myself. This was on him, not me. Tossing my book aside, I crossed my arms and scowled beneath the floppy brim of my sun hat.

That's what his problem is. He's mad at himself, and he's taking it out on me. This isn't just about weddings on the farm. This is about him being unable to handle the fact that he's attracted to me—someone he sees as a spoiled rotten rich city girl who always gets what she wants. And even if he hated all my ideas, that doesn't give him the right to be rude.

Even a swim in chilly Lake Huron couldn't take the hot edge off my anger. That asshole owed me an apology—and he needed to hear what I had to say! Maybe the old Margot would have stayed cool, brushed it off, taken the high road, but she had been replaced of late by New Margot. And New Margot didn't hold back! She spoke her mind. She threw scones. She stood up for herself.

So after spending the entire day dying to tell Jack Valentini just what I thought of him (and the entire evening drinking wine and eating leftover French toast casserole), I showered off the sand and sunscreen, threw on some clothes, and stomped through the dark to his house to do just that.

CHAPTER FIFTEEN
JACK

I was lying on the couch, drowning in misery, when I heard someone approaching the cabin. Immediately on edge, I sat up and listened. My windows were open, and I heard a voice. A female voice.

It was quiet at first, as if she were muttering to herself, but grew a little louder as she got closer. "…so you can go to hell, asshole. I've never been so mad at anyone in my entire life. How dare you say those things to me after what you did yesterday? You should be ashamed of yourself."

Margot.

Was she coming here to tell me off?

If so, I deserved it. I'd been way out of line this morning. But she had me so fucking worked up—I'd tried so hard to do what I said, look her right in the eye and feel nothing, and I'd failed. Everything about her got to me—the long blond hair, the blue eyes, the fair skin, the pearl necklace, the graceful hands. I couldn't see her legs beneath the table, but they drove me crazy anyway. Then there were other things, not even physical—the lilt of her voice, the excitement in her smile, the confidence she had in herself and her ideas, the genuine enthusiasm for our farm. Other than a few nervous glances early on, she'd hardly seemed rattled by my presence. And I'd been a fucking mess.

So I'd taken it out on her, on all of them. Tried to make them feel guilty for distorting my dream, when I knew they were just trying to build on it. But dammit! I didn't want things to *change* around here. I didn't want the farm to be something new and different. *I* didn't want to be someone new and different. And Margot, who'd never been told no in her life, didn't understand what it was like to feel like you were losing control of what mattered to you. None of them did! This wasn't just about weddings at the farm. It was about everything in my life feeling so slippery all of a sudden. About being unable to hold on to what mattered.

I sighed, closing my eyes as she drew closer.

But I shouldn't have treated her that way. It wasn't her fault I was so drawn to her. She had no idea that she was part of what was making me feel so unsteady. I owed her an apology, but after that, I needed to stay away from her.

I opened the door before she even knocked, and her mouth fell open in surprise. I was surprised too—she looked so different. Her hair was wet, and although she wore a flowery summer dress, she had no makeup or jewelry on. My heart knocked against my ribs. *She's so beautiful.*

Beautiful and fucking furious.

Her mouth snapped shut, her eyes narrowing. "I have something to say to you."

"So say it." I joined her on the porch, shutting the door behind me so the cat didn't try to get out. I figured I owed it to Margot to let her bitch at me. What could she say that I hadn't said to myself?

First, she parked her hands on her hips and then she poked a finger in my chest. "You're not nice."

I almost smiled. "No?"

"No. I don't know what you have against me, but I'm not here to make you miserable, I'm here to do a job. And I'm just as sorry about yesterday as you are, but you did not have to be such a jerk to me today."

"No, I didn't. And I'm sorry."

"And you—" She blinked at me. "What?"

"I'm sorry. You're right. I was a jerk today. You didn't deserve it."

She looked to the side and then back at me. "That's it? You're not going to argue with me?"

"Did you come here looking for a fight?"

She huffed. "I don't know. Yes."

"Well, there's nothing to fight about. I was a dick." I stuck my hands in my pockets and took a small step back. Margot sweet and bubbly in broad daylight was tempting enough—Margot feisty and looking for trouble in the dark was downright dangerous.

"Why'd you do it?" she asked.

"That's hard to explain."

"Were you getting me back for spying on you?"

"No."

She chewed her lip for a second. "What about that stuff about my shiny hair and blue eyes fucking with you? What about telling me *I'm* your problem?"

"You're not my problem. That came out wrong." *My problem is the way I feel standing so close to you.*

She didn't appear convinced. "What about what happened yesterday? In the barn. Are we ever going to talk about that?"

I shrugged. "It was a mistake."

That earned me an eye roll. "No shit."

"Then why'd you ask?"

Her brow furrowed. "I don't know. Because you confuse me. I never know whether I'm coming or going with you. One minute we're kissing, the next you're yelling at me to get out. This morning you're an asshole, tonight you apologize." She slapped a hand to her forehead. "I can't keep up."

"You don't have to. Aren't you leaving soon?" *Please say yes. I can't go on like this, wanting you this way.*

"In about ten days."

Fuck. I wasn't sure I'd make it.

Suddenly she clapped her hands over her face. "God, what am I *doing* here? I must be crazy. You're a *client*." She stepped off the porch and started hurrying down the path away from the cabin.

"Margot, wait!" I was relieved she was leaving, but I couldn't let her go alone. "I'll walk you to your car."

"I didn't drive," she called, heading into the trees.

My chest got tight, and I sped up, following her into the dark. "Margot, stop! I'll drive you back. You shouldn't walk alone at night."

"I'm *fine*."

"Hey." Catching up to her, I grabbed her elbow and spun

her around. "I'm not letting you walk anywhere near that highway in the dark, do you understand me?"

Just enough moonlight spilled through the tops of the trees that I could see her eyes glitter with angry tears. "Let go of me."

"No." I started trying to drag her back toward the cabin so I could get my keys, but she fought me.

"Let go of me," she said through clenched teeth.

"No!" I roared, gripping her by the upper arms and drawing her in. "I can't."

And without even thinking about it, I crushed my mouth to hers.

She wiggled around in my grasp for a second, and I thought she was still trying to escape, but when I loosened my grip, she threw her arms around me.

I reached under the bottom of her dress and grabbed the back of her thighs, lifting her right off the ground. She wrapped her legs around me, threading her fingers through my hair, fingernails raking across my scalp. Chills swept down my arms and back. It felt so good to be touched this way again, wanted this way—I'd forgotten how good, and the heat of it ignited a fire inside me that had long been out. She stroked my tongue with hers, kissed my jaw, my forehead, my neck, and my entire body thrummed with the need to be inside her, to be surrounded by the warmth of her desire. It was enough to shut off my brain—all I did was feel.

Moving off the path, I put her back against a thick tree trunk, pinning her there, pressing the bulge in my jeans between her legs, rocking my hips to rub against her. She used her legs to pull me closer. Minutes flew by as our breathing grew heavier, our bodies more demanding. "Yes," she whispered. "I want it. I want it."

Ten seconds of fumbling around with clothing later, I was sliding into her, my hands beneath her ass, her forearms braced on my shoulders. Her mouth was open, just above mine. "Oh God," she whimpered as I lowered her onto my cock. "I want it, but don't know if I can take it."

"You're going to take it," I told her.

Her eyes closed as I buried every last inch inside her tight, wet pussy, her head turning to the side. "You're so big it hurts."

"Want me to stop?" *Don't say yes, don't say yes, don't say yes.*

Her eyes flew open and she stared me down. "Fuck you. I want this. I don't even know why I want this so badly, but I do."

It was enough for me. Because I *needed* this—needed to be this close to someone, needed to hear her sighs and moans, needed to feel her heat and softness, needed to release all the tension inside me. I needed it so desperately I couldn't see straight.

Pushing her back against the tree again, I drove into her, hard and fast and deep. She cried out at the peak of each thrust so loudly I put a hand over her mouth so that anyone within hearing distance wouldn't think someone was being attacked by an animal.

But I felt animalistic in my desire—almost bloodthirsty.

She gasped for air against my hand, her eyes wide and wild. But I felt her tongue stroke my fingers, and when I slipped my thumb into her mouth, she sucked it, licked it, bit it. Every muscle in my body was tight and tingling, and I knew I couldn't hold out long. I put both hands beneath her again and concentrated with all my might on being less selfish, holding her tight to my body and flexing my hips to give her the best angle, rubbing the base of my cock against her clit. I'd missed this too—making a woman come, feeling that surge of power and pleasure.

"Yes! Just like that," she cried, her eyes closed. "Don't stop, please don't stop..." She dropped her head to my shoulder and sank her teeth into my flesh, one hand fisted in my hair, the other clutching my bicep. Her legs tensed up, her entire body going still, and I pulled her even closer, using my hands to move her in little circles on my cock. Her pussy pulsed rhythmically around me, and I lost control.

I rasped and growled through clenched teeth, my orgasm tearing through me with brutal force. I fucked her barbarically, passionately, like I hated her, like I loved her, like a man completely driven by instinct and not reason or emotion. And when I came, exploding inside her with violent bliss, her face buried in my neck, everything went silent and black.

Stumbling backward, depleted and dizzy, I sank to my knees taking Margot with me. She yelped and clung to my neck like a child, sending me tumbling onto my back in the dirt.

And I laughed.

CHAPTER SIXTEEN
MARGOT

I ended up straddling him, my knees in the dirt, my arms around his neck.

He was laughing.

Laughing.

I had to smile. *So that's what it takes? An orgasm?*

And speaking of orgasms, my whole body was still humming from the one he'd just given me. I'd never felt anything like it—so deep and intense I couldn't even move while it happened. And it had happened so fast! I usually had to concentrate pretty hard to come during sex, and certain conditions had to be met for me to relax enough to let it happen. (Total darkness, soft sheets, complete privacy. Also, I didn't love being on top because it forced me to see a man's O face, and they were never dignified. It also made me feel sort of like being on display during a vigorous treadmill workout.)

But with Jack, it had struck me like lightning.

The reality of what had just happened started to sink in. I'd just been fucked against a tree. By a farmer. Without a condom.

Oh, God.

My sandals were missing. He'd seriously fucked me right out of my Jack Rogers. And tree bark had probably torn up the back of my Lilly Pulitzer shift.

But damn, that was good. Rough. Messy. Frantic.

Totally un-Margot, yet I'd loved every second.

I sat up, laying my hands on his chest and peering down at him. He looked so *different*. It was dark, but I could see the way his facial muscles had relaxed—no furrow in his brow, no tension in his jaw. His full mouth looked even more sensual, one side of it hooking up in a wry grin.

"That the fight you were looking for?" he asked.

I smiled ruefully. "Not exactly."

"You were pretty mad."

"I'm still mad."

He laughed again, and my toes tingled. I loved the sound of it—deep and warm and gratifying.

"But embarrassed too," I admitted.

"Why are *you* embarrassed? *I* started it." Some of the tension returned to his face. "Are you OK?"

"I'm fine."

"We didn't use anything…"

I pressed my lips into a line. "No, we didn't. But we're OK." I was on the pill, although I'd never had sex without a condom before.

Don't think about that.

Or with a client.

Don't think about that either.

"OK." He took a breath, his chest moving under my

palms. His hands were still on my hips. "God, Margot, I'm sorry. I don't know what came over me."

"Don't be sorry." I started to get up, feeling like things were about to get awkward. "Really. It just…happened."

He helped me to my feet, located my shoes, and while I tugged my panties back into place (they were still looped around one ankle), he did up his jeans. "I guess I just…" He ran a hand through his thick dark hair. "Lost control. It's been so long."

"How long?" I asked before I could stop myself. "I'm sorry—you don't have to tell me that."

"Since Steph."

My jaw dropped. "That long? *Three years*? Wow, I thought I had you beat. But it's only been just over a year for me." Not that sex had ever been anything like what we'd just done. I hadn't even missed it, to be honest.

"That's a long time, too."

I lifted my shoulders. "Guess that explains it. We just needed to get something out of our systems."

He nodded, sticking his hands in his pockets. "Yeah."

We stood there for a moment as the crickets chirped around us. My heart was beating a little too fast for comfort as I looked at him in the dark, knowing I was the first woman he'd been with since his wife. It was messing with me… I wish I'd known. I might have tried to make it nicer or something, maybe not screamed so loud. Or bit him.

I mean…*the first woman since his wife.*

That *meant* something to me.

But I had no idea what to do with it.

"So," I said briskly, as if we were wrapping up a business meeting, "I think the best thing would be to pretend this never happened."

He nodded again. "I think so too."

"We'll just agree it was a moment of insanity, fueled by pent-up frustration," I suggested, needing to file this in my brain somewhere, and not in my heart.

"Right."

I put on a smile, but I didn't feel happy at all. "And now that the moment of insanity has passed, I'd better get going."

"Please let me drive you." His voice was quiet and serious. "I won't sleep tonight if I don't, not that I sleep very well anyway."

"You don't sleep well?"

"No."

It was something small but personal, and I was grateful for the admission. Still, I hesitated, glancing toward Pete and Georgia's house. "Won't someone see us and wonder what we're doing?"

"No. It's late. Pete goes to bed early, and Georgia is working tonight."

I nodded. "OK, then."

"I just have to get the keys. Come with me?"

"Sure." We walked toward the cabin in silence, Jack's hands still in his pockets and my arms crossed over my chest. I thought about asking to use his bathroom to clean up a little, but something about it didn't feel right. Instead I waited for him on the porch, and then we retraced our steps back through the trees toward Pete and Georgia's.

In the driveway, Jack opened the passenger door of his pickup for me and I climbed in. He got in the driver's side just as I was pulling the bottom of my dress down as far as I could. I thought about asking Jack if he had a handkerchief, but he didn't look like the type.

"What are you doing?" He gave me a funny look.

"Trying not to get the seat sticky," I said, feeling heat in my cheeks. So much about sex was embarrassing.

He chuckled and started the truck. "Don't worry about it. Really. Tell me where you're staying?"

I gave him directions, and we were silent again on the two-minute ride. *Thank God*, I thought. Because the more he talked to me in that sweet, serious voice or smiled or laughed or showed me there was a gentleman inside that rough exterior, the more I liked him.

I didn't want to like him.

When he pulled up next to the cottage, I opened the door. "Thanks for the ride."

"Margot, wait." He put a hand on my leg. "Don't go yet."

It's better if you don't touch me, Jack.

"Yes?"

"It's not personal, my objection to your ideas for the farm. I can tell you're good at what you do."

"Thanks."

He took his hand off my leg and rubbed his jaw. "I just don't want things to change."

"Even if the changes make sense? If they'll bring in more money eventually? If they'll make people happy?"

He didn't answer, but I saw the stubborn set of his jaw return.

Sighing, I pushed the door all the way open and got out. "Goodnight, Jack. Thanks for the ride." I shut the door and walked to the door, and he waited until I was safely inside before pulling away.

Another display of courtesy.

Damn him.

Later, I lay in bed, listening to the waves through the screens and struggling to process tonight's surprises. The way Jack had apologized. The way he'd agreed he'd been mean and unfair. The unexpected—and vehement—insistence that he drive me home. The shock of that first kiss, when he'd grabbed me by both arms, his frustration giving way to passion all at once.

You're going to take it.

My stomach hollowed as I recalled the way he'd driven deep inside me, so deep it had hurt. Never in my life had I experienced anything like the way that sharp twinge had started to feel good. How could pain accompany pleasure like that? How had two opposite sensations merged inside my body, so seamlessly that I couldn't tell where the pain stopped and where the pleasure began? Which was which?

And I'd screamed and panted and gasped and clawed at him like an animal. He'd drawn something out of me, a part of myself I didn't even know was there, a part that existed only to *want* so ferociously, I could think of nothing else—not our crude surroundings, our nonexistent relationship status, not even our privacy. I never once worried about how loud I was or felt ashamed of my desire or stopped to fret that well-bred ladies should not appear to enjoy sex so unabashedly. (Bet I was the first Thurber woman to fuck a farmer in a forest.)

I'd loved every minute of it. Even his O face.

Was sex with Jack always like that? I wondered if the mad desperation of it was due to the fact that it had been so long for both of us or if he was always so rough and aggressive.

You'll never know. Understand?

Out of nowhere, Old Margot made an unwelcome appearance.

You both agreed it was a one-time thing. Leave it alone.

I frowned, waiting for New Margot to speak up and defend my right to another mind-blowing orgasm, but that scone cold bitch said nothing.

See? Even she agrees. There is no universe in which you and Jack Valentini make any sense whatsoever. Fine, he's not the jerk you thought he was this afternoon, but the reasons you need to forget about him still exist, not to mention that he's made no secret of the fact he'll be glad to be rid of you when you're gone. Finish up your work here and get back where you belong.

Sighing, I rolled over onto my stomach and closed my eyes. Old Margot was right. In ten days, I'd be back in my world, and this would just be that craziest-thing-I've-ever-done story I looked back on and laughed about.

Or cried about. One of the two.

CHAPTER SEVENTEEN
JACK

I lay in bed that night, waiting for the guilt to assault me. For my conscience to prick me. For my ghosts to haunt me. For regret, for tears, for a bitter taste in my mouth. All the familiar things that usually accompanied a sleepless night.

But it didn't happen. Even Bridget Jones lay beside me, content and purring. Didn't she know what a horrible person I was?

Come on, I thought angrily. Someone needs to scream at me for this. Make me feel bad. Demand to know how I could do such a thing. *Make me answer for this, God. I shouldn't come away unscathed.*

But God was silent tonight.

Instead the voice in my head was Margot's. *I don't even know why I want this so badly, but I do.*

It was a mystery to me, too, this explosive chemistry between a beautiful, sophisticated city girl and a rough-around-the-edges country guy like me. Where did it come from? And why did it have such a grip on me? It drove me insane the way I couldn't stop thinking about her. All I could do was pray that giving in to that desire would get her out from under my skin.

I was likely out from under hers, anyway. She'd been pretty quick to decide we should just pretend it never happened. Not that I disagreed—I didn't need anyone in my family to know about it, and I certainly didn't want to pursue any kind of relationship with her. I wasn't free to do that.

My heart would always, always belong to someone else. I'd made a promise to Steph, and I intended to keep it. Not only that, I wanted to be the kind of man she'd be proud of. I wanted to honor her memory. I wanted to honor *her*.

Thinking about how to do that kept me up long into the night.

In the morning, after checking on the animals, I went up to Pete and Georgia's for coffee. I could have made it at the cabin, but I owed them both an apology and wanted to get a few things off my chest.

I knocked twice on the back door before letting myself in. "Morning."

Georgia looked over her shoulder at me from where she sat at the kitchen table helping Cooper with his breakfast. "Morning." Neither her tone nor her face was particularly welcoming.

I'd expected that. "Pete around?"

"He's out front."

"OK to have some coffee?"

"Help yourself."

I poured a cup, ruffled Cooper's hair, and went out to the driveway, where Pete was changing the oil on an ATV.

"Hey," I said.

He glanced at me. Barely. "Hey."

"Almost done?"

"Not really."

"Can you take a break?"

"For what?"

"I have something to say, and I want to say it to you and Georgia at the same time."

My brother laughed, but it wasn't a happy sound. "I think you said enough yesterday."

I took a deep, slow breath, fighting my instincts to get angry and snap back. "I was wrong yesterday, and I'd like to apologize."

"You should apologize to Margot."

"I did."

He looked up at me in surprise, shielding his eyes from the sun. "You did?"

"Yes."

Turning his attention back to the oil filter, he was silent for a few seconds. "I'll meet you inside in five minutes."

"Thank you." I went back into the kitchen and sat across from Cooper, making goofy faces at him so he'd giggle. His little laugh was my favorite sound in the world.

"Jack, I'm trying to get him to eat," Georgia complained, but she was smiling too. "You're making it difficult."

"I'll do it. Go get some more coffee." I went around the table and nudged her out of her chair, then sat. "Cooper's gonna eat for me, aren't you buddy?"

"Bunny!" he said happily.

"I said *buddy*. Now open the barn door, because here comes the horsie!" I did my best at the horse, motorcycle, and airplane tricks to get him to open his mouth and managed to shovel in the rest of his blueberry pancakes by the time Pete came in.

"Good enough," Georgia said, taking away the little plastic plate and wiping his mouth and hands with a washcloth. "Thanks."

"Anytime. I can take him to the park later, if you want."

"That would be great." She set him down on his feet and I laughed when he took off running at full speed, face planted in the hall, then got right back up again. Kids were so resilient.

"You guys have a few minutes for me?"

Georgia nodded and sat down across from me, and Pete took the chair next to her. "So what's up?" he asked, bringing his coffee cup to his lips.

"I need to apologize for yesterday. I had a bad attitude right from the start and I was rude to a guest in your house. I'm sorry."

"And you apologized to her already?" Pete still sounded like he didn't believe me.

I nodded. "I did. Last night."

They exchanged a glance. "Last night? Where?" Georgia asked.

Be careful. "The cabin. She came over to talk about the meeting, and I told her I was sorry for being such a dick about things. I tried to explain myself better." *Then I fucked her right out of her shoes.*

"What reason did you give her?" Pete asked.

"I told her I can tell that she's good at what she does, but that I'm reluctant to make any changes on the farm that weren't part of my original vision."

"But Jack, her ideas can be in addition to your vision," he said. "No one wants to take the farm from you or stop you from doing what you love and what you're good at. This place is your dream. We know that."

Pressing my lips together, I forced myself to say what I'd come here to say. "You two deserve the same shot at *your* dream. So I won't stand in your way."

They were stunned silent for a moment. Then Pete said, "Are you serious?"

"Yes." I took a breath. "I did a lot of thinking last night. And if the situation were different, and it was Steph sitting here, not me, I know she'd tell you to go for it."

Georgia smiled, her eyes getting misty. "That's so true. She would have."

"And the best way to honor her is to do what she would do."

Pete cleared his throat. "That's great, Jack."

"I'm not promising to go along with just anything," I said quickly, "and I don't want anything to interfere with what I'm doing, but I'd be willing to discuss the possibilities of a restaurant, maybe look into buying the Oliver place. If that's impossible, I'd *consider* finding space on our property to put up a tent or barn for weddings or whatever. But you guys will have to do the legwork. Convince me it won't be horrible."

Georgia squealed and jumped up, coming around the table to throw her arms around my neck. She kissed my cheek and squeezed so hard I nearly choked, but inside I felt good. Deep down, I didn't think there was any way we could afford the Oliver place, and I still hated the idea of strangers trampling around my beloved farm, but something Margot had asked me last night stuck with me. *Even if the changes make sense? If they'll make people happy?*

The truth was, it wouldn't matter what changed or didn't on the farm—*I'd* never be happy, not after everything that had happened. So if they could, then I shouldn't hold them back. They didn't need to suffer for my sins.

"I'll call Brad," Pete said. "Maybe he can send us some info on the Oliver listing."

"I better get back to work. Thanks for the coffee." Rising from the chair, I took my cup to the sink before heading out the back door.

A few seconds later, I heard Pete's voice. "Hey, wait a sec." He jogged to catch up with me. "Thanks, man. Georgia is beside herself."

I shrugged, sticking my hands in my pockets. "I hope it works out."

"So why the change of heart?" he asked, lifting his cap off and replacing it. "I'm curious."

"I don't know."

"You get laid last night or what?"

I rolled my eyes, but my cock twitched. "Jesus, Pete."

"OK, OK. Just asking." He held up his palms. "You seem different today, that's all. More relaxed than you've been in a long time."

"So quit bugging me before I get tense again," I said, resuming my walk across the yard. Actually, I did feel more relaxed. A sense of relief and even peace had eased the tension in my mind and body. My steps were lighter. My shoulders looser. My fingers free of the urge to curl into fists.

Whether that was because of the sex I'd had or the conclusions I'd drawn or the apologies I'd offered, I wasn't sure. I had yet to suffer any debilitating guilt about having sex with Margot, which shocked me—I'd actually felt worse after the kiss. It had seemed more *personal,* somehow. Fucking her in the woods felt more like blowing off steam than anything else.

At least, that's what I told myself.

But the real relief would come in nine days, once Margot was gone for good.

CHAPTER EIGHTEEN
MARGOT

I was on edge the next morning. Too much coffee had me jittery, too little sleep had me restless, and too much time thinking about Jack had me unsettled. I didn't feel right in my skin.

I spent the morning trying to catch up on work for other clients, but I struggled to focus. The tenderness between my legs, the soreness in my stomach muscles, the memory of my legs wrapped around his waist distracted me endlessly.

Stop it! It never happened!

After lunch, I took a walk on the beach, hoping a little exercise and Vitamin D might help.

It didn't.

I tried to take a nap, which was a disaster since what I actually did was lie there and picture every inch of Jack's naked body (good thing I'd gotten that view from the tree), and replay in my mind every second of The Fuck That Never Happened.

Irritated, I sat up and grabbed my phone. I felt like talking about it to someone, but I hesitated before calling Jaime for two reasons—one, I'd told her I wouldn't bang the client, and two, I was supposed to be pretending I hadn't. Telling her about it was *not* a step in that direction.

I could always call Claire instead, I thought. I'd have to start from the beginning since she didn't know anything about Jack yet, but—

My phone buzzed in my hand. *Mom calling.*

I cringed. My mother was the *last* person I wanted to talk to right now, but I dutifully took the call.

"Hello?"

"Hello, Margot. This is your mother."

No matter how many times I told her she didn't have to announce herself, she never failed to do it. "Hi, Mom. How are you?"

"Fine. I played tennis this morning and I'm about to meet Aunt Dodie for lunch."

"Sounds nice." *Nothing ever changes in her world.*

"So I have to run," she breezed on, as if she hadn't been the one to call me, "but I wanted to let you know you can come home whenever. Tripp was caught *in flagrante delicto* with a waitress at the country club. In the men's locker room, of all places! Why any woman would want to go in there is beyond me."

My jaw was hanging open. "Really?"

"Yes, it's all anyone can talk about. Mimi Jewett's beside herself, but if you ask me, she had it coming, the way she gossiped about you and The Incident."

"Right."

"So I don't know what your plans are, but do be back for the Historical Society fundraiser at the end of the month.

We're hosting, and it's important for Daddy's campaign."

"What's the theme?"

"Gatsby."

"Again?"

"People like tradition, dear."

I sighed. It was useless to argue with Muffy on the subject of tradition. Her life was ruled by it. Mine was too, for the most part. "I'll be there. Bye, Mom."

I put my phone down and looked out the window at the lake. So thanks to Tripp (what an idiot), I could show my face again at home. And even though I was paid up here for nine more days, I knew hanging around any longer than necessary was probably a bad idea.

Because the more I thought about Jack Valentini, the more I wanted to see him again, get to know him better. Kiss him again. Touch him. Feel him inside me. Hear him whisper to me in the dark. Figure out why the chemistry between us was so good. Was it simply a case of opposites attract? Or was there more to it?

Sighing, I gave up trying to solve the riddle and admitted the truth.

There's no way this can work. I should just leave.

I tidied up the cottage, packed my bags, and called Georgia, explaining that due to a family emergency I was leaving earlier than planned, but I'd be available by phone or FaceTime or Skype or whatever she wanted to use to keep in touch moving forward. She thanked me for my time and said she'd contact me as soon as they'd had a chance to discuss everything.

I also contacted Ann, the property manager for the cottage, and told her I was leaving sooner than expected, but I understood I wouldn't get my money back.

"I'm sorry to hear that. I'll mail you a check for the security deposit."

"Thank you. I'm about to get on the road, so I'll leave the key on the counter."

"You're not leaving tonight, are you?" she said. "At least wait until morning. There's a huge line of storms coming through."

Frowning, I looked out the window but saw no evidence of impending doom. Maybe Ann was like my mother, who thought every drizzle was a monsoon. But I did drive an old car, whose windshield wipers weren't the best. I could wait until morning. "I suppose I could wait until tomorrow."

"I think you'd better, dear. If you shoot me a text when you leave, I'd appreciate it."

"I'll do that. Thanks."

Faced with an evening alone and no food in the fridge, I decided to walk into town and grab a bite to eat and a glass of wine. On my way out the door, I thought about grabbing an umbrella, but a quick hunt for one in the cottage turned up nothing. Oh, well. At this point, the skies looked relatively clear, the water was calm, and only a slight breeze ruffled the curtains. I wouldn't be out long, anyway.

I walked into town, proud of myself for remembering the way, and purposely chose a restaurant other than the one I'd seen Jack at two nights ago. It was right on the water, busy with a summer dinner crowd, and the hostess seemed a bit put out having to seat a table of only one. "I can sit at the bar," I told her. "It's not a problem."

She looked grateful. "Perfect. It's right through there in the next room."

The moment I walked in, I saw him. I might have turned right around and left, except he saw me too. Sitting at the bar, a beer in his hand, he turned and looked right at me, like he knew I was there. Our eyes met, and he slowly lowered the bottle. My pulse galloped.

Dammit. Now what?

CHAPTER NINETEEN
JACK

Pretend it never happened.

I knew that's what I was supposed to do, but the sight of her had caught me off guard, and I found myself staring at her, dumbfounded, my beer halfway to my lips.

I'd purposely chosen this place because she'd been at The Anchor last time, and I wanted to avoid seeing her. But I'd been sitting there thinking about her, when all of a sudden I'd looked up and seen her reflection in the mirror behind the bar—as if I'd conjured her up. I glanced over my shoulder, and sure enough, she was real.

Real and beautiful and walking right for me, a surprised smile on her face. "Well, hello. Guess we think more alike than it would seem."

Pretend those legs were never wrapped around your body. "Hey. How's it going?"

"Good. I was going to get a table," she said, gesturing behind her toward the dining room, "but they weren't too keen to seat just one person."

Pretend those hands were never in your hair. "Yeah. Busy in here tonight."

"Is there room for one more at the bar?"

Pretend you didn't come inside her so hard, your knees buckled. I recovered enough to look around, and noticed the chair next to me was empty. *Fuck.*

My hesitation flustered her. "I'm taking off tomorrow, and I already cleaned out the fridge at the cottage, so—"

"Tomorrow? I thought you were here longer than that." If she was leaving tomorrow, I'd be OK. Maybe.

"I was supposed to be here longer, but my mother called this afternoon, and there are some family issues…" She waved a hand in the air. "Anyway, I won't bore you with it. But yes, leaving tomorrow. So this is my last night."

"Oh." Some of my nerves evaporated, and I nodded toward the empty chair. Now I simply had to keep it casual. Light. No touching. "No one's sitting here. If you're not still mad at me, you can sit."

Laughing, she slid onto the seat and set her purse at her feet. "I'm not mad. You apologized. We can be friends."

"Friends, huh?" I side-eyed her. "I don't know if I can be friends with a city girl."

She smiled. "If I can be friends with a cocky, know-it-all farmer like you, you can handle a sweet little city girl like me."

"Sweet—ha." I took a long pull on my beer, and damn if she didn't stare at my mouth the entire time.

"Can I get you something?" the bartender asked her.

"Uh." Her cheeks grew a little pink as she realized what she'd been doing. "Can I see a wine list? And a menu?"

While she chose a drink and some food, I studied her

covertly. She wore the sandals from last night, this time with pink shorts that made her legs look even longer, and a white blouse. Her hair was loose and wavy around her shoulders, and I had to stop myself from leaning over to smell it.

"Have you eaten already?" she asked me.

"Yeah. Earlier at home. I just came up here to get out of the house a little. Every now and then I have to remind myself to do it."

She nodded. "I get that."

"You live alone?" I asked her, feeling braver since her departure was imminent. No harm in getting to know her a little better at this point, right?

"Yes." She swirled her wine around in her glass. "But my family lives close. Not as close as yours," she said, grinning, "but close."

"They do live close—too close sometimes." I grimaced and lifted my beer again. "But I love having my nephew there. He's so fucking cute. I took him to the park today."

She placed a hand over her heart. "Awww. Did you?"

"Yeah, he loves the park. He never wants to leave."

"So cute. And you're so good with him—I heard you have the magic touch."

Our eyes met. "The magic touch, huh?"

The blush in her cheeks deepened.

I looked at her lips, and my thoughts strayed into dangerous territory. *It would be so easy to kiss her right now. So easy.* My entire body tightened up, and I gripped the beer bottle tight.

I couldn't. We were in public, this was a small town, and

rumors would fly. They'd probably fly already, just because we were sitting together. I tossed back the rest of my beer, the moment passed, and she cleared her throat before taking a sip of wine.

Just talk to her, asshole. "You'll be glad to know I apologized to Pete and Georgia. Told them I'd be willing to consider their ideas. *Your* ideas."

She gasped as she set her glass down. "Did you really? That's great—I bet they were so happy."

"They were."

Her head tilted. "Can I ask about the change of heart?"

I took some time with my reply. "I did a lot of thinking last night. Some of the things you said sort of sank in."

"Really?" She sat up taller, her face lighting up. "What did I say?"

"You said something about changes making people happy, and I realized I didn't want to be responsible for standing in the way of their dreams." I studied the label on my empty beer bottle. "And I thought about what Steph would do if she were in my place."

"Oh."

I kept my focus on the bottle in my hand, tilting it this way and that. "I know she'd support them. She was completely unselfish."

Margot took another drink of wine and said, "Tell me more about her."

I blinked at her. Seriously? She wanted to hear about my late wife? Not only did it seem strange in light of what we'd done last night, but no one *ever* asked me about Steph.

"What do you want to know?"

Margot shrugged and smiled. "Anything. I know she was short and cute and loved her boots, but what was she *like*?"

Exhaling, I tried to come up with words that would do her justice. "Feisty. Energetic. So damn smart. She was accepted at three different medical schools. Granted scholarships at all of them."

"Wow! I didn't realize she was a doctor."

"She wasn't. She didn't go to med school, said she'd changed her mind." Which her parents had always blamed on me, even if they never said it outright.

She drank again. "Tell me more."

"She was stubborn as hell. Once she made up her mind about something, she never wavered. None of us could talk her into going to school."

"She must have wanted something else more," Margot said pointedly.

"I guess." I shrugged, feeling guilty again. "Me. The farm."

"I take it you feel bad about that?"

I rubbed the back of my neck. "Sometimes. But she had me convinced it really was what she wanted. And if she wanted something, she never gave up, and she didn't care what people thought. She was a firecracker."

"Ha. I like her."

"Everyone liked her."

She smiled again, a little sadly. "Were you high school sweethearts?"

"No. She was two years younger than me, and I thought

she was a pest. I'd known her since we were kids, though. And I knew she had a crush on me, but I never looked at her that way until I was out of school."

"Did *you* go to college?"

I nodded as the bartender offered me another beer. "For a year, but it wasn't for me. I hated being in a classroom. I was restless and bored. Then 9/11 happened, and I joined the Army."

"*Really*," she said, as if she'd never heard of such a thing. "And how long were you in the military?"

"Eight years."

"Wow. And she waited for you?" Her eyes went wide.

I nodded, smiling ruefully at the memory of her insisting she'd wait for me, even though I told her not to. "She did. Swore she would, and she did. I mean, she went to college while I was gone, but we kept in touch, saw each other when we could."

"And you got married when you came home?"

I nodded, taking a sip of the new beer. "We got married after my dad died. About five years ago."

She propped her elbow on the bar and her chin in her hand. "Tell me how you proposed."

I grinned at the memory. "Actually, she proposed to me."

Her head came off her hand, her lips opening in surprise. "Now way. Really?"

"Really. She knew we were right for each other and I wasn't one for ceremony. I'd probably have just asked her in the chicken coop or something."

Margot rolled her eyes. "You and that chicken coop. Thank goodness she had more of a sense of romance than you."

"You don't think the chicken coop is romantic?" I slapped a palm to my cheek. "I'm shocked."

"No, I don't." She poked me in the chest. "Now go on."

"About what?"

"The proposal!" She slapped my shoulder this time, rolled her eyes. "Sheesh!"

"Oh, right." But I was distracted by the way she kept touching me. "Uh, she asked me at the cabin. Brought me breakfast in bed on my birthday and there was a little note on the tray that said 'Marry Me.'"

Again she put a hand over her heart, and her expression went wistful. "So sweet."

I felt some heat in my face, remembering how things had gone after that. I'd said of course I would—promised to love her and take care of her forever, the way she'd been taking care of me. We'd made love over and over again that day, on the bed, on the floor, in the shower, on the kitchen table. I never felt safer or more sure of myself than when I was lost inside her. I missed that feeling so much. And I missed taking care of someone. "Yeah. It was."

"Was she your first love?"

I hesitated before going on. It felt a little odd to be talking about this with Margot, but it was also kind of nice. And as long as conversation stayed on the topic of Steph and our marriage, I was safe from other, less honorable thoughts. "Definitely. I was a typical guy in my teens, totally uninterested in any emotional attachments. But when I joined the Army, it kind of forced me to reevaluate what mattered in life. I realized what I had in her. And when I got out…" I paused, nervous to reveal too much of myself but unable to deny that it felt good somehow. *Just keep it focused on Steph.* "I kind of struggled to adjust, and losing my dad made it worse. Steph was there for me. She pushed me to get better."

"She must have been really special," Margot said softly.

"She was. She saved my life, I have no doubt." I took a long drink. "But I couldn't save hers."

Margot's face fell, and she studied the base of her wine-glass.

I groaned and set my bottle down. "What the fuck—I'm sorry, Margot. I didn't mean to unload that on you."

"No, no, it's OK," she said, touching my arm. "I'm glad you did. I'm sorry if asking about her made you sad."

"Don't apologize. I'm glad you asked. You know what?" I ran a hand over my scruffy jaw, wishing I'd trimmed it up a little. "No one does. No one ever talks about her in front of me."

"Maybe they're worried it's too painful."

"I guess. But I'd much rather talk about her than myself." I looked at Margot and realized I'd monopolized the entire conversation. "Actually, I don't want to talk at all, I want to listen. Tell me about you."

She smiled. "What do you want to know?"

I thought for a second. "Tell me about the horse you had growing up."

Her eyes lit up, and she told me about Maple Sugar, the thoroughbred she'd owned from the time she was eight years old until she left for college. When she teared up, she apologized and said it was silly to get sentimental about a horse she hadn't seen in more than ten years, but I understood the bond between humans and horses and told her so.

I learned about her family, her father's Senatorial race, the company she'd started with her friend. "Did you always want to go into marketing?" I asked.

"No. Not really." She smiled. "Actually, I'd have liked to be a social worker, but Muffy said that was out of the question."

I made a face. "Muffy?"

"My mother's nickname. You see, all the first-born daughters in her family, the Thurbers, are named Margaret or some variation thereof, the middle name has to be her mother's maiden name, and woe to anyone who tries to defy this tradition."

"Oh yeah?"

"Yes. You can go traditional, like Margaret or Marjorie. French like Margot or Marguerite, and you can even get away with changing up the spelling, like M-A-R-G-R-E-T, but don't you dare get cutesy and American and do something like Maisie or Maggie or Greta, at least not on the birth certificate. My cousin Mamie named her daughter Marley, and Great-Grandma Thurber died before she spoke to her again."

"Wait." I put out one hand. "Mamie and Muffy are OK, but Marley isn't?"

She giggled, flushed from two glasses of wine. "Mamie and Muffy are only nicknames, not on the birth certificates. We have to have nicknames, see, otherwise it would be mass confusion all the time. Plus WASPs love nicknames."

I propped my arm on the bar. "What's yours?"

She brought her hands to her mouth, laughing uncontrollably. The sound was girlish and playful, and sent a wave of heat rushing through me.

"Come on, tell me," I said, unable to keep a smile from my lips.

She dropped her hands in her lap and tried to keep a straight face. "It's Gogo."

"Gogo?" I burst out laughing, leaning back in my chair. "Seriously?"

"I'm afraid so." She looked at me, and her eyes were full of something good—wonder and warmth and affection.

My laughter died down and I found myself looking at her the same way. I loved that she could laugh at herself. *If only things were different.* I cleared my throat. "So Muffy said no to social work, huh?"

"Yes. She said, 'Don't be ridiculous, Margot. Thurber women go to Vassar and major in English.'" She shrugged. "So I did."

"Were you happy with that decision?"

"I guess. I never really thought about it. I got my degree, came home, took a job working for my father…and that was that."

"Did you like what you did?"

"Yes." She thought for a moment. "A lot of what I did

involved charity work and fundraising, and I liked knowing I was helping people."

"How'd your parents take it when you left to start your own company?"

She chuckled. "They were kind of baffled by everything I did last year—I broke up with my boyfriend, took up yoga, quit working for my dad, started Shine PR…"

"Yoga?" I arched a brow at her.

She shook her head. "Didn't take."

"And the boyfriend?"

"Still gone. And he'll stay that way." Her dinner arrived and she laid her napkin across her lap.

"Why's that? Let me guess—Muffy didn't approve?"

She hesitated, her fork hovering above her planked whitefish. "That's a long story. Let's just say we've both moved on. I'm looking for something better."

"Like what? What is Margot Thurber Lewiston looking for in a man?" I was teasing, but I was also curious. "A certain number of zeroes in his bank account? A Rolls Royce? A house in the Hamptons?"

"*No,*" she said. "I'm not *totally* shallow and pretentious, despite what you might think."

"So?" I prodded. "What then?"

She put a forkful in her mouth and chewed as she thought. "I don't know exactly," she finally said. "I'm still figuring that out."

"Fair enough."

"I know I want to get married and have a family. Actually, I sort of thought I'd have one by now, but…" Her voice trailed off and she shook her head. "But I was wrong."

"Life's full of surprises." I tried not to sound bitter.

She glanced at me. "What about you? Think you'll get married again?"

"No," I said, and I meant it. "I know what I had. And it doesn't happen twice."

"Fair enough."

We chatted a little more about the farm, about my family and hers, about places we'd traveled. She liked visiting big cities, and I preferred small towns, but we both agreed Mackinac Island was beautiful, perfect for a summer getaway. The more we talked, the easier I found it. Margot had definitely grown up in a different world, but she wasn't a snob. And she was so damn pretty. Even the way she ate and drank was graceful. I found myself mesmerized by little things—the curve of her wrist, the straightness in her back, the arch of her foot. She had the kind of beauty that resides in the bones. The creamy skin, perfect lips, and big blue eyes were just a bonus. Then there was the body—the endless legs, the narrow waist, the small round breasts that sat high on her chest.

What did they look like? I hadn't even gotten to see them last night. Were they even more pale than her face? And what about her nipples? Pale pink like cotton candy? Dark pink like a raspberry? Or maybe even deeper, like a cherry. As she chattered on about Mackinac Island fudge, my cock started to rise as I imagined licking my way up her vanilla skin to the cherries on top. *I can practically feel them under my tongue. I can taste her.*

God, why hadn't I done it last night? Why had I raced to the finish like a fucking teenager afraid of being caught? Why hadn't I taken my time with her? For fuck's sake, I'd barely touched her *anywhere*. I dropped my eyes to the napkin on her lap.

"Jack?"

"What?" I looked up sharply to see her slightly amused face.

"Do you want another beer?" She nodded toward the bartender, who was standing there waiting.

"Oh, sorry." I was completely torn. On one hand, I was having a nice time, and when was the last time I'd done something like this and enjoyed it? On the other, the longer I sat here with Margot, the more attracted I felt to her. "I shouldn't."

"Oh, come on. I will if you will. And then we can go our separate ways and you'll be rid of me forever."

I shook my head. "You really don't like to be told no, do you?"

She grinned devilishly, her blue eyes lighting up.

Sometimes I wonder if it was that smile that did me in.

CHAPTER TWENTY
MARGOT

I'd thought it would be awkward, pretending it had never happened. I'd thought it might be difficult, making conversation with him. I'd thought it would be safe, talking about his wife—I'd thought hearing about her would help me remember that he was off-limits.

But it was fun. And easy.

And deliciously, drastically dangerous.

When I'd first walked in, it had been slightly uncomfortable, not knowing exactly how it would go pretending we hadn't done what we did. But then he'd invited me to sit, and made a joke, and eventually, he'd smiled. And laughed—God, his laughter made me so happy. I wanted to roll around in it, get it all over me, like a pig in the mud.

He looked so *good*. I could hardly take my eyes off him. I loved the wayward curl of his hair, which I noticed for the first time had a little bit of gray. I loved the shape of his full mouth and had a hard time looking away every time he brought his beer bottle to his lips. I loved the way the cuffed-up sleeves of his blue shirt showed off those tanned, muscular forearms. He even wore a wrist watch tonight, with a large round navy blue face and a brown leather band with white stitching.

He also wore his wedding ring. And when he brought up Steph, I'd taken it as an invitation to ask about her, although I was surprised at how forthcoming he was. I got the feeling he was surprised, too, by how much he was revealing about himself, but it made me happy to think he felt comfortable confiding in me.

But instead of shutting down my attraction to him, the opposite happened—after hearing about their romance, I found myself even more intrigued. Here was this big, brawny, tough-as-nails ex-soldier talking about his first love, how grateful he was for her, how she'd saved him. And when he'd said he couldn't save her, my heart had cracked, and feelings for him had started to seep in.

Maybe if he hadn't asked about my horse. Maybe if he hadn't been curious about my family. Maybe if he hadn't told me he'd enlisted after 9/11 or talked so lovingly about his nephew or laughed so joyfully at my nickname. Maybe then, I'd have been safe.

But instead, I found myself wanting him again—badly—and regretting the circumstances that made it a terrible idea.

I tried not to flirt. I tried not to touch him. I tried to "pretend it had never happened," but by the time he paid the bill—he'd insisted on treating me to dinner—we were both half drunk and unable to remember the rules.

"OK, Magellan," he teased, turning me around after I headed the wrong way, looking for the exit. "Neither one of us should drive home tonight, so I'm going to walk you back to your cottage. Then I'll walk home."

"You don't have to walk me back!"

He held up a hand. "Please. If I don't help you, you'll probably end up in Deckerville."

I giggled. "What about your truck?"

"It'll be fine. Oh, shit." Thunder rumbled as we stepped out onto the sidewalk in the dark, the air warm and humid and smelling faintly metallic, but it wasn't raining yet. "We better hurry."

I had to work to keep up with him, and I was out of breath by the time we'd walked a block. "Slow down," I panted, then laughed. "You're always so fast at everything."

He groaned and grabbed my hand as we crossed the street, like he was the parent and I was the child. "Last night was not representative of my sexual skills."

"Hey, no complaints here," I said, stumbling up the curb.

He caught me by the elbows, and his touch electrified me. It must have had an effect on him too, because he let go of me as soon as I had my balance and put some distance between us. "Well, good."

"And anyway, it never happened." I bit my lip to keep from laughing.

"Nope, it didn't," he said.

"Not in a house."

"Not with a mouse."

"Not in a box."

"Not with a fox."

"It did not happen here or there."

"It did not happen anywhere." Lightning flashed, and he grabbed my arm and started to jog, dragging me alongside him. But he was laughing.

And I was giggling so hard, I could hardly breathe—the fact that Jack could recite Dr. Seuss was hilarious to me. Did he read to his nephew?

"Oh God, I have to go to the bathroom," I moaned,

trying to run in sandals while squeezing my legs together. "Who told me to have that fourth glass of wine. Was it you?" I pointed at him accusingly.

"Don't blame me, Miss I Will If You Will. If you wet your pants, it will not be my fault. And I don't have a bathroom to offer you this time."

I groaned. "This is really embarrassing."

"I know. You're a mess." He looked both ways and led me across another street.

"I am, aren't I?"

"Yep. Look at you. Unattractive, not too clever, uneducated, *hopeless* at farm work, a Peeping Tom, and *serious* bladder control issues."

"Ouch." I made a face.

"And you're slow," he complained, tugging me along.

"Sheesh, I don't have much going for me, do I?" A few raindrops started to pelt us as he yanked me up the walkway to my cottage.

"Oh, I don't know." We stood at the door and faced each other as the drops fell heavier. "You might have a few things going."

"Like what?" The air around us hummed with electricity. He was so close I could smell his beach bonfire scent, feel his breath on my lips. *Kiss me, Jack.*

He slid his fingers into my hair, cradling my head in his hands. "You have beautiful eyes."

"Thank you."

"And lips." A flash of lightning lit his face briefly before thunder growled above us.

"Thank you." My voice trembled.

"And if things were different…" He closed his eyes as

the rain made the metal gutters sing. "If I were different…"

"I don't want you to be different." Rising on tiptoe, I lifted my chin, let my eyes drift shut, waited to feel his mouth on mine.

But he pressed his lips to my forehead instead. "Good-bye, Margot."

One second later, he was racing away from me in the rainy dark.

I stood there in shock, stomach jumping, hands shaking, rain dripping from my hair and clothes. *He's gone. That's it.*

Disappointed, I let myself into the cottage and locked the door behind me. A lump formed in my throat, and I tried to swallow it away. *What did you expect? He is who he is, and you are who you are, and the two of you do not belong together.*

I used the bathroom and washed my hands, talking back to the voice of reason in my head. *Of course we don't belong together. I know that. But it was such a nice night, and I thought maybe…*

No. There is no maybe.

Sighing, I switched on a lamp in the front room and stood by the windows looking out at the lake. The rain drummed hard on the cottage roof, and I shivered again as lightning lit up the dark. The lamplight flickered, and I wondered what I'd do if the power went out.

Three sharp knocks made me jump. I hesitated for a second, then raced toward the sound. Was it him?

I yanked open the door, and there he was—dripping wet, breathing hard, body tense with restraint.

A second later, we lunged for each other.

Our mouths slammed together as his hands moved into

my hair again, slanting my head as his tongue plunged between my lips. I ran my hands up the damp front of his chest and gripped the back of his neck. *He came back! He came back!*

He walked me backward without taking his lips off mine, kicking the door shut behind him. Frantically, we tore at wet clothing, our hands working as fast as the rain was falling. My fingers fumbled with the buttons of his shirt until I could push it from his shoulders. He broke our kiss only for the half-second it took to whip my blouse over my head. I undid his jeans and shoved my hand down the front of them, both of us moaning as I wrapped my fingers around his cock. It was hot and hard and grew thicker inside my fist. He unbuttoned my shorts and slid his hands down the back, inside my underwear, squeezing my ass.

Oh, God that *feeling* was back—that desperation to clutch and claw, to lick and bite, to scratch and pull. The way I wanted him gnawed at my insides like it was captive, determined to escape.

Part of me was dying to know what had made him change his mind, but no way was I about to stop and ask. And nothing about his actions suggested he wasn't sure about this—not the stroke of his tongue, not the strength in his hands, not the thrust of his cock through my fingers. The force behind his desire heightened my own, because I *knew* what it had taken for him to come back here tonight, to admit that we'd failed to smother the spark between us, to give it another chance to burn.

Howling winds pressed against the windows as we shoved off shoes and jeans and shorts and underwear and tumbled onto the rug. He caught himself above me, and I stretched out on my back, his hips between my thighs. For the first time, we stopped kissing and looked at each other. Lightning flashed a split second before a loud crack of thunder shook the floor beneath us. Then the power went out, leaving us in the near dark.

Jack looked sharply toward the corner of the room where the lamp was, and his body tensed. In my mind I saw him hit the ground after the branch I was standing on snapped.

"Hey." I took his face in my hands, forcing his eyes back to mine. "It's OK." I kissed his lips, his cheek, his lips again. "It's OK. Stay with me."

He pressed his mouth to mine and reached behind me with one hand, and I arched my back so he could unclasp my bra. The moment he'd tossed it aside, he descended on my breasts, kissing them, licking them, sucking them, kneading them with his hands. I wove my fingers into his hair, fisted them tight when he took one nipple between his teeth and flicked it with his tongue. The ache between my legs throbbed, and I sighed with pleasure when he slipped one finger inside me, then two. As his mouth traveled down my ribs and stomach, I rocked my hips against his hand, melting into his touch. His thumb moved gently over my clit, slow, rhythmic circles that made my skin hum and my stomach muscles tighten.

He moved down further, settling his head between my thighs. I closed my eyes and held my breath. No one had done this to me in *years*.

After what seemed like a lifetime, he treated me to one long, slow stroke of his tongue from bottom to top, his fingers pushing deeper inside me. I moaned louder than I intended to and caught my bottom lip in my teeth. But when he did it again, this time lingering at the top to tease my clit with the tip of his tongue, I cried out with even more abandon. Propping myself up on my elbows, I looked down at his dark head between my pale thighs. Was this even real?

"I had to taste you." His voice was low and gravelly, and I struggled to hear him over the storm. "I was halfway home, soaked to the bone, and determined to put you out of my head, but all I could think about was tasting you."

"I'm so glad you came back," I whispered. "I didn't want you to go."

"You taste as sweet as you look," he went on, pausing to circle his tongue in a slow, decadent spiral. "Like strawberries in June." He flicked my clit with quick, hard strokes. "Cherries in July." He sucked it into his mouth. "Peaches in August."

"Christ, you can even make fruit sound sexy."

"It's you." He tilted his head in a different direction, swirled his tongue from a new angle. "It's all you."

I wanted to tell him it wasn't—it couldn't be—wanted my hands on his body, wanted to lick him and suck him and taste him, wanted to drive him insane like he was doing to me—but I couldn't talk, couldn't move, couldn't breathe. Higher and higher he took me, until I teetered at the edge of bliss and then sailed over, my clit throbbing against his tongue.

Desperate to feel his weight on me, I grasped at his shoulders, trying to pull him up. He took his time, lingering between my thighs like I was his favorite dessert and he didn't want anyone to take the plate away, even though it was empty.

"Come up here," I said. "Please."

Reluctantly, he crawled up my body, his mouth hot and wet as he kissed a path up my stomach, between my breasts, up my throat, until his elbows were braced above my shoulders. I reached between us, positioned the tip of his cock between my legs, rubbed it over my clit, slipped it inside me. My entire body vibrated with need for him.

He lifted his hips, pulling out. "I didn't plan for this. I don't have—"

"It's OK."

"You're sure?"

I nodded. "Please. I want to feel you there again."

"Feel me where?" He slid into me, slow and controlled.

I smiled wickedly and moved my hands to his ass to pull him closer. "So deep it hurts," I whispered in his ear. "I want you to tear me apart. Leave me bruised. Mark tonight on my body."

"You shouldn't say that to me."

I gasped as he plunged in deep, the sharp twinge making me jump. "God, I love the way you move. Like you want me so badly you can't hold back."

"I can't. No matter how hard I tried—and fucking hell, I tried." He moved a little faster, rolling his hips over mine. "But you're under my skin."

Then I couldn't talk anymore because his mouth was on mine, and I let my desire take over—I raked my nails across his back, took his lower lip between my teeth, pulled his hair, writhed and panted and gasped. Pleasure zinged along every nerve ending in my body like a live current. When I came again, I cried out his name as my body pulsed around his driving cock, my fingers digging into his ass. I felt wild, untamed, untethered—free to say and do and feel *everything*.

As the rippling waves tapered off, Jack pulled out and flipped me over. "Get on your knees."

Heart still pounding against my ribs, I got on my hands and knees, wincing when he grabbed my hair. He yanked my head back as he pushed inside me—*yes*. He gripped one hip, holding me steady as he fucked me so hard, I could hear his hips smacking my ass—*yes*. He came fast, his body going stiff, a growl escaping his throat, his cock throbbing again and again inside me—*yes*.

He let go of me and fell forward, catching himself on his hands outside of mine. His forehead rested on the back of my head, his breath was warm and soft on my neck, and the rain still drummed against the cottage roof. Neither of us spoke.

A moment later he wrapped one arm around my stomach, holding me close to him.

My throat squeezed shut. I wanted to say things. I wanted to tell him that he was the best I'd ever had. I wanted to ask if he was OK. I wanted to know if I'd eased anything inside him. I wanted him to know how badly I too wished things were different. I wanted him to know I'd never regret this, I'd never forget him, I'd never stop wondering *what if*.

I opened my mouth, but he spoke first.

"Don't go home tomorrow, Margot," he said, tightening his arm around me. "Please. Don't go."

CHAPTER TWENTY-ONE
JACK

Her body went still beneath mine. *She's holding her breath.*

She swallowed. "You want me to stay? Are you sure?"

"Yes." I pulled out of her, and turned her gently onto her back. The way she looked up at me made my chest tighten. "If you want to."

"Jack." Her hands flew to my face, her thumbs brushing my cheekbones. "Of course I want to."

I smiled, feeling as if a massive weight had been lifted off my chest. "Good."

"But I know things are complicated."

"They are." I wouldn't lie to her. "And I can't make any promises."

"I don't need promises," she said quickly. "I don't have conditions, don't need to put a label on this, don't have to know how it ends. I just like being with you."

I kissed one of her palms. "Thank you."

She smiled, letting her hands trail over my shoulders. "You know, it's funny. This is the first time in my life I'm giving myself permission to just do what I want to do without worrying about how it fits in to the grand scheme of my life. Without caring if it's what Thurber women do."

That made me chuckle. "I'm gonna guess Muffy would not approve."

She giggled and shook her head. "Probably not. But guess what? I don't care." Her face lit up the dark. "I don't care. I just want to stay here for a while and enjoy myself."

"Me too." Although for me, *here* wasn't a physical place. It was a state of mind that allowed me to enjoy some time with Margot without feeling like I owed anyone an apology. Without feeling like it was a complete betrayal. Without the guilt. It was a place I'd reached as I'd run through the rain toward home, realizing that I could either spend another sleepless night alone and tortured by thoughts of her, or I could allow myself a brief reprieve from the loneliness.

And maybe for Margot, it was the same—a break from the expectations, the rules governing her behavior, a chance for her to indulge her less...*polite* side. Get her hands dirty. I could definitely help her with that.

But that's all it could be—a respite, a temporary relief. Anything more was out of the question.

"Wonder when the power will come back on." Margot came out of the bathroom carrying the candle we'd lit. She was still naked—I loved that. "Think it's on at the cabin?"

"No idea." The prospect of spending the entire night in the dark did not thrill me. Did I have candles to burn? I tried to remember as I buttoned up my shirt.

"Is it still raining?" We listened for a moment, and sure

enough, the downpour hadn't let up.

"Yeah." Frowning, I glanced around the room for my socks, which were probably still soaked. Fuck, I hated wet socks.

"Want to stay here tonight?"

I looked at her, hesitated. Sex was one thing, but spending the night with another woman seemed like too much. Lying next to her. Watching her sleep. Waking up with her. *But I want to. Just this once would be OK, right?*

"No pressure." Margot walked toward me, the candle lighting her face from below. "But the invitation is there. Thinking about you trying to get home in the pitch dark makes me nervous."

Our eyes met, and I wondered if she was thinking about the highway. *It was raining that night too.* For one insane second, I wondered why the hell I shouldn't tempt fate. Would I get what I deserved?

"You wouldn't let *me* walk home in the dark, remember?"

The concern on her face moved me. "I remember."

"So stay." She set the candle on an end table and twined her arms around my waist. "For me. I know you're a big strong soldier and you're not afraid of the dark, but I'll be too scared here all alone."

I smiled and wrapped my arms around her. *You have no idea.* She rested her cheek on my chest, and I kissed the top of her head. Even her hair smelled sweet. *A whole night surrounded by her scent. By the sound of her breathing. By the knowledge I wasn't alone.* "OK. I'll stay."

"Good." She wriggled happily in my arms. "God, I love getting my way."

I pinched her butt. "You're a spoiled brat. Did you just trick me?"

"Maybe."

"Jesus, you could sell water to a drowning man. You should go into politics."

"No, thanks. But I was pretty good at fundraising, or at least getting rich people to write checks for good causes."

"I have no doubt." She yawned, and I hugged her tighter. "Tired?"

"Yes. You wore me out. Or maybe it was the wine."

"Let's say it was me."

She looked up at me and smiled. "It was totally you."

She went into the bathroom to brush her teeth, taking the candle with her, but she left the door open so I could find my way into the bedroom. By the time she came out, I was undressed again and under the covers.

Setting the candle on the bedside table, she slipped in next to me and then blew it out. We lay there for a moment, the rain softer now, the scent of smoke from the candle lingering in the air. Both of us were on our backs, no parts of our bodies touching.

"Is it strange?" she asked.

I looked over at her. "Is what strange?"

"Being in bed with someone else."

Returning my eyes to the ceiling, I put my hands behind my head. "Yeah. It is."

She turned onto her side to face me, tucking her hands

beneath her cheek. "I'm glad you didn't lie and say it wasn't."

I focused on her again. "I won't lie to you, Margot. I promise."

"OK." Her voice was soft. "I was brushing my teeth and thinking that I shouldn't have pressured you to stay. I didn't think about it being strange for you that way. I feel bad."

"Hey. Come here." I reached for her, and she moved close, tucking herself along the side of my body. Her skin was warm and soft and smelled like vanilla. My cock stirred beneath the sheets. "I stayed because I want to be here with you tonight. Yes, it's the first time I've spent the night with anyone other than Steph in a lot of years, and yes, it's a little unfamiliar, but it's not uncomfortable."

"OK." She kissed my chest, slinging an arm over my torso. "Since we're being honest, I have to tell you how much I love your chest."

I smiled. "Yeah?"

"Yes." She rubbed her lips back and forth on my skin, slid her hand up my ribcage. "From the moment I met you."

I thought for a second. "In the kitchen?"

"Yes. You were so grouchy and mean, but you had this amazing body. I felt like you could snap me in half, and you looked like you wanted to." Her fingertips brushed over my nipple, and my dick jumped so high it made the sheets move.

"I think I did." Oh fuck, now she was circling my other nipple with her tongue, flicking it gently. Heat rushed through my body, prickled over my skin.

"Maybe you still will." She pinched the nipple beneath

her fingers, and I inhaled sharply. It felt so fucking *good,* and it was one of those things I'd never ask for but loved. Her hand moved slowly down my stomach. "I've never seen a body like yours before. So tight and muscular. All these ridges and lines." She let her fingers ripple lightly over my abs, making them clench. "It's incredible how strong you are. It makes me think of all the things you could do to me."

Keep going, I thought, *and keep fucking talking.*

Her hand closed around my cock, now fully hard and aching. "And this," she said, her voice low and fluid. "When I saw you on the dock, dripping wet and completely naked, my eyes went right here." Working her hand up and down my shaft, she picked up her head to speak softly in my ear. "I had thoughts I've never had before."

"Like what?"

"I wanted to watch you get hard. I wanted to get my hands on you. I wanted to taste you."

"Fuck," I rasped, one hand seeking her breast, the other snaking down her lower back.

"I was *so bad,*" she whispered. "I wanted you to touch yourself, and I wanted you to catch me watching you. I wanted you to punish me for it."

"Yeah? How would I do that?" I pinched her nipple hard enough to make her gasp and slid my middle finger along the crack of her ass.

She went still. "Actually, I don't know. I didn't get that far."

"Never mind. You couldn't dream up anything close to what I'd have done."

"Tell me," she begged. "I want to hear it."

"Nope. I'll let it come as a surprise."

A slow, sly grin stretched her lips. "Fair enough."

I moved fast, flipping her onto her back across the bed and pinning her wrists to the mattress, anchoring her body with my hips. "I don't always play fair."

The grin vanished.

But her eyes glittered.

When we were finally sated—no easy feat, Margot had an appetite for sex that nearly matched my own—we collapsed on top of the twisted sheets, her head on my chest, one arm and leg draped over me. I wrapped an arm around her shoulder and kissed the top of her head.

"This OK?" she asked. "I don't know if you're a cuddler or not."

"It's OK."

"Night," she murmured sleepily.

"Night."

She fell asleep in minutes, her breathing deep and rhythmic, her body relaxed. I lay awake for a while, listening to the rain, in awe of her and this night and myself. It hadn't been an easy decision, coming back here. It hadn't been easy asking her not to leave tomorrow. It hadn't been easy climbing into bed with someone other than the woman I'd married.

But everything else…everything else had been *so* easy. Talking to her. Touching her. Listening to her. Being inside her. Why was that? How was it possible I was this comfortable with someone I'd only met days before, someone so completely different from me? It didn't seem real.

So let it be a dream, then. Don't analyze it. Don't scrutinize it. Don't look for meaning that isn't there.

I closed my eyes, content to be with her in a temporary dream world where I wouldn't be judged—where neither of us would be judged—for what we wanted.

For the first time in years, I fell asleep in the dark.

And slept through the night.

CHAPTER TWENTY-TWO
MARGOT

The mattress shifted, and I reluctantly opened my eyes. Blinked. In the pale gray morning light, I saw Jack sitting on the bed, dressed. His hair was a disaster.

I smiled. “Hey.”

“Hey. I have to go.”

“Are your animals missing you?”

He mussed my hair. “Yeah. And I have to get my truck still.”

“Oh, right. What time is it?”

“Just after six.”

The conversation we’d had last night filtered through my wake-up haze. “I need to tell them I’m not leaving today.”

“I was hoping you’d still want to stay. How much longer do you have?”

I had to think for a second. “What day is it?”

“Wednesday. The twentieth.”

“I’m here until the twenty-eighth. So eight more days.” When I’d been faced with the prospect of eight more days here having to stay away from him, it had seemed an interminable amount of time. Now it seemed short.

"Good." He leaned down and kissed my cheek. "Don't get up. I'll let myself out and catch up with you later, OK?"

"OK."

After I heard the front door shut, I tried to go back to sleep but couldn't. Was it possible things had changed so much in just twenty-four hours? If Jack hadn't been here when I woke up, I might have thought I'd dreamt the whole thing.

Rolling onto my back, I stretched out my arms and legs, pointed and flexed my feet. I was sore in places I didn't expect to be—my back and arms and neck. I was also sore in the expected places. Holy moly, that man could fuck a woman into next year! And his tongue, oh my *god*, he was good with his tongue. I'd had four orgasms last night—four! That was more than I'd had in the last *six months* of my relationship with Tripp!

I had to tell someone. I had to.

My phone was still in my purse from last night, which meant it was probably dead. Was the power back on yet? Hopping out of bed, I darted naked into the front room, grabbed my phone and the charger, and plugged it in next to the bed. It took a minute, but eventually it buzzed on and began charging. As soon as it would let me, I hit Jaime's name in my recent calls.

"Hello?" She sounded nervous.

"It's me."

"Are you OK?"

"Yeah, I'm fine. Why?"

"Because it's not even seven."

"Oh! Sorry. I didn't think."

"Why are you awake? Aren't you supposed to be on a semi-vacation?"

"Yes. And I'm awake because I can't sleep. And I can't sleep because of what happened last night."

"What happened last night?"

"I had four orgasms!" I burst out. "Onetwothreefour!"

She gasped. "Hold on, let me go in the other room."

"But I want to hear about the four orgasms," I heard Quinn say.

"They're not for you, now hush." There was a pause and some muffled breathing before she spoke again. "OK. Go. Tell me everything."

"I will, but first…" I chewed on one knuckle. "Promise you won't get mad."

She sighed. "I'm going to pretend the fourgasm was from someone other than a client. Does that work?"

"Good idea." I filled her in on what had happened since I'd last spoken with her, everything from the disastrous meeting—she groaned—to the tree sex—she gasped—to the fourgasm—she sighed.

"That's awesome, Gogo. I'm happy for you. I'm also in shock."

"Believe me, I am, too." And I couldn't even tell her about some of the most shocking things—the bruises on my body, the bite marks on his skin, the scratches on his back. The way I'd begged him to be rough. The way he'd used his size and strength to subdue me. The need in me to explore a different side of myself. The need in him to lose control without fear. That took *trust*—and somehow we had established it in the short amount of time we'd known each other.

Maybe that was the biggest surprise of all.

"So now what?" Jaime asked. "Will you see him again?"

"God, I hope so. When he left, he said something about catching up with me later."

"Why'd he leave so early?" She laughed. "Is he a bolter like I was?"

"Ha. No, he had to go feed the animals, I think."

"I keep forgetting he's a farmer. You're fucking a *farmer*."

"I know, and he's so hot," I said seriously. "I mean, I don't know if there are others like him, but women seriously need to start checking out the farmers markets around them just in case."

"Hm. Maybe we should tell Claire."

"Yes! Do it! What's she up to this week?"

"House hunting, actually. I'm supposed to go look at one with her later today."

"Any more dates with the hockey player?"

"Not that I know of. I'll get the scoop tonight."

"That's right, it's Girls Night." I felt a little sad about missing our standing date. "I'm sorry I can't make it."

She burst out laughing. "Shut the fuck up, you are not. And I wouldn't be either."

I grinned. "OK, I'm not."

"Just give us all the juicy details when you get back. We'll forgive you."

"Scout's honor."

She sighed. "I better get in the shower. Keep me posted on the work end of things please. I'm going to keep pretending you're not sleeping with the client, though."

Guilt made me cringe a little. "Is there anything else you need me to be working on while I'm up here?"

"No, don't worry about it. I have things handled. Take a few days off."

"You're the best." I blew her a noisy kiss. "Bye."

"Bye."

I hung up and sat there for a moment, trying to decide if I was tired enough to go back to sleep. But I was wired —I felt like I'd already had six cups of coffee and a bowl of Froot Loops with a sprinkling of cocaine on top. Where was this energy coming from? I couldn't have gotten more than six hours of sleep, and I usually liked eight. I wondered if Jack was tired or if he felt the same kick I did this morning. Had he slept OK? I remembered how he said he didn't usually sleep too well. Had being in my bed made it better or worse? He'd seemed happy enough this morning, hadn't he?

Finally I decided I was too keyed up to lie around thinking about him. I got up, dressed in jeans and a t-shirt, and figured I'd head over to the farm and help him out today, or at least make the offer.

I had to laugh as I tugged on my boots, still caked with mud from the other day. If anyone would have told me I'd be spending a vacation day doing farm chores a year ago—even a month ago—I'd have said they were crazy.

But everything about me felt different.

Well…almost everything.

I still wore the pearl necklace, of course.

Since it was light out and not too hot, I decided to walk over to the farm. It had stopped raining, but the skies were cloudy and the air was muggy. On my way up the sloped, cottage-lined street toward the highway, I called Ann and was surprised when she answered, since it was still early.

"Oh, hi, Ann. I was just going to leave you a message and tell you that I've decided not to go home early."

"Oh good!" she said. "I'm so glad. You survived the little blackout last night?"

"I certainly did. I lit a candle and had a perfectly enjoyable evening." *Want to hear about my fourgasm?*

"Happy to hear it. You enjoy the rest of your stay, and let me know if you need anything."

"I will. Thank you."

I crossed the highway right in front of the Valentini house, and saw Georgia come out the front door, coffee cup in her hand.

"Good morning!" she called from the porch with a wave.

"Good morning!" I waved back and headed up the gravel path toward her.

"I saw you crossing the road. What brings you here so early?" She smiled at me over the brim of her mug.

Damn, what should I say? My cheeks warmed before I could formulate a response. "Uh, I thought I'd offer Jack a hand again." I gestured over my shoulder in the direction of the lake. "Not much of a beach day."

"Nope." She looked a little amused. "Jack know you're coming?"

"No." I stuck my hands in my jeans pockets. "Truthfully, he might have told me not to bother. Not sure I was that much help the other day."

She laughed. "Any extra pair of hands is a help. But why don't you come in for a cup of coffee first? He doesn't know you're coming, so he won't miss you yet, right?"

"Right." I smiled, even though I was kind of anxious to see him. "OK, thanks. Coffee sounds good." I followed her into the house and down the hall to the kitchen, where Cooper sat on the floor playing with plastic containers and lids.

I ruffled his curls. "Hey, cutie."

"Cream and sugar?" Georgia asked, pouring me a cup.

"Yes, please."

I took a seat at the counter, and she placed a steaming cup of black coffee, a pitcher of cream, and a sugar bowl in front of me. "There you go. Doctor it up."

I added some white stuff to my coffee until it was a shade of beige I could handle, and took a sip. "Perfect. Thank you."

Holding her cup in two hands, she leaned on her elbows across from me and smiled like the cat that hasn't eaten the canary yet, but knows where it lives.

She suspects something.

Again my face warmed, and I tried to hide the blush behind my coffee cup.

"I'm not good at keeping secrets," she blurted.

"Oh?"

"No, not when I'm this curious." She set her cup down and straightened up. "Last night when I came home from work, I noticed Jack's car wasn't there. Then this morning I saw him driving home. And I'm just wondering where he might have spent the night." The glint in her eye told me she had a pretty good idea.

I shifted in my seat, my eyes dropping to the ivory Formica countertop. "Uh…I'm not really, um, at liberty here to…" Shit! We hadn't talked about this at all. Did Jack want to keep our little fling a secret?

"It's OK." She held up one hand. "You don't have to tell me anything specific. Let me just say that yesterday when he came over to apologize, both Pete and I sensed something different about him. He was more relaxed, more willing to listen, less stubborn and crotchety."

"Interesting." I played it cool with a big sip of coffee.

"It was. Very." She smiled as she toyed with her cup. "Pete asked him flat out if he'd gotten laid."

I swallowed the mouthful of coffee too fast and ended up coughing. "And what did he say?" I asked when I could speak again.

"He neither confirmed nor denied."

Lifting my cup to my lips again, I struggled to keep my expression neutral.

Her grin was huge. "OK then. Moving on."

"Moving on."

"Did Jack tell you the exciting news? We're going ahead with plans for catering and the restaurant—I mean, at least with exploring the options."

"That's wonderful," I said.

"I'm so excited. And I was thinking, once the new website is in place, I could start blogging about the project."

"Perfect! That's exactly the kind of story to put out there."

"Brad is supposed to call us today to tell us if we can get in to see the house this afternoon." She made a face. "But we usually do the Frankenmuth farmers market on Wednesdays from three to seven, so I'm not sure how that's going to work. We might have to wait."

"Can't someone else do the market?"

She shrugged. "It's not really Jack's thing, at least it hasn't been since—"

The kitchen door swung open and he appeared. My pulse raced. My arms and legs tingled. My stomach was wild with butterflies. I couldn't keep the smile off my face, especially when I saw his hair. He hadn't put a hat on, probably because it wasn't sunny today, and it was still a mess from last night. *From my hands.*

I crossed my legs.

"Hey," he said, offering a small smile, but a smile nonetheless. "What are you doing here?"

I smiled back. "Thought I'd see if you wanted some help today."

"Oh. I came in for some coffee." He gestured toward the pot but didn't move, just stood there looking at me with that little smile on his lips.

Georgia looked back and forth between the two of us.

"Can I get you a cup, Jack?"

"Ah, I got it." He started for the cupboard but caught sight of Cooper and leaned over to scoop him up. "Hey, buddy!"

"Pahk!" Cooper said as Jack set him on his arm.

"You want to go to the park *again*?" Jack teased. "Aren't you tired of the park?"

"Never," Georgia said. "But no more ice cream when you take him. He refused to eat dinner yesterday."

Jack set Cooper down and tweaked his nose. "Don't worry, buddy. We can sneak the ice cream. That's what uncles are for."

Georgia flicked him on the shoulder as he passed her on his way to the coffee pot. "I was just telling Margot that Brad is trying to get us in to see the Oliver place later today."

He muttered something unintelligible as he poured himself some coffee, and Georgia and I exchanged an eyeroll.

"But there's a conflict because they're supposed to do a farmers market somewhere," I said.

"Frankenmuth." Georgia turned to Jack. "From three to seven."

"I was thinking, why don't we do it?" I said brightly. "I've never been to a farmers market before, and I'd like to learn more about them."

Jack turned around and leaned back on the counter. "No. I don't like those things."

"Why not?" I demanded.

"There are *people* there," he said in his grouch voice.

"Oh, for goodness sake. Of course there are—they're called *customers*," Georgia said. "I think it's a great idea! You should do it, Jack."

He brought his coffee cup to his mouth and mumbled into it before taking a sip.

"Please?" Setting my cup down, I clasped my hands and gave him my best smile. "I'll be good."

He exhaled, narrowing his eyes at me, but I saw a smile threatening. "I suppose I have to buy you an ice cream, too."

I clapped twice. "Yay! Ice cream!"

"This is great. Thank you," Georgia said. "I'll let you know for sure once I talk to Brad."

"Let's just plan on it!" I said excitedly. "No matter what, Jack and I will do it."

"Really?" Georgia blinked and looked at her brother-in-law. "That OK with you?"

"It's fine." Jack tipped up the rest of his coffee and set his cup in the sink. "I'd better head back out if I'm only getting half a day in. Is everything ready to go for this afternoon?"

"No, but I'll sort, wash, and package this morning, and maybe Margot will give me a hand getting the tables and signage together. That way I can show her how I set up. All you'll have to do is load the truck."

"Of course," I said. "Anything you need."

"OK." Jack looked at me. "Want to give me a hand with the egg collection before you do that?"

I wrinkled my nose. "Do I have to?"

"Yes."

“Have fun, you two,” Georgia chirped, giving me a secret thumbs up while Jack was opening the door for me.

As we walked toward the coop, my boots sank in the mud, my nostrils were assaulted with the smell of manure, and my anxiety about reaching beneath an angry hen returned. But my heart tripped with excitement for the day ahead.

CHAPTER TWENTY-THREE
JACK

As soon as we got around the side of the barn, out of sight from the house, I grabbed Margot's hand, spun her around, and kissed her. Our arms wrapped around each other, our bodies straining to get closer, as if it had been a lot longer than just a few hours since we'd seen each other. She smelled like last night—vanilla and sex.

Fuck, that's hot.

I hadn't thought of anything but this since I'd left her in bed. I was distracted as hell, too, moving slowly or standing still staring off into space when I was supposed to be getting shit done. "What the hell is with you?" Pete had asked me an hour ago when he found me standing like a statue in the barn, a length of rope in my hand. *Oh nothing, just thinking about tying up the nice lady who's working for us, maybe blindfolding her too. Fucking her mouth. The usual.*

Then when I saw her in the kitchen, my heart had knocked fast and hard against my ribs—a feeling I hadn't counted on. How long had it been since I'd felt so happy to see someone? She'd looked so pretty sitting there, with her hair off her face and no makeup, a simple white t-shirt. It would be filthy by day's end, but I didn't think she'd care.

"Wow," she said, coming up for air. "Is this because I said I'd help you with the eggs?"

"Nope. It's because I'm glad to see you. And also for the sleep I got last night."

Her face lit up. "I was going to ask you. You told me you don't sleep well the other night."

"I don't, not usually. But last night I did." I was trying not to think too much about it and simply enjoy the feeling of being well-rested. If I let my mind dwell on the *why* behind the *what*, I'd have to ask myself some questions I wasn't ready to answer.

"That makes me happy." She bounced on her toes.

I kissed her again, slow and soft this time, wanting to stretch out this moment in time as far as it would go. But when my hands started to wander and the crotch of my pants grew tight, I figured we'd better stop. "I'd much rather do this than work today, but I should probably get some things done before we have to leave."

She smiled. "I'm all yours. Put me to work."

Margot was still hopeless at gathering eggs ("I can't take that one under the hen…it seems personal, like she really wants to keep it."), but she remembered lessons from the other day and definitely worked faster. After that, Pete and I went out to check the fences and Margot stayed with Georgia to get things ready for the market. I hadn't done one in years, and when I had, Steph had been there to make everything look nice. Hopefully Margot would remember everything Georgia told her.

Just before noon, we loaded everything in the truck—including a picnic basket Georgia had packed for our lunch—and set off for Frankenmuth. "What kind of music do you like?" I asked her as we headed west. The sun was just starting to shine through the clouds, and it looked like we'd have good weather, which always meant a better turnout.

"Oh, I like whatever."

"Whatever, huh?" I played with the radio to see what stations would come in. "We'll see what we can find, but this truck is old and completely lacking in frills, like, say, a Mercedes."

She poked me in the ribs. "My Mercedes is from 1972. Frills as we know it weren't really an option then."

"True. And who needs 'em, anyway?" I turned up the radio and rolled down the windows, since the A/C didn't work. "Scratchy Hank Williams in a beat-up Chevy truck, driving down a back road, wind in your hair…" I thumped her on the leg and drawled, "It don't get more country than that, sweetheart."

She laughed and threw her head back. "Yeehaw!"

I laughed too. I hadn't felt this good in a long, long time.

We arrived at the pavilion around one-thirty, located our vendor spot, and unloaded the truck. Margot gamely did a bunch of the heavy lifting, wiping the sweat from her forehead with the crook of her elbow, and began setting up once we had everything ready.

"I can do that," I told her as she struggled to get a stubborn table leg unfolded.

She straightened up, blew a wayward piece of hair out of her face, and gave me a dirty look. "I'm not totally helpless, Jack. I can handle a folding table."

"OK, OK." I turned away from her to hide a smile as I unpacked the scale.

When the tablecloths were on and the displays done exactly how Georgia had specified, Margot stood back and eyed it critically. "I wish we had some different levels on the table. And more depth."

I frowned. "Depth?"

"Yes. I love the different-sized baskets on the ground and the old barrels. But on the actual tables, I think we could use something more." She tapped her chin with one finger. "The banner needs to be redone once you have your new logo, and we should also get it on the tablecloth front. I'd like to see it be a little modern and a little old-fashioned at the same time. On-trend but authentic."

"What difference does it make? Shouldn't the quality of the product be what attracts people?"

She smiled indulgently at me. "That will bring them *back*. But look at how many people are setting up here right now. How are you going to stand out? People make decisions about first impressions in under a second, Jack. You need to catch their eye with something visually stunning. Lure them in."

I scratched my head. I had no idea how to do that, but if anyone knew visually stunning, it was Margot.

She came around the tables and grabbed her purse. "I'll be right back."

"Where are you going? Don't you want to eat lunch before it opens?"

"Give me ten minutes," she called over her shoulder as she hurried off.

She was back in five with potted herbs and flowers at varying heights, which she set up on the table, rearranging things to make room. Standing back, she studied it again and nodded. "Better. And that basil smells so good. Once we sell some things, I'll use the empty boxes to sort of prop up the little crates along the back of the table, but this will work for now."

I arched a brow at her. "You're the boss. Ready to eat?"

"Yes. I'm ravenous, actually."

We ate lunch at our stand, scarfing down the sandwiches, pickles, and cookies Georgia had packed. "I hope they get to see the house today," Margot said around a mouthful of cookie.

I uncapped my water bottle and took a drink.

She kicked my foot. "Hey. Don't you?"

"I guess."

She clucked her tongue. "You're such a poop. Well, *I'm* excited for them. It's their dream!"

"I know," I said grudgingly. "And while I can't say I like the prospect of them buying that peeling, splintering old heap, I do like knowing it's making Pete and Georgia happy."

"That is because underneath your grouchy exterior beats

an actual heart." She gave me a superior look. "Admit it—you're really a softie."

I made a face. "A softie? I'm not sure I like the sound of that."

"Don't worry, Farmer Frownypants, your secret is safe with me." She patted my leg. "I won't tell anyone how sweet you really are."

I leaned over to whisper in her ear. "And I won't tell anyone how *dirty* you really are."

She gasped and giggled. "You better not."

"Jack?"

I looked up at the woman who'd spoken, and for a terrifying second, I thought I was seeing a ghost. *Holy shit.* "Suzanne." Immediately I sat back in my chair and moved it away from Margot's a little.

"I thought that was you. I saw the banner and expected it would be Pete and Georgia." Steph's younger sister looked at Margot and then back at me. "Haven't seen you here in forever."

"Yeah, I don't usually do them." Fuck, the older she got, the more Suzanne looked like Steph—same coloring, same height and build, even the same voice. They were three years apart, so Suzanne had to be thirty now, the age Steph had been when she died.

"Well, come here, you big lug." She opened her arms, and I stood up, coming around the side of the stand to give her an awkward hug. She went up on tiptoe the way Steph used to do to get her arms around me, and my stomach turned over. "It's good to see you."

"You too," I lied, letting her go and retreating behind the stand as quickly as I could. At least she didn't smell like Steph. Suzanne was wearing flowery perfume, and Steph had never touched the stuff.

"Hi. I'm Margot Lewiston." Margot stood and offered Suzanne her hand and a smile.

Did Suzanne hesitate before taking it? Maybe I only imagined it. My equilibrium was off, and I'd started to sweat.

"Suzanne Reischling." She shook Margot's hand, and though she wore sunglasses and I couldn't see her eyes, I sensed her sizing Margot up from heel to hair.

"Nice to meet you," Margot said.

"You too." Suzanne took her hand back. "Are you a new employee at the farm?"

Margot laughed. "Sort of. I'm doing some marketing work for them. Helping them with branding and PR, that kind of thing."

"Interesting." Suzanne folded her arms. "Are you from around here?"

"No, I'm actually from Grosse Pointe, which is just north of Detroit."

"I know where it is."

Suzanne's reception of Margot was so cool, it jolted me back to my senses. "Margot is visiting for a week or so and getting to know the business better," I said, feeling an odd need to defend her.

"Yes, and I just tagged along today to see what this was like. I've never been to a farmers market before." Margot's smile remained genuine, her tone friendly. Sticking her hands in her back pockets, she rocked onto the balls of her feet. "I'm excited."

"How nice," Suzanne said flatly.

"What about you? Are you here with your mom?" I turned to Margot. "Mrs. Reischling sells homemade jellies and jams and baked goods at these markets sometimes." Yet another reason I avoided coming to them. She never said as much, but how could she not blame me for everything that had happened? Wasn't she dying to scream at me? I knew exactly what she'd say: *If it weren't for you, she'd be a doctor right now, probably married to another doctor, living in a nice big house with a baby on the way.*

She'd be right about all of it.

"I *am* here with Mom, and I know she'd love to see you. Come over and say hi?" Suzanne cajoled.

I glanced at Margot. Did she realize who this was? If she did, her face didn't show it. She was so good at keeping calm, at holding her tongue. *I could use a lesson in that.* "Maybe later. We need to finish setting up here."

"OK. Don't forget, though. We're still your family, aren't we?" It almost sounded like an accusation.

"Sure." I stuck my hands in my pockets, hoping she wouldn't try to hug me again.

She smiled with Steph's mouth, and it made my spine stiffen. "See you later, then." Without another look at Margot, she ambled off.

When she was out of hearing range, I exhaled and dropped into my chair. Picked up my water bottle. Took a long drink.

Margot slowly lowered herself to the edge of her seat. "Steph's sister?" she asked gently.

"Yeah."

She nodded. "Thought so. They look alike, huh?"

"Yeah."

"That's gotta be tough."

I shrugged. "Steph was really different than her sister."

"How so?"

"Different personalities. Different interests." I looked at her. "And Steph never would have treated you that way."

Margot's lips tipped up in a sad smile. "I got the feeling she didn't like my being here with you."

"Probably because this is something I used to do with Steph."

Margot tilted her head side to side. "So her reaction is understandable."

"Maybe. That doesn't make it OK, though." I sighed, closing my eyes for a second. "You know, when Steph was alive, her family never even liked me that much."

"Really?" Margot sounded shocked. "Why?"

I shrugged. "They felt she could have done a lot better than stick around here and marry me. Fuck, she could have done better. I told her that a million times." Angrily, I chugged my water again, wishing it was whiskey.

"I find that hard to believe."

"I don't know why," I said bitterly. "You've seen first-hand what an asshole I can be."

"Because you're a good man, Jack. Yes, you get angry

and lash out. You get pushed, you push back. And hell yes, I've seen you be an asshole." Her voice softened. "But I've also heard you apologize. I've seen you treat people and animals with love and kindness. I've seen you treat *dirt* with love and kindness."

I almost smiled, and she caught me.

"Plus," she said, leaning over to whisper in my ear. "You've got good hands, an *amazing* tongue, and a big dick. What more could a girl want?"

Reluctantly, I allowed a small grin and shook my head. Did she really believe a big dick made up for everything I couldn't offer? Margot, of all people? "Uh, stability? Financial security? A nice car? A big house? Expensive jewelry?"

"You told me yourself she didn't care about those things."

"But you do." It came out of nowhere. Why the hell would I compare Steph to *Margot*? "Fuck. Forget I said that."

"No, listen." She put a hand on my leg. "You're not wrong. I do care about those things. I've never lacked for them, or anything else money can buy. But you know what?"

Christ, we are so different. "What?"

"Something is missing from my life."

I looked at her. "Like what? What could possibly be missing from your life when you have everything you ever wanted? And if you don't have it, you can go out and get it?"

She rolled her eyes. "I hate to break it to you, but they don't sell happiness at Bloomingdale's, Jack. Plenty of wealthy people are miserable and plenty of poor people are content."

"I guess."

"Were you and Steph rich?"

I snorted. "No."

"But you were happy."

"Yeah, we were. Too happy."

She cocked her head. "What do you mean?"

Jesus, why had I said that? Working off sexual tension with her was one thing, but I didn't want to reveal too much of myself. "Nothing."

"You meant *some*thing, Jack. Tell me."

I exhaled, feeling weight return to my shoulders that hadn't been there all day. "I just meant that it can't last, the kind of happiness that we had."

"Why not?"

"Because it was too good to be true. I didn't deserve it." *Shut your goddamn mouth, Valentini! What the hell are you doing?*

She studied me a moment. "Why not?"

"Christ, Margot. Can we drop this, please? I really don't want to talk about it. You won't understand, and it has nothing to do with you." *And I can't start telling you things. I just can't.*

"But I—"

"Drop it, I said! Steph and I are none of your fucking business!" And because my temper was threatening to get the best of me and I had a habit of running my asshole mouth when that happened, I jumped out of my chair and stomped off.

I had no idea where I was going, I just wanted some

distance between us. Marching past other vendors in a blind rage, I strode through a public parking lot and took off down the street.

Goddammit, why did she have to get into it with me? I'd been in such a good mood today. Happy, even. Why did she have to ruin it by prodding at my pain with a fucking hot poker? Just because I was fucking her didn't mean she had the right to ask me about my feelings. She and I weren't going to do feelings—it was sex for the sake of sex and that was it! We didn't need to complicate things by talking about our pasts or our pain or what was missing from our lives. The moment we started to do that meant this was turning into something else, something I didn't want and she didn't need.

Taking a few deep breaths, I stopped walking and locked my hands behind my head. Waited for my heart rate to slow. For my agitation to ease. For my raw edges to smooth over.

After a few minutes, I was calm.

And ashamed of myself.

I was the one who'd said too much. What was it about her that made me spill my guts like a slaughtered animal? I couldn't fucking do that. And again, I'd gotten mad at myself and taken it out on her. When would I learn that lashing out at people who were trying to help only made me feel worse? Margot didn't have any idea how guilty I felt about Steph's death or why I felt responsible. And I wasn't about to tell her—not only would it burden her unnecessarily and cast a pall over what was supposed to be an uncomplicated good time, but it was too big a betrayal. Sex was one thing, but our connection had to remain purely physical.

Friendly was fine, but romantic was pushing it, and intimate was out of the question. *The less she knows about me, the better.*

I had to be more careful. For both of us.

On my way back, I stopped to buy some flowers for Margot. Unsure what kind of blooms were her favorite, I chose a small arrangement of blue hydrangeas because the color reminded me of her eyes. They were nicely wrapped in brown paper and tied with twine, but when I saw her sitting alone at our table, looking a little nervous and a lot sad, I felt like I should have bought a bigger bunch.

I walked around the stand and dropped down beside her chair, balanced on the balls of my feet. "Hey."

"Hey." She kept her eyes on her hands, which rested in her lap.

"These are for you." I handed her the flowers. "I'm sorry."

She looked at the bouquet and then at me. Took a breath. "Me too."

"You've got nothing to be sorry about."

"I do, I do..." She shook her head. "I shouldn't have bugged you about what you said. I've never lost anyone like you have, and I don't know what it's like. I've never even *loved* anyone like you have." Her eyes met mine. "I have no business trying to give you advice. I don't blame you for getting mad."

"It wasn't you I was mad at. I know it seemed like it," I said quickly when I saw the doubt on her face, "but I promise you it wasn't. I was mad at myself and let it get the best of me. I apologize."

"Apology accepted." She smiled and then buried her nose in the flowers she held. "I love hydrangeas. Thank you."

"I'm impressed you know what they are."

Over the blooms, her matching eyes glittered. "Good."

"The color matches your eyes. That's why I chose them."

She lowered the bouquet and looked at me in surprise, her cheeks going pink. Her mouth opened slightly like she might say something, but then she closed it again.

Looking at her, my heart started to beat a little too quickly for comfort, so I checked my watch and saw it was coming up on three. "Market's about to open up. You ready?"

"Yes." Smiling, she set the bouquet gently under the table and stood. "What should I do?"

"Don't let them walk away without buying something." I straightened up, my joints cracking.

She grinned. "Easy peasy. I could sell water to a drowning man, remember?"

"I remember," I said. "And I'm counting on it."

She gave me a thumbs up as a few people approached the stand. I watched her charm them, smiled and shook hands when she introduced me, and gave her a high five after they left with a bag full of eggs and vegetables.

It happened again and again.

Margot was a natural. People were drawn to her. They listened to her. Talked to her. No wonder she was so good at her job—she was beautiful and sweet and sincere. People wanted to please her. And I could tell she'd done her research on sustainable farming and the benefits of organic eating. She even dazzled *me* with her knowledge, especially because I knew she'd acquired it in such a short time. She was smart. And was she really doing all this for free?

"This is awesome," I told her. "I just have to stand here and take money while you do the work."

"Don't be silly, this is nothing. You do the hard work growing everything! Honestly, I can't believe I never thought about where my food was coming from before, or what was on it." She blinked those blue eyes at me. "I'm in awe of what you do. Plus, I think this is fun!"

She turned her attention toward the next customers, and I couldn't resist catching her around the waist from behind. "Careful, city girl. I'll want to keep you."

She laughed as I let her go.

But the scary thing was, I was only half joking.

CHAPTER TWENTY-FOUR
MARGOT

After the market closed and we'd loaded the truck, Jack wanted to take me out for dinner to thank me for working today. I told him it wasn't necessary, that I'd truly enjoyed myself, but he insisted. I think he still felt bad about the little blow-up, too, although he didn't mention it again.

I still felt bad about it. I'd only been trying to reassure him that he was good enough for Steph and deserved to be happy, but I shouldn't have pushed like that. He'd asked me to drop it. It was so sad, though—why did he think he didn't deserve to be happy? I'd never heard anyone talk about himself that way. It made my heart ache.

After he'd left me at the table, I'd felt like crying. Here I'd practically forced him to come to the market, something he used to do with his wife, and he'd run into her sister, which had dragged up painful memories, and then I'd made it worse by digging where I didn't belong.

And what an asshole I was, offering platitudes like *money doesn't buy happiness*!

How could I compare my situation, which was probably just boredom, to his tragic loss? What a spoiled brat I was, complaining about "something missing" from my life. I'd never wanted for anything. God, I wanted to kick myself! I could just imagine how that sounded to someone like Jack, who knew what it was to fight and struggle and suffer. What did I know about any of those things?

And his apology was so sweet. I'd gotten roses from Tripp before, but he'd always had them delivered. And while I appreciated the classic formality of the gesture as much as any woman, there was something so endearing and personal about the way Jack had handed me the bouquet today. The way he wanted to take the blame. The way he hunched down next to me and offered the flowers. The way he'd chosen them because they matched my eyes. It meant something to me.

He meant something to me. I just wasn't sure what.

He never did go over and say hello to Steph's mother, which I was glad about. I believed in social niceties, but after seeing the way Suzanne had acted toward me, I didn't feel he owed her any favors. She'd made things uncomfortable for him when she could just as easily have been nice. After all, I was no threat to her sister's memory. I just wanted to make him smile and laugh and feel good, even if it was only for a little while.

"I know a place you'll like in town," he said as we left the parking lot.

"And how do you know I'll like it?"

"Because it has things on the menu like charcuterie and fromage and craft cocktails." He put his pinkie in the air. "Very chic."

I slapped his hand down. "Oh, stop. I'm fine with anything. And I certainly don't belong in a place that's chic." I held my shirt away from my body. "I'm sticky and sweaty and gross."

"On your worst day, you couldn't be gross."

I smiled. "Thank you. But are you sure we're dressed OK?"

"I'm sure. Not too many places have a dress code around here."

We opted to eat on the restaurant's patio, and we were seated at a table under a string of party lights and a black and white striped umbrella. It was a table for four, and I was glad when Jack sat next to me instead of across. We ordered drinks—a martini for me and a whiskey on the rocks for him—and while those were being made, we looked over the menu and chose some charcuterie, cheese, and other small plates to eat.

Our drinks arrived, and the logo on the cocktail napkins reminded me of something I wanted to ask him. "Hey, what does a beet look like when it's picked?"

He arched a brow at me over his whiskey glass. "Why?"

"Because I need to draw one." I flipped the napkin over and took a pen from my purse. "Show me. Draw three of them."

He gave me a funny look but sketched a trio of beets on the napkin. "Like this?"

"Perfect." Biting my lip, I added a little banner across them and inked the words *Can't Beet Valentini Brothers Farm* on it. A little shyly, I turned it to face him.

He groaned, but he smiled too. "What is that?"

"Just an idea for a logo. Wouldn't that be cute on your tablecloths and your banner? On t-shirts? Shopping bags?" I was getting excited.

"Are those beets me, Pete, and Brad?"

I nodded happily. "We could even give the beets little faces!"

"You're killing me."

"I'm branding you." I took the napkin back and stuck it and the pen in my purse. "And I had lots of ideas today."

"I had some too. But none of them involved beets."

Our eyes met, a hot little current passing between us.

He still wants me! My heart beat faster. I'd been nervous that seeing Suzanne today and the blow-up afterward might dampen the fire between us, but it still burned.

We ate quickly.

On the way home, I asked Jack what his favorite meal was. I had this crazy idea I'd try to cook it for him—that would probably give him a laugh.

"Hmm. Probably a steak on the grill. Twice baked potatoes. Some kind of vegetable from our garden."

Damn. That was a tall order. I'd have to learn to grill. And twice-baked potatoes? What the heck was that? Why would you bake a potato twice? Wasn't once enough?

He glanced at me. "Why do you ask? Are you going to cook for me?"

"You don't have to sound so amused." I frowned slightly. "I think I could do it, but I'm not sure how to work the grill at the cottage."

"Why? Is it complicated?"

"I don't know. I asked the property manager how to turn it on but she started talking about charcoal and lighter fluid." I shook my head. "That sounded dangerous to me."

He burst out laughing. I'd never get tired of that sound, even if it was at my expense. "Jesus. You really have led a sheltered life."

"Not *that* sheltered," I said defensively.

"Oh no? Let's play a game." He gave me a sidelong glance. "I'll name something, and if you've never done it, you have to take off a piece of clothing."

"What?" I said indignantly. "OK fine, but if I *have* done it, you have to."

"Fine with me," he said.

"OK, then. Go."

"Changed a flat tire."

"Oh, come on!" I scoffed. "Start with an easier one. Who does that for herself?"

"Plenty of people. You should learn how. You've got that old car, what are you going to do if you get a flat tire?"

"Call triple A."

"What if you don't have a phone?"

I sighed.

"One piece of clothing." He said it like a warning.

"Fine." I tugged off one boot. "Next."

"Pumped your own gas."

"Ha! I've totally done that." I pointed at him. "Take something off."

He grinned. "Take the wheel."

I did, and he whipped off his t-shirt. My mouth watered. Even in the shadowy dark of the truck's cab, I could see the bulges in his arms, the lines on his stomach.

He grabbed the wheel again. "Waited tables."

"Oh, Jesus." I took off the other boot. "I didn't have summer jobs. We traveled abroad."

Jack thought that was hilarious. "OK, OK. An easier one. Plunged a toilet."

Off came one sock.

"Mowed a lawn."

Off came the other.

"Smoked a joint."

There went my t-shirt.

"Slept in a tent."

I shimmied out of my jeans.

He was smiling. "This is fucking fun as hell."

"I hope we don't get pulled over," I said, crossing my arms.

"I might pull over anyway."

My bare toes tingled.

"Been in a fight."

I thought for a second. "Like what kind of fight?"

"A fight. Where punches are thrown."

"Punches, huh? Not scones?"

"What?" He glanced at me. "What the hell are you talking about?"

I started to laugh. "My weasel ex came over a couple weeks ago at two AM and proposed to me. I can't even believe it now, but I sort of said I'd think about it. The very next night, he and his stupid girlfriend showed up to a fundraiser for my father's campaign, and she was wearing the very diamond ring he'd proposed with. He'd gone right from my house to hers."

"That is *fucked up*."

"Yeah. Come to find out, his father said he had to quit dicking around with his life and get serious, and I guess getting married would show he was serious. If he didn't, he wouldn't inherit his trust fund, which he needs to pay off gambling debts."

"Man." Jack shook his head. "Guess having money doesn't solve your problems."

"Nope. Anyway, I was so mad that night at the fundraiser that I started screaming at him and throwing scones."

He looked at me. "Scones? That was the best you could do? There wasn't a vase or something? In movies, rich people throw vases around."

I slapped his bare arm. "I knocked over a vase. Does that count? Oh! I also accidentally set fire to a table cloth."

Jack shook his head again, but he was grinning. "Did you ever hit the target?"

"Once or twice."

"How many scones did you throw?"

I shrugged. "Maybe a dozen or so?"

The grin widened. "Hopeless. And it doesn't count as a fight."

Sighing, I reached behind my back and unclasped my bra. It dangled off my arms a moment while I looked around.

We were on a rural highway that wasn't well lit, and I hadn't seen a lot of other cars, but still. I could just hear my mother saying *Thurber women do not disrobe in moving vehicles*.

"Well, come on, city girl. Show me what you've got."

I slipped off the bra. Struck a sex kitten pose. "Happy?"

A quick glance my way, and he frowned. "Oh, fuck. I didn't think this through. I don't know if I can drive with you naked."

"Ha! Should have thought of that before you started this little game."

Next thing I knew, Jack slowed the truck and made a sharp right turn down a narrow dirt road between two fields. He switched off the car, and everything went dark and silent. "Come here."

But before I could move, he slid toward me on the seat and flipped me onto his lap, my legs on either side of his thighs. Our mouths crashed together as his hands snaked down my back. He grabbed my ass and pulled me against the bulge in his jeans. I rocked my hips over him, feeling my panties go damp.

My hands moved over his chest and arms and abs, my head filled with the scent of him. I felt drunk with the idea of him, of us, of doing this crazy, spontaneous, probably illegal, definitely ill-advised thing on someone else's property. We could be seen. We could be caught. We could get in trouble.

I'd never really been in trouble.

"My cock is so fucking hard." He flexed his hips, lifting them off the seat.

"I love it." Words I'd never uttered before tumbled out

easily, breathlessly. "I want you to fuck me with it. Right here." I reached for his belt.

Inside a minute I'd wiggled out of my panties and he'd shoved his jeans down just enough for his cock to spring free. I lowered myself onto it, watching his eyes close, feeling his fingers gripping my hips.

I felt powerful and solid and *physical*. I'd never been so aware of my body or felt so driven by its need. Never experienced hunger or thirst or exhaustion to the point where my body craved food, water, or sleep the way it craved to be filled by this man. Connected to him. Anchored by him.

When he was buried deep inside me, I stayed still for a moment, wanting to commit the feeling to memory.

He opened his eyes. "Sex in a car?"

I smiled as I began to move. "Never."

"Good. I'm a fucking pioneer." He moved his hands and mouth to my breasts as I rocked my hips above him, making me arch and gasp with his fingers and tongue and teeth.

I wasn't very experienced being on top, but somehow my body knew exactly what to do, how to circle and grind and writhe above him, rubbing my clit along the base of his cock, angling so he'd hit that perfect spot inside me. And when I came, it was unlike anything I'd ever felt—deep, hard, surging contractions as my entire core tightened around him, the world turning to gold behind my eyes.

"I can feel you." Words whispered against my chest. "I can feel you come, and it drives me fucking crazy."

"Let me feel *you*." I could hardly talk.

He took over, grabbing my hips and sliding me up and

down his cock as he stabbed into me. Then he switched it up, holding me tight to his body and working me back and forth, making my clit start to hum once more. "Come again for me. Now."

Fuck, I loved it when he gave me orders like that, his voice as hard as his cock. "Yes," I breathed, letting him move my body like he owned it, surrendering completely. "Make me."

It was like magic, the way he knew how to move with me, the way my body asked and his answered. The way his body commanded and mine obeyed. We shared everything—the spiraling ascent, the dizzying peak, the spinning free fall…and as we clung and cursed and kissed and caught our breath, something in me began to unravel.

The slight sense of unease stayed with me as I dressed myself and we got back on the highway. But what was it? The sex had been incredible—each time was better than the last. Each time, I felt more comfortable letting instinct take over. Each time, I felt more pleasure in giving myself to him and taking what I wanted. What I needed. Was I worried he didn't feel the same way?

No, that couldn't be it. He was enjoying himself every bit as much as I was—I could hear it in the way he talked, see it in the way he looked at me, feel it in the way he moved. We felt free with each other. It was as if the temporary nature of our arrangement gave us permission to be as wild as we wanted to. We had nothing to worry about, no relationship drama, no complications.

But we did have a deadline. An expiration date. In a week, this thing between us would be over.

I looked over at him, and my stomach flipped.

What if I didn't want it to end?

CHAPTER TWENTY-FIVE
JACK

As the truck sped down the highway through the dark, I kept my eyes on the road but my mind was all over the place. Questions I'd avoided asking myself this morning now refused to be ignored.

Why was this so easy with her? Why was the sex so hot? Why did being with her feel so good? What was it about Margot Lewiston, rich city girl who didn't even know how to light a grill let alone use one, that appealed to me so much? When I looked at her, why did I feel like I *had* to have her?

Sex with Steph had been amazing, but it hadn't been like this. I hated to even compare because the two women were so different, and it wasn't as if I felt sex was *better* with Margot, but it satisfied a different need in me. Sex with Steph was passionate because we loved each other, understood each other, took care of each other. It was a physical expression of our emotional connection and our history. We'd been through so much, and I'd wanted to shelter her, protect her, cherish her, even during sex. I'd never even thought about being rough with her, pulling her hair, leaving bruises on her body. Maintaining control had never been an issue, because I always felt I had it.

Sex with Margot was passionate too, but in a completely different way—if being with Steph was like diving into a beautiful blue sea, being with Margot was like going over Niagara Falls without a barrel. It was rough and turbulent, fraught with panic and desperation. At any given moment, there might be pleasure or pain, fear or relief, stillness or chaos. I had to fight for control, assert myself over her, combat the feeling that I was powerless. Thankfully, that dynamic worked for her too. She liked that I didn't treat her as if she were delicate, breakable, and when I issued commands, she obeyed.

I loved the contradiction between the Margot everyone else saw and the person she was with me. I loved every dirty word she whispered, every scratch and bite mark she left, every animalistic moan and cry.

Maybe that was it—maybe it was so good between us because we could be someone with each other that we couldn't be with anyone else. Or maybe it was the short-lived nature of this thing, sort of like how vacation sex feels better than everyday sex. And maybe I'd been able to sleep next to her because for the first time in years, I'd been able to forget for a while, let go of some of the pain. That was OK, wasn't it? Because it was only temporary? I'd take it all back again as soon as she was gone. For now, I'd stay focused on the present. On her.

I looked over at her and saw her chewing on a thumbnail. "So serious. Are you worried about what I'm going to do next to unshelter you?"

She smiled, giving me a sidelong glance. "Should I be?"

"Definitely."

"Whips and chains?"

"Ha. You wish. I'm taking you camping."

The grin melted off her face. "What."

"You heard me."

"Like…camping where you sleep outside on the ground in the woods?" she asked, like she might not entirely understand the concept.

"Yes. Scared?" I reached over and poked her in the side.

"Yes! There are creepy-crawly things on the ground! And there are no bathrooms! Or room service! Or plush hotel bedding!"

I laughed. "Nope."

"And there are animals in the woods." She whispered it, like she didn't want to alert them she was coming.

"Sweetheart, the only animal in the woods you'll have to worry about is me." I glanced over at her. Her eyes were wide, her expression half-pleased, half-terrified.

"Couldn't we just go to a nice, quaint little B & B around here?"

"What fun is that?" I turned into Pete and Georgia's driveway. "No, I want to take you camping for real for one night. You can manage one night without luxury, can't you?" I put the truck in park and looked at her.

"One night?" she asked shakily.

"One night."

She thought for a second, then sat up straighter. "OK.

Yes. I can handle camping for one night. And you," she went on imperiously, "can handle a black tie Great Gatsby-themed fundraiser for the Historical Society."

"Black tie?" I pretended to think. "I don't think I own one of those."

"Black tie means you wear a tuxedo."

"Well, I sure as fuck don't own one of *those*."

She patted my arm. "I'll take care of everything."

"No way. I'm not going to any fundraiser."

"Scared I'll throw a scone at you?" Cocking her wrist back, she pretended to take aim.

I laughed and opened the driver's side door. "Actually, I'd like to see you do that."

She jumped out and met me around the back of the truck, and we began to unload it. "Come on, please? It will be fun."

"You don't really think that."

Her turn to laugh. "Not really. But I don't think camping will be fun, either." We started to walk through the dark toward the shed, arms loaded with empty crates and boxes. "Actually, you know what? I think we would have fun at the fundraiser."

"Oh yeah, why's that?"

"I think we would have fun anywhere."

I smiled, wondering who'd feel more out of place—Margot in a sleeping bag or me in a tux? It was a close call, but I think I'd win. Plus, I was only comfortable spending this time with her because whatever was between us would end when she left. I didn't want to make any promises that extended beyond that day. "I'm sorry, Margot. But no."

She sighed. "You're so unfair. I have to leave my comfort zone for you, but you won't leave yours for me?"

"You're going to leave your comfort zone for *you.* I'm going to teach you valuable survival skills. Like how to light a match."

"And when is this happening?"

"Let's see. Today's Wednesday, tomorrow night I'm watching Cooper, so how about Friday night?"

"Deal. Do I need a certain kind of clothes for camping?"

We reached the shed, and I laughed as I pulled the door open, picturing her decked out head to toe in some kind of designer camping gear, all in white. "Nope. You can wear anything. Or nothing's fine too."

"Hey, you two."

I jumped, nearly dropping the armload I held, my nervous system kicking into high gear. It was Georgia walking toward us, and she hadn't meant to startle me, but it took a moment to breathe normally again.

"Hey, Georgia." Margot greeted my sister-in-law, but her eyes were on me.

"How'd it go?" Georgia asked, hands in her back pockets.

My heart was still beating too fast as I moved inside the shed and stacked boxes against the wall.

"Great," Margot said. "I had a ball."

A second later I felt her hand on my back—a brief, reassuring touch. She didn't say anything, didn't even make eye contact, but I knew what she was doing…and I appreciated it.

"A ball?" Georgia laughed as we came out.

"Yes. And I have a bunch of ideas for you."

We began to walk back to the truck, and Georgia followed. "Margot was a natural," I told her. "We sold out of everything we brought."

"Really? Wow!"

"Did you get to see the house?" Margot asked.

Georgia shook her head. "Tomorrow at ten. Want to come along?"

"I'd love to!" Margot looked at me. "Unless Jack needs me for something."

Fuck, she was cute. I smiled at her. "No, you can have tomorrow off."

We reached the truck and Georgia peeked in the back. "You really did sell well today, huh?"

"It was all Margot," I said. "I'm telling you. She's got some kind of magic in her smile. No one can say no to her."

Margot beamed. "That's very flattering, but all I did was sell what you grew. That's the real magic."

Georgia looked over her shoulder at us, and my face felt hot. Why had I said that about her smile? Now Georgia probably suspected something.

"Come on, let's get this done." I tried to sound businesslike, but I was positive my sister-in-law's mind was ticking. She stayed quiet the rest of the time it took us to unload the truck, and she's *never* quiet.

"Well, goodnight, you two," she said breezily when we were done. "Thanks again for working the market today. See you tomorrow. Oh Jack, you still on for babysitting tomorrow night?"

I nodded. "Yeah."

"Great, thanks. Night!"

"Night, Georgia," Margot called. As soon as we were alone, she looked at me. "She knows."

"Seems like it."

"Are you OK with that?"

Rubbing the back of my neck, I thought for a second. It wasn't so much I minded Georgia knowing, but I didn't want her telling my brothers. They'd have a field day. They'd ruin it. But that wasn't Margot's problem. "Yeah, I'm fine. Georgia gets me."

She nodded. "Seems like it."

We stood there for a moment while the crickets chirped and wind rustled through the birch trees nearby. Lonely, nighttime sounds. *But I don't want to be alone tonight. More than that—I don't want to leave her.*

"So." I took a step closer to her.

She smiled. "So."

"What would you like to do?"

"Honestly? I really need a shower."

I cocked a brow. "What a coincidence."

I stared at the tub. "Really? A bubble bath? I don't think I've taken one of these in thirty years." We'd stopped in at the cabin—Margot had waited on the porch—so I could grab clean clothes, then gone back to her cottage, where she'd filled up the bathtub with hot water and bubbles.

Margot giggled. “Then you’re due. How old are you, anyway?”

“Thirty-three. You?”

“I’ll be thirty next month.”

“And you still take bubble baths?”

“As often as possible. And I never travel without my bath foam.” She breathed in, closing her eyes. “Doesn’t that smell good?”

I inhaled the scent of lavender. “I have to admit it does.”

“See? A little luxury is nice sometimes.” She looked pleased with herself.

We peeled off our clothes, and Margot got in, leaving me standing there staring at the tub. “There’s no way I’m going to fit in there with you.”

“Yes, there is.” Scooting toward the back of the tub, she looked up at me and splashed the bubbles. “Come and play.”

Somehow I managed to get in without falling, and we spent the next five minutes scrubbing up and rinsing off with some kind of fancy shower gel she’d also brought from home. It smelled delicious, just like her skin, but I couldn’t resist giving her a hard time. “I’m going to smell like a girl tomorrow. What’s the matter with plain old manly bar soap?”

She frowned. “It’s not good for your skin.”

“Oh.” I started washing my hair with the gel and she looked appalled.

“Jack! That isn’t shampoo!”

“What difference does it make? It made suds. I’m sure my hair is getting clean.”

She reached for a bottle on the tub ledge. "Rinse that out. I'll do it."

I rolled my eyes but let her wash my hair with her fancy shampoo, which frankly didn't even foam up as well as whatever cheap shit I had in my shower. I told her so.

Sighing with exaggerated patience, she began to massage my scalp. "That is because your cheap shampoo has chemicals in it called sulfates that make it suds up. Frankly, I'm surprised at you, Jack. You know about avoiding chemicals in your food but you don't pay any attention to them in your skin and hair care products?"

I could hardly speak, her fingers on my head felt so fucking good. Every nerve ending in my body tingled, and my cock started to swell. I might have moaned.

"OK, turn around and tip your head back."

I had to stand up to turn around, and she started to giggle.

"What?"

"Your…" She pointed at my dick, which stuck straight out at her and was covered in foamy white bubbles. "It looks so funny."

I stuck my hands on my hip. "For fuck's sake, Margot. You can say dick. Just don't say it looks funny."

"I'm sorry," she said, laughing uncontrollably. "But I just never pictured you like this—standing in my tub all covered in lavender bubbles with half a hard-on—oh, God." She shook her head and tried to compose herself while I stared her down.

"I'm going to remember this when we're deep in the

woods." Turning around, I sat down again and tipped my head back.

"No! I'm sorry. Don't torture me in the woods." She used a cup to pour water over my head, rinsing off the shampoo. "There. Now stand up again."

"Why? So you can laugh at me some more?" But I stood and faced her, making sure this time there were no lingering bubbles on my junk.

"No." Scrambling to her knees, she slid her hands up my legs. "I'm sorry." She kissed my right thigh. "Your dick isn't funny." She kissed my left. "It's very serious." She kissed the tip of my cock, making it jump like it wanted to kiss her back. "It's perfect."

My breath caught when I felt her tongue on me—soft, sweet little licks that made my insides quiver and leg muscles tighten. I was fully hard in seconds, and she ran her tongue from bottom to tip. Good fucking God, it had been so long…

I glanced down to see her look up and smile at me, that naughty little grin that always proved to be my undoing. "My turn."

"Your turn to what?" I managed as she took me in her hands, angling my dick toward her mouth.

"To taste you." She swirled her tongue around the tip. "To drive you crazy." She took the head between her lips, sucked gently. "To make you come with my mouth."

I groaned as her lips moved down my shaft, half my cock disappearing inside her mouth before she pulled back. Then she did it again, and again, never sucking too hard, never moving too fast, never making any sound.

Her tongue felt incredible on me, her mouth was hot and wet, and I loved the way she kept her hands on what she couldn't get in her mouth, but Margot was giving the most polite blowjob I'd ever had.

In contrast to the way she moved during sex, it almost seemed like she was scared of hurting me. Or maybe she was scared of *being* hurt. A girl like Margot probably hadn't done this very much. Maybe she didn't even like it and was only offering to please me.

Well, fuck—now what should I do?

My hands slid into her hair, and I forced myself to maintain control, to hold back, but every instinct in my body wanted to take over.

No, asshole! Let her be in charge! Just because she likes rough sex doesn't mean she wants to choke on your dick.

Oh fuck, now I'm thinking about that. I need to calm down.

I let go of her head, stared at the ceiling, counted to ten.

She knew what I was doing.

"Jack," she drawled. "Are you holding back on me?"

I looked down at her and saw those blue eyes gazing up accusingly as she rubbed the tip of my dick playfully against her lips. Her skin was wet, and her nipples were hard. Fuck, she was gorgeous. And sweet. What the fuck was the matter with me that I wanted to choke her with my dick? Was I an animal? "I don't want to hurt you."

"You won't."

"You don't know what I want to do to you right now."

"Tell me."

I groaned, knowing I was unable to say no to her.

"Teach me, Jack." Her cheeks colored as she placed her hands on my thighs. "I don't have much experience with this. But I want to learn. I want to make you feel good. Tell me what to do. Tell me what you want."

I swallowed hard. Tightened my fists in her hair. "Open your mouth." She widened her lips, and I pushed inside, as deep as I could go. "I want your mouth so full of my cock you can't breathe."

She jumped when I hit the back of her throat, and I thought she'd try to back away.

But she didn't.

She wrapped her fingers around my shaft again and looked up at me expectantly.

"Good girl. Now listen to me. I want you to stop being so fucking polite. Use your hands. Get messy. Make noise. Forget about being queen of the prom and suck me off like the greedy little slut under the bleachers. Got it?"

She got it. Oh my fucking God, she got it. She went at me like a porn star.

Five minutes later, I came so hard I saw galaxies born on her bathroom ceiling and thought my body might rocket into space, and she eagerly swallowed every last drop.

"So," she said, breathing hard. "Was that greedy enough for you?"

I reached under her arms and pulled her up to sit on the edge of the tub, then I dropped to my knees and pushed her legs apart. "Fuck yes, it was." Lowering my head between her thighs, I stroked her clit with my tongue. “But I’m about to get greedier.”

CHAPTER TWENTY-SIX
JACK

"Tell me about these." Margot's hands brushed over the ink on my side, sending a shiver down my spine. We'd probably been in this tub for an hour, the bubbles were gone, and the water wasn't even that hot anymore. But I was reluctant to get out. *It's not raining tonight. I have no reason to stay.*

"They're swallows," I said.

"Can I look at them?"

I turned around and sat so my back was to her.

"You have two of them." She traced them with her fingers.

"Two tours of duty."

"Ah. Did they bring you good luck?"

I closed my eyes. Heard shots fired. Saw bodies in the front seat. Smelled blood.

Swallowing hard, I clenched my gut and forced the ugly memory from my head. *Here and now. Here and now. Here and now.* "I didn't get them until I came back."

"So they're more of a symbol of a journey completed than a good luck charm?"

"Something like that."

"Are you glad that you did it? Joined the Army, I mean?"

"I've asked myself that question a lot. And I guess the answer is yes. I mean, if I had it to do over again, I know I'd still join up when I did."

"You know, you're the first person my age I've ever met in the military."

I looked at her over my shoulder. "Seriously?"

"Yeah. I think someone in my graduating class went to the Naval Academy, but I've never personally known a real soldier unless you count Veterans of World War II or something."

"Wow." Her life had been so different from mine. So different.

She kissed my shoulder blade. "I've never met anyone as brave as you."

I snorted, but I liked the compliment. "Thanks."

"Or someone who works as hard or knows so much about things I don't."

"Or someone whose hands get as dirty as mine do every day. I bet most people you know wear suits to work. Have their shoes shined. Get regular haircuts." *Own boats, golf clubs, and stock portfolios.* It was hard not to compare myself to those guys.

"Hey." She poked me in the back. "I like that you get your hands dirty every day."

I didn't quite believe her. "Yeah?"

"Yeah. It makes you different from other guys I know. Same with your tattoos." Sighing, she looped her arms around my neck and leaned back against the tub, taking me with her. "I don't have any tattoos."

My back rested against her chest, my head in the crook of her neck. The tension drained from my muscles. *If only I never had to leave this bathtub.* "I didn't think you would."

"Why not?"

"You just didn't strike me as the kind of girl who'd have them is all."

"I'm not," she said after a moment. "You're right. The truth is, I think they can be beautiful, but they seem very exotic and forbidden to me. Something for people who are braver than I am."

"Why? Are you scared it will hurt?"

"No, not exactly. More like I'd be scared of what people would think about me."

"Fuck people."

She sighed again. "Muffy would die."

"No, Margot. She wouldn't."

"Maybe not. But she'd think I'd gone crazy."

"So let her. Don't spend your life worried about what people think of you, Margot. That kind of fear is like a cage —it will trap you forever if you're not careful."

She didn't speak right away. Then a question. "What are you scared of?"

I didn't answer, because I knew I'd say too much. She was too soft, too sweet, too warm tonight. It would be too easy to tell her things she didn't need to hear, too selfish of me to reveal things just to share the burden of my truths. She'd only try to reassure me I wasn't the monster I thought

I was, just like Steph had done.

But it would feel so good.

"Probably nothing, right?" She squeezed me. "You're a big tough soldier. Not scared of anything."

I spoke without thinking. "I'm scared of becoming unrecognizable."

A pause. "What do you mean?"

"Nothing," I said quickly. What the fuck was I doing? I even tried to get up, but she held me in place, wrapping her legs around me from behind.

"What would make you unrecognizable, Jack?"

Exhaling, I allowed myself to surrender, just a little. Just this once. "Letting go."

"Of what?"

"My past."

"You don't have to let go of your past—it will always be part of who you are. But you don't have to let it shackle you, or prevent you from moving on."

Yes, I do. She didn't know, didn't understand.

"Hey." She squeezed me again. "Talk to me."

God help me, I wanted to. My secrets were pushing up against the underside of my heart so hard I thought my chest might burst open with them. I wanted to admit my guilt. Open my wounds. Bleed for her.

The temptation overwhelmed me. "The accident. It was my fault."

"I don't understand."

I tried to swallow but couldn't. "Steph's accident."

"What are you talking about? You weren't driving the

car that hit her."

"No. But…there was a different car." My voice was weak, and my body started to tremble. "Years ago. In Iraq."

Margot's hand began rubbing my chest in slow, soothing arcs. "I'm listening. Tell me."

My throat was dry and tight, but the story forced its way out. "My convoy was moving through the country and we'd stopped to rest. Three of us set up a checkpoint. Cars were being used as rolling bombs, so we had to stop every vehicle from coming into the zone where soldiers were resting."

She shivered, as if she knew what was coming. Pressed her lips to my head.

"We had signs in Farsi instructing drivers to stop, and if a vehicle didn't stop, we fired warning shots at six hundred meters. It was rare that cars tried to go through, unless they carried IED's. But one night…" I paused. Inside my head was a voice screaming at me to stop talking, but I couldn't. Every word out of my mouth relieved some kind of pressure inside me. I had to get it all out.

"One night someone didn't stop?" she prompted. "Was there a bomb in the car?"

I shook my head, swallowing the sob threatening to choke me. "No. But it's possible the driver thought the warning shots were coming from behind, because the car sped up as soon as they were fired. So I fired directly at the vehicle. I didn't even think twice."

"Of course you didn't." Her voice was strong. "Jack, no one would ever blame you. You did your job. You protected people."

"I didn't even see who was in the car until morning and it was time to move from that position." My eyes filled.

She went completely still. "And?"

"The driver was a woman. And there were children with her."

"Oh, my God."

"Three of them." My voice cracked, and tears dripped from my closed eyes.

"Oh, Jack." Margot's voice was splintering too. She held me tight. "That must have been horrible for you."

I inhaled, regaining control. "You know what? It wasn't. It barely registered. At the time, I remember feeling proud for doing what I had to." The words were bitter in my mouth. "Later, after I got home, it hit me what I'd done. I was a wreck. I couldn't talk to anyone, didn't feel safe, couldn't make myself feel normal. Every single minute I was just waiting for the retribution, you know? I was positive there was no way what I'd done could go unpunished. I *wanted* the retribution. I nearly brought it on myself."

She hugged me even tighter, and I felt the trembling in her body as she wept. Kissed my shoulders, my head, my neck. Ran her hands over my chest and stomach, as if she had to reassure herself I was still here. "I'm so sorry. And I'm so glad you're here. You didn't do anything wrong."

I didn't deserve her sympathy or her tears.

"Do you know how many fucking nightmares I've had about that woman?" I touched my thumb and index finger to the insides of my eyes. "She's right there in front of me and I'm begging and begging her to stop, and she doesn't. I wake up shaking and screaming."

"Do you still have the nightmares?"

"Sometimes. For a while, they got better, after I went to the doctor. I started taking meds that would make me forget what I'd dreamt. I didn't dread going to sleep so much. But I stopped taking them after Steph's accident."

"Why?"

"Because it was my fault." I retreated into the truth that tortured me, repeated the words that haunted me. "'Just as he has done, so it shall be done to him.'"

"No, Jack. You're wrong." She sniffed and sat up taller. "What you did saved lives, and it had nothing to do with Steph's accident. You are *not* responsible."

I closed my eyes. "It's the only way I can make sense of it."

"No one could *ever* make sense of a tragedy like that."

"Sometimes I dream about the checkpoint, and it's Steph driving the car," I whispered. "In my subconscious, they're connected forever."

Gently she rocked me, her words laced with quiet sobs. "It wasn't Steph, Jack. She was the love of your life, and you never would have harmed her. You made her happy."

"I wanted to. God, I wanted to."

"You did. And if she were here right now, I *know* she'd be saying the same thing to you that I am—it wasn't your fault."

I knew she was right—Steph would say that, and she *had* a thousand times in my mind. But I just couldn't believe her.

"And she'd probably be angry that you blame yourself," Margot went on. "She'd want you to forgive yourself so you could be happy again. Don't you think?"

Of course she would. She'd stand right there and argue with me just like she used to. But forgiving myself would mean giving myself permission to move on, to be happy when I didn't deserve it. I'd never make that mistake again. "I can't."

She rocked me again, her arms wrapped around me, her lips pressed to my skin. When she spoke, her voice was soft. "Have you ever told anyone about this?"

I hesitated. "Steph and my therapist knew about Iraq. But I've never talked to anyone about feeling responsible for her death until you."

She let that sink in—both of us did. I'd just shared a part of me with her that I hadn't shared with any other living soul. I wasn't even sure why I trusted her so much, but I did. Again, I figured it had to do with her temporary presence in my life. It freed me to be my real self around her.

"I wish there was something I could do for you," she said.

I exhaled. The truth was out. And while I didn't exactly feel better or hopeful, I did feel less alone. I put my hands over hers on my chest. "You're here. You're listening. That's something."

"I *am* here. And I'm glad you told me."

"I am too." It was startling to realize I meant it. I hadn't intended to reveal so much of myself, but it had been so long since I felt this kind of closeness to someone, the kind that compelled you to share your secrets.

She sighed as she leaned back again. "Want to hear something ridiculous?"

"Sure."

"The entire reason I took the job up here was because my mother made me leave town after the scone-throwing incident."

I craned my neck so I could see her face. "What?"

"It's true. I had to leave town until the rumors died down."

"Jesus. And have they?"

"Yes. She called yesterday and said I could show my face again."

"That's why you were going to leave yesterday, huh?"

"Yes."

God, I was glad she hadn't. "But you're still here."

"I'm still here," she whispered.

I kissed her, felt her fingers stroking my jaw. Her lips were warm and soft and tasted like lavender, and I wanted nothing more than to live in that kiss with her forever, to trap it under glass and stay safely inside, cut off from memories that haunted me and a future that could never be.

I wanted it so badly I didn't stay the night.

CHAPTER TWENTY-SEVEN
MARGOT

The next morning, I walked to Pete and Georgia's house just before ten. I hadn't slept well, so I felt a little groggy as I made my way, but the sunshine felt good on my arms. Inhaling deeply, I hoped the fresh air would succeed in perking me up where three cups of coffee had failed. But I caught the scent of manure on the breeze, and wrinkled my nose. Was that fertilizer? Ugh, how did people who lived near farms ever get used to that smell? *That's one thing I will not miss when I go home.*

But there was something I would miss—being with Jack. The last twenty-four hours had been incredible. Something had changed between us. What we shared no longer felt like a meaningless little fling. I felt close to him. Protective of him. Proud of him. Fascinated by him and how he made me feel.

I was falling for him so fast, everything around me was a blur.

It was mind-boggling. We weren't even dating! In the past when I'd developed feelings for someone, it had taken a while. And those feelings had stemmed from times spent together enjoying common interests rather than intense physical attraction. For heaven's sake, it had taken me six months to sleep with Tripp! And I'd never even had a one-night-stand, let alone an extended fuckfest with someone *not* my boyfriend. I'd never had an extended fuckfest, period!

And last night had been *insane*. I could still hear him telling me to act like a greedy little slut—was it terrible that it turned me on so much? How had he known that's what I'd needed—permission to act that way *with the lights on, while he watched?* That's what had made me nervous. Prior to that we'd always been in the dark, and letting that other side of me take over hadn't seemed so daunting. I'd gotten stage fright, especially since I wasn't that experienced with oral sex to begin with. But I'd wanted to do it for him. I wanted to make him feel good in every possible way.

And the things he did to me... I stopped walking for a moment. Put a hand on my stomach. Caught my breath.

Everything felt different with Jack. Now I knew what Jaime had been talking about when she said things like *mind-blowing physical chemistry*. And since I'd gotten a taste of it, I didn't want to let it go.

It wasn't just physical either. Not anymore. When I thought about the way he'd opened up to me last night, sharing something with me he'd never told anyone else, shedding tears in front of me, making himself that vulnerable...God, I just wanted to hold him and kiss him and cry for him, make everything better for him, make him happy.

But how?

I'd been hoping he might stay over again, especially since he'd said he'd slept well in my bed the night before, but I hadn't wanted to pressure him. I'd asked, he'd said no, I dropped it. He'd revealed so much of himself to me, he probably needed the time alone to come to terms with that. I understood that about him, and I'd learned not to push his buttons that way—he snapped and pulled back when I tried to get too close, almost like a skittish horse.

So after kissing him goodbye, I'd said goodnight and climbed into bed, hugging the pillow he'd used the night before. Sleep eluded me for hours, which I spent replaying every moment of the day and night in my mind, struggling to keep my feelings under control, and choking up all over again when I thought about what he'd told me.

By morning I had to face the truth.

I had feelings for him, and I didn't want this to end.

I wanted there to be a way for us.

Was it out of the question? People dated long distance all the time, didn't they? Two hours was practically nothing! I could work from anywhere most of the time, and I liked this little town. It didn't have designer shops or three-star restaurants or glamorous salons, but Main Street was charming, the beach was uncrowded, and the farms were beautiful. I could even start riding again! Being with the horses the other day reminded me how much I'd missed it.

As I waited for highway traffic to clear so I could cross, I thought about an even bigger problem than distance: Jack didn't want to get married again. Didn't think he could love someone again. Didn't want to let go of his past. Part of me thought I was crazy to even worry about getting married, since I'd met the guy less than a week ago, but another part of me insisted.

Look how intense things were between us after just five days. What if we started dating, and things continued to go well? Did I really want to invest time and energy and feelings in someone who didn't want what I wanted in the end? And I was almost thirty—I didn't want to wait that much longer to start a family. If there was no chance of that, what was the point?

As I hurried across the two lanes and started up Pete and Georgia's drive, I saw that wedding band on Jack's finger, heard his voice in my head.

I know what I had. And it doesn't happen twice.

My heart dropped. How on earth could I argue with that?

Jack was right about the Oliver house in many ways—it needed a lot of work, including a new roof, but Brad was right, too. Like all aging beauties, it had great bones beneath layers of dust, mold, peeling wallpaper, flaking paint, smelly carpet, and rot. It would take time and money and loving care, but it could be restored.

Georgia was beside herself as we walked back. "I knew it. I knew I'd love it that much." Brad and Pete were up ahead, Cooper in his dad's arms.

I smiled at her. "It could be great. And so easy to bump out the back wall, extend the kitchen."

"Pete and I have been talking about making it a bed and breakfast in addition to a restaurant," she said.

"A B and B, I love it! And it totally makes sense if you host weddings on the property."

"Exactly. And if we bumped out the back wall for an extended kitchen, we could put living space for us above. That would leave the five bedrooms in the old part of the house for guests."

Her enthusiasm was contagious, and I found myself brimming with new energy. "Yes! Oh, Georgia, that's perfect. Just imagine decorating that place—it could be so beautiful."

"I know!" Her eyes lit up. "Antique beds, a big old table in the dining room, vintage dishes and silver pieces…" Then she sighed. "But that takes money. And we haven't got it."

"What about selling your current house?" I asked.

Georgia shook her head. "We couldn't. It's been in the family too long. Plus it's mortgaged with the farm, which is owned equally by Pete, Brad, and Jack. Any money we got for it would technically have to be split between the three of them."

"Would Jack move into it if you left?" I wondered where he was working this morning and if he was thinking about last night as much as I was. "Maybe he'd buy you out."

"I don't think so. He doesn't have the cash, and he loves that damn cabin."

"You'd think he might want to leave, though, given the chance. Aren't the memories kind of painful there?" As soon as I said it, I realized that it wouldn't matter—staying in that cabin was one of the ways he prevented himself from letting go of his past.

"Yeah." She sighed as we reached the path leading to their front porch. The others had gone inside already. "He baffles me sometimes, you know? The way he refuses to move on? He chooses to be unhappy, and I don't know why."

I dropped my eyes to the ground. I knew why, but Jack trusted me with his feelings. I couldn't betray him.

"I mean, Steph's clothes are still in the closet."

I gasped and met her eyes again. That was a detail he hadn't mentioned. "Wow."

She shook her head. "I've offered to get rid of them so many times, but he won't let anyone touch them."

"God, it's so sad." My hand covered my heart. "How can he live like that?"

"He says that's how he wants it. And whenever any of us try to help, he lashes out."

"He does do that," I agreed, remembering how he'd snapped at me yesterday at the market. "But it's hard not to try, because once you get to know him, you see how sad he is. And you want to help."

Georgia looked at me for a moment. "I will say this. He's been different since you've been here. Better."

"Me?"

She rolled her eyes. "Yes. You guys were like two googly-eyed teenagers when you got back last night. Let's not pretend there's nothing there."

"What could be there?" I tried for innocent, but it came out more coy than anything.

Georgia laughed. "I don't know exactly what it is you're

doing, but he's never called *my* smile magic. I haven't seen him that way in years. It's a shame you live so far away."

"Yeah." Frowning, I played with the braid trailing over one shoulder. "But I don't know if it would make a difference anyway. I mean, does he ever date?"

"Never," she admitted.

"And he told me the other night he'll never get married again. Doesn't want a family."

"Yeah, that's what he says to us too, any time we suggest he try getting out there again. It's sad, because he'd make such a great father. And he's still young."

Exhaling, I dropped my hands to my sides. Tried to cover up my disappointment with a lie. "Oh, well. I don't think I'm his type anyway, and he's not really mine."

"Oh, I don't know," she said airily. "I think you two could be good together. And sometimes opposites attract, right? Maybe you can change his mind."

I smiled. Opposites attracted, sure, but attraction wasn't our problem. We had *all* kinds of that. Our problem was that the attraction was getting stronger. It was bringing us closer. It was making me feel things with my heart and not just with my body.

But he wasn't interested in my heart.

Georgia and I chatted a little more about the branding and social media strategies I'd outlined for them, and I was happy to hear they'd contacted a web designer and had filled out her project questionnaire. Again she asked me to please send her a bill for my time, but I politely refused. "You're going to need every extra dollar to buy that house," I told her. "Consider it my donation."

She hugged me and went inside to discuss things with Pete and Brad. Presumably Jack would be in on the discussion eventually, but he hadn't come to see the house. I hoped he'd be reasonable on the subject of buying it.

I also hoped I'd see him today. We hadn't made any plans, but he had put my number in his phone before leaving last night. Maybe he'd call.

In the meantime, I didn't want to sit around doing nothing, since that would just mean more time spent fretting over him. Instead, I researched some of my ideas for their market stand and displays, then drove to the nearest craft store for materials. I hit the grocery store too, buying fresh items for the next few days. When I saw the potatoes, I wondered again about baking them twice and made a mental note to look that up. Maybe I could take a cooking class or something—that would be getting out of my comfort zone for sure.

Learn to cook. Start riding again. I started a mental list of things I could do to change up my life, be happier and more fulfilled. *Stop obsessing over my thirtieth birthday. Get involved with the food justice movement.*

After a peanut butter and jelly sandwich lunch, I spent the early part of the afternoon working on the display projects and mulling over possible solutions for Pete and Georgia's cash flow problem. A small business loan maybe? But I knew next to nothing about the loan process since I'd never needed to take one out.

I was printing a price list on a chalkboard when my cell phone buzzed with a text. **Hey you. It's Jack. Want to meet Cooper and me at the park?**

I picked up the phone, grinning at it like a goofball. **Sure. What time?**

Twenty minutes?

That was perfect—I'd have time to finish what I was doing first. **See you then!**

I set the phone down and hummed a tune as I completed the list, then held it out to make sure the writing was even and legible. When I was satisfied, I quickly put everything away, used the bathroom, brushed my teeth, and touched up my makeup. At the last minute, I decided to wipe off the lipstick I'd applied and put on some honey lip balm instead. It looked more natural and tasted better.

As I walked to the park, my feet felt a hundred times lighter than they had this morning. Nothing had changed since then, but just the prospect of seeing him was enough to excite me. And when he came into view, standing behind Cooper, pushing him on a swing, the butterflies in my stomach multiplied. *This feeling*, I thought as I crossed the playground toward him. *I don't want to lose it.*

He looked up as I approached and the smile he gave me turned my legs to jelly. "Hi."

"Hi."

He glanced over his shoulder. "Didn't you come from the cottage?"

I cringed. "Yes, but I walked one block too far, so I came from the other side. I wasn't paying attention."

He laughed, shaking his head. "It's like three blocks away. Only you could screw that up."

"I know, I know." I'd let him tease me as much as he wanted as long as I could stand there watching him push his nephew on that swing. His fitted black t-shirt showed off his arms and chest, the tight jeans hugged him in all the right places, and his aviator sunglasses worn without the usual hat made him look a little more polished, a little more military. It did things to me. In the panties.

"Did you hear about the house?" I asked.

He harrumphed and mumbled.

"I take it that's a yes."

"I heard about it. They've got some crazy idea about running a motel there?"

I rolled my eyes. "Oh, Jesus. It's not a motel, Jack, it's a bed and breakfast."

"Whatever. I won't stand in their way, but there's no way they'll come up with the money they need."

"That's what Georgia said. Could they get a small business loan or something?"

"I guess they can try." He didn't sound too hopeful.

"I wish there was a way I could help," I said wistfully. How terrible to have your dream within reach and not be able to afford it. I'd been so spoiled my entire life. Not that I'd spent frivolously or irresponsibly, I hadn't—but I also didn't know what it was like to go without something I really wanted because I couldn't afford it.

"That's nice of you, but they'll figure it out. *We'll* figure it out."

"So you have Cooper tonight?" I ruffled the little boy's hair as he swung near me.

"Yeah. Pete and Georgia are both working."

"What will you do with him?"

"Feed him ice cream for dinner, buy him a bunch of candy, let him watch a bunch of TV until he falls asleep." He smiled at me. "The usual uncle stuff."

"Sounds like fun."

"Want to join us?"

My heart stuttered. "Sure. I'd love to."

We spent another hour at the park, and I was amazed at how good Jack was with Cooper. He went down the slide with him, spun him on the merry-go-round, helped him climb up the old-fashioned jungle gym. When Cooper fell and scraped his knee, Jack brushed him off, dried his tears, and hugged him close. When it was time to leave and Cooper insisted on one more time down the slide, Jack raced him to it. When we walked to the ice cream parlor, Jack swung the little boy up onto his shoulders and held his tiny hands the whole way there.

Later, I watched him make dinner for Cooper and spoon-feed him every bite. I watched him give his nephew a bath—we'd exchanged a fun look as he started to fill the tub—careful not to get any water in his eyes when he rinsed the shampoo from Cooper's hair. I watched him put a diaper and clean pajamas on the tired toddler, brush his baby curls off his forehead in an adorable imitation of his own hair. "There," he said. "Just like your Uncle Jack."

All I could think was, *This man should be a father.*

When it was time to turn off the light and put him in bed, I said I'd wait downstairs, said goodnight to Cooper, and headed down to the kitchen.

As soon as I entered the room, I heard Cooper fussing for "Mama" and then Jack's voice on the monitor. "OK, Buddy, time to settle down. Let's get Bunny." Smiling, I stood in front of the little screen and watched Jack grab something from the crib and cradle the weepy Cooper against his chest.

"You want to rock a little bit? OK, OK." He disappeared from view. A few seconds later, the fussing stopped. And the singing began.

It was soft at first, and I leaned toward the monitor to hear it better. At first, I didn't recognize the song—something about a whippoorwill—but after another line or two, I clapped a hand over my mouth, my heart pounding. It was the Hank Williams song that we'd heard in the truck yesterday on the way to the market. He'd sung along then, too. He had a nice voice—deep and melodic with just the right amount of grit.

Goosebumps blanketed my arms. I put a hand over my heart, surprised my chest was still flesh and bone since I felt as if I were melting. I'd never heard anything so sweet.

A lump formed in my throat.

Give me a chance to make you happy, Jack.

Let me try.

CHAPTER TWENTY-EIGHT
JACK

I rose to my feet, careful not to jostle my sleeping nephew. Cursing the wood floor that creaked beneath my feet, I tried to avoid the spots I knew made noise as I made my way to the crib. After laying him down on his back, I kissed my fingertips, touched his forehead and quietly slipped out of the room.

I found Margot sitting on a kitchen chair, one hand over her heart. When she saw me, she clapped the other one over it. Looked as if she were about to burst into tears.

"Fuck. I forgot to turn off the monitor, didn't I?"

"I can't talk, I'm a puddle."

Groaning, I went to the fridge and grabbed a beer. All I wanted to do was get my hands on her (and various other body parts) but it didn't feel right in Pete and Georgia's house, so I needed to find something to occupy them.

"Don't worry, don't worry. Your secret sweetness is still safe with me."

I eyeballed her as I uncapped the bottle and took a drink. "It better be. Want a beer?"

"No, thanks."

"Glass of wine?"

She hesitated. "I hate to drink Pete and Georgia's wine."

"Why? They got free babysitters tonight." I pulled a bottle down from the rack above the fridge and showed it to her. "This OK?"

"Looks great. Thank you."

I uncorked the bottle and poured her a glass. "You hungry? I was going to order pizza."

"Pizza sounds perfect." She smiled, and it was perfect. Her hair in that long blond braid was perfect. The way she held her wineglass was perfect. The way she'd kissed my shoulder last night and told me I was the bravest person she knew was perfect. Pizza was fucking dough and sauce and cheese. It didn't even taste as good as she did.

I'd lain awake the entire night thinking about her. About us. I thought I'd feel good that I hadn't given into the urge to stay with her again, that I'd been strong enough to resist that temptation, but instead I just felt miserable. Restless. Lonely. In the past I'd found a kind of solace in those feelings, but not last night.

Last night, I'd just missed her.

I thought about the days we'd spent together, the way she made me laugh, the way she listened to me. I wondered when I'd see her again, what she'd be wearing, what we'd do. There were places I wanted to take her, things I wanted to show her, songs I wanted her to hear, foods I wanted her to taste. There were curves on her body I wanted to kiss, filthy words I wanted to whisper to her, things I wanted to do to her. But I wanted to listen to her, too. Wanted to know about her dreams, her hopes, her memories. And I didn't have a lot of time—a week, that was it.

I made up my mind not to waste any more of it.

Because when she left, that would be it. I'd sleep alone again every single night for the rest of my life. I'd suffer for my sins. The loneliness would be all the worse for having had these days and nights with her, so in a way, *she* would become part of my punishment.

A friend in the Army once lent me a copy of *The Prophet* by Khalil Gibran, and it resonated with me so much, I'd bought my own copy when I came home. I thought about this one particular line a lot: *The deeper that sorrow carves into your being, the more joy you can contain.* At the time, it had brought me hope.

Later, I realized the reverse was also true: The greater your joy in something, the deeper your sorrow will be when it's gone.

And loss, I'd learned, was inescapable.

After we ate, I dug out a deck of cards and taught Margot to play gin rummy. In contrast to her egg-gathering efforts, she was a quick learner at cards and improved fast. A few times my mind waded into deeper waters, imagining how nice it would be to have her around during the winter, when nights were long and cold and there wasn't much to do but light a fire and play cards or curl up on the couch and watch a movie. I'd had to scold myself.

Don't. She's leaving next week, and it's for the best.

If Pete and Georgia were surprised to find her there with

me when they got home, they didn't say it. We chatted with them for a few minutes, then said goodnight and exited out the back door.

"Come here." I pulled her into the shadows behind the house, away from any windows, and crushed my mouth to hers. Her arms came around my neck, and I lifted her right off her feet. Her lips on mine felt like rain after a drought.

"Wow, you been saving that up?" she asked once I let her catch her breath.

I set her down. "Yes. I was afraid if I started in there, I wouldn't be able to stop."

"Mmm. Don't stop," she whispered, rising up on her toes and kissing my neck. Her tongue on my skin sent bolts of lust straight to my cock, which twitched uncontrollably. It was as if my body knew the clock was already counting down the hours we had together. She moved one hand to my crotch, rubbing the bulge through my jeans while she sucked my earlobe, licked her way down my throat, sank her teeth into my shoulder.

"Oh, fuck." I grabbed her arm and took off across the moonlit yard. I barely even thought about where I was going, I just knew I had to get her somewhere alone before I came in my pants like a teenager.

We ran through the trees to the cabin, pounded up the porch steps. It wasn't until I opened the front door and pulled her through it into the darkened front room that it struck me I'd brought her to a place full of memories. I froze, my fingers still clasped around her wrist. Could I do this?

"Hey." She spoke softly. "It's OK."

I turned to her, my chest a battleground. "Fuck," I whispered.

She put a hand on my jaw. "It's OK. I understand."

"Margot, I'm sorry."

"Don't be. I know this is hard."

Exhaling loudly, I circled both her wrists and tipped my forehead to hers. "It shouldn't be this hard. I want you so badly."

"I want you too." Her voice was strained.

The dark was so thick I couldn't see anything in the room. But I heard her breathing, sensed the rise and fall of her chest. Felt her skin, warm beneath my palms. Smelled her hair, the scent evoking memories of last night. And then my mouth was on her throat, because I had to taste her.

"Jack," she whispered. "We don't have to—"

"I don't want to be alone tonight," I heard myself saying. "I'm so fucking tired of being alone."

"You don't have to be." She slid her fingers into my hair, covered my face with kisses. "I won't leave you."

Her words stayed with me as we hurriedly removed clothing and tumbled to our knees. *I won't leave you.* As I laid her down gently on the rug and stretched out above her. *I won't leave you.* As I moved my hands and lips and tongue over her breasts, her ribs, her stomach. *I won't leave you.* As I buried myself inside her, rhythmic and deep, her arms around my neck, her lips a whisper away.

I won't leave you.

God, what would that be like? What would it feel like to

let go of the guilt, let go of the pain, let go of the fear? To look forward, and not back? What would it feel like to be happy again? To believe that I deserved it? To think that it could last?

I fought back against the crazy seed of hope taking root inside me, but its hold was already frighteningly deep and strong.

Something that had long been closed off inside me was opening up, and I felt a rush as it was filled with her presence, her trust, her understanding. The idea that she could feel something for me. The hope that all would be forgiven. The promise of a new life. A new beginning. A new love.

No. This is not about love. It's not absolution or even acquittal. It's a temporary stay, a bandaid on a wound. Soon it'll be ripped off, and you'll bleed again. Oh, God...

I felt like two halves of me were splitting apart—one wanted so badly to be granted that second chance at loving someone and allowing myself to be loved, while the other demanded I serve out my life sentence alone in the prison I'd built for myself.

Desperate to regain control, I focused on the heat and friction between us, on the sound of her voice saying my name, on the sting of her nails raking down my back. I concentrated on making her come, grinding against her the way she liked, whispering dirty words in her ear. I was rough with her, like I had been before.

But it was different this time—how could it not be? I'd told her everything. I was vulnerable to her in a way I'd never been to anyone. Everything was bare to her now, all my secrets, all my suffering, all my scars.

And she still wanted me.

I felt myself falling.

Frantically, I fought off my orgasm, panicked that coming together would only strengthen our sexual chemistry and bring us closer. But she held me so tightly, like she'd never let me go, and she took me so deep, and her cries were so helpless and my cock was so hard and I couldn't hold back, couldn't hang on, couldn't stop myself from crashing through the gates and careening over the edge with her, my willpower no match for my feelings.

Don't leave me, I thought with every thrust and throb inside her trembling body, every pounding beat of my heart. *Don't let me go. I need you to feel alive.*

As our bodies stilled and our breathing slowed, I opened my eyes—and realized what I'd done.

I'd let her in. I'd let her get close. I'd let myself feel again.

Worse, I'd brought another woman into sacred space. I'd broken a promise. I'd dishonored a vow.

I had no right. No right.

The hope I'd felt moments ago was crushed by the weight of shame.

I forced myself to stop justifying my behavior and admit the truth.

This had to end. Tonight.

I didn't say anything as we put ourselves back together. My chest felt like a cannonball had lodged within it, and my throat was tight.

"Can I use your bathroom?" Margot asked timidly.

"Of course." Already my voice was stiff.

While she was in the bathroom, I sat on the couch in the dark, hating myself for letting it come to this. *I never should have kissed her. Never should have touched her. Never should have asked her to stay.*

Now I had to get her to leave, and I only knew one way to do it and make sure she left for good—put up walls around my heart and be a complete and utter asshole. Blow her off. Hurt her. *Make her hate me like I hate myself.*

She came out of the bathroom, leaving the light on, and sat next to me on the couch, but not touching me. "You OK?"

Fuck, Margot. Don't be sweet to me now. "Yeah."

"That was kind of…intense."

I shrugged. My stomach churned.

"You didn't think so?" She looked at me, probably trying to read my expression.

"Not really."

Her body deflated. "Oh. Well…maybe it was just me then."

"Maybe." I couldn't bear to look her in the eye, so I stared at her knees, which were pressed together tightly, her hands clasped around them. Someday, some rich bastard with a trust fund and a Porsche would put a big fat diamond on her finger. She'd have the huge, fancy wedding of her dreams, followed by a luxury honeymoon. After that, he'd buy her a mansion, which they'd fill with beautiful children who went to private schools and called her Mummy. She'd have everything she wanted. *She'll be where she belongs, and she'll be happy.*

I looked down at my wedding band. *And I'll be here.*

"Jack, what's wrong? Something is off, I can tell."

"Nothing." I stood up. "I'll take you home."

I grabbed my keys from the shelf and went out the front door, so she didn't have much choice but to follow me. I pulled it shut behind her and started down the porch steps, but she grabbed my arm.

"Hey. Wait a minute."

I steeled myself and looked at her. "What?"

"Are you mad at me?"

"No." *I'm mad at me.*

"Are you mad that we…did what we did in there?" She dropped her hand. "Because we didn't have to do it. I told you I understood."

"It's not that."

"Well, it's something." She stuck her hands on her hips. "I know you're moody, but this is like a complete one-eighty. An hour ago you couldn't keep your hands off me, and now you're freezing me out. Tell me what I did."

"You didn't do anything," I snapped.

"Then tell me what you're thinking. Tell me what went wrong. Tell me something, Jack!" Her voice broke. "You can't just shut down on me."

"Yes, I fucking can!" I yelled, furious with myself for letting my guard down and with her for penetrating my defenses. "This is me, Margot. This is who I am. And it's why we never should have gotten involved in the first place."

Her body seemed to wilt. If I could have seen her eyes, I knew they'd be shiny with tears. "This isn't you. I know you."

I put up another wall. "You think because we fucked a few times that you know me? You don't. It was just sex."

She shook her head again, like she couldn't believe what she was hearing. "Why are you doing this?"

"Because it's time, OK?" My hands were shaking. "We both knew this thing couldn't go on, so we might as well end it now."

"Why couldn't it go on? I don't live that far away, and…" She took a breath. I had the feeling I wouldn't want to hear what she said next, and I was right. "I feel something for you, Jack. I don't want it to end."

I had to be ruthless. Rip off the bandage. "Well, I do."

She started to cry. "Don't you feel anything for me? Have the past few days meant nothing to you?"

I shrugged, and she cradled her stomach as if I'd struck her. She believed the lies so readily. Fucking hell, this was torture.

"God," she wept, rushing past me down the steps. "I was so wrong about you."

Cursing myself, I followed her through the trees, past the spot where we'd first combusted, and into Pete and Georgia's yard. I saw her glance at the spot where I'd kissed her so passionately just a couple hours ago, and wanted to put my fist through a wall. *Godammit, you weren't wrong about me. But I can't handle my feelings for you. I have no place to put them, they don't fit inside me, don't fit inside the life I have to live. I have no choice, Margot! Can't you see?*

She didn't even try to walk home—she knew me too well, another punch in the gut—but marched right to the driveway and got into my truck, slamming the door so hard I thought it might fall off.

Moving slowly, as if the air around me was mud, I got behind the wheel and started the engine. She sat as far away from me as she could, arms crossed, legs together, jaw set. How insane that an hour ago, I'd been inside her, and she'd welcomed me in. I'd never feel that again.

My walls started to crumble.

"Margot, look. I—"

"Don't. Don't say my name, don't talk to me, don't even fucking look at me."

Exhaling, I put the tuck in reverse and backed out of the driveway. I should have been relieved that she wasn't crying anymore, that she wasn't going to make this any harder for me, that she was going to go back to her pretty world and forget I ever existed.

It was exactly what I wanted, wasn't it?

CHAPTER TWENTY-NINE
MARGOT

The ride back to the cottage was agony. I couldn't believe the way he'd turned on me. My head was spinning!

It was just sex.

It was?

But he'd waited three years. He'd come after *me*. He'd asked me to stay. He'd confided in me. He'd shared deeply personal feelings. It wasn't just sex! So what the hell was this sudden withdrawal? I racked my brain, trying to piece it together.

Had he just pretended to be a good guy? Was this asshole next to me the real Jack Valentini? Had the entire week been one big charade just to get in my pants? I found that hard to believe, but I was reeling. A couple hours ago, we'd been laughing and kissing and talking.

What had gone wrong? Were all men just manipulative bastards? I couldn't accept that Jack was like Tripp.

Maybe having sex in the cabin had been too overwhelming. Maybe it felt like cheating for him. Maybe he felt guilty for enjoying it so much. Despite what he'd said, there *had* been something different about it tonight. Something intense and real and big. Something *good.* I'd felt it, and he must have, too.

I stole a glance at him and caught the usual stubborn body language and expression out of the corner of my eye. But there was something else…his right hand was nervously tapping on his thigh. I'd never seen that before. Something had him wound up. Something was making him nervous—scared, even.

That's it.

It hit me all at once. His biggest fear—letting go of his past.

Maybe he started to let go. And it terrified him.

A little sadness tempered my anger. Why did he torture himself this way? Why wouldn't he forgive himself and move on? Why wouldn't he let me help? Why was he so fucking *loyal* to his pain? And after everything he'd told me, did he think I couldn't see what he was doing?

I wanted to shake him. Hug him. Scream at him. Plead with him. Hurl accusations at him until he admitted the truth—he felt something for me.

But what good would it do? He'd never admit it. In fact, pushing him like that would only make him retreat further. It was hopeless. Until he made a conscious decision to move on, there was nothing I could do. And if the last few days hadn't been enough to convince him, I had to face the fact that maybe it wasn't going to happen. Blinking away fresh tears as he pulled up at the cottage, I had my hand on the door handle before the truck even stopped moving.

"Margot."

I froze. Refused to look at him.

"I just…want you to know. I've…" He struggled for words. "I've had a good time with you."

"Oh my God." Now I glared at him. His words felt like a slap in the face. "Really? That's what you have to say to me right now?"

He jerked his chin at me. "What do you want me to say?"

"I want you to admit the truth, Jack!" I yelled, cursing these damn tears that wouldn't quit. When had I become so emotional? "You feel something for me, and you're scared of it."

"Don't tell me what I feel," he said angrily, fidgeting in his seat. "You have no idea what it's like to be me."

"You're right, I don't. But I know you're *choosing* to be that way. Closed off. Miserable. Lonely." I wiped my nose with the back of my wrist and softened my voice. "It doesn't have to be that way, Jack. We could be good together if you'd let yourself move on."

He started to say something, then stopped. His right hand clenched into a fist. "The night I asked you to stay, you said you didn't need promises."

"I didn't! And I don't—I'm not asking for a promise, Jack. I'm asking for a *chance*. That's all. A chance." My heart beat frantically in my chest as he weighed my words against his misguided convictions. His lips trembled and slammed shut. His forehead creased. His fingers curled and flexed. I could see the struggle in him, the temptation to give in to me versus the strength of his guilty conscience. Which would prevail? Our eyes met, and for a second, I thought he'd choose me.

But he didn't. He looked away. "I've got no chance to give you."

Devastated, I got out of the truck and ran into the cottage, choking back tears. When the door was closed behind me, I locked it and ran to the bedroom, throwing myself onto the bed. Gathering his pillow in my arms, I sobbed into it for what felt like hours.

I cried for Jack, for the life he lived and the life he was wasting. I cried for myself, because I hadn't been enough to change his mind. I cried at the thought of going home and trying to forget we'd ever met, kissed, touched each other.

And I cried for what would never be, a chance that would never be taken.

CHAPTER THIRTY
MARGOT

I was up the entire night. Even after the tears ran dry, question after question nagged me. Was this my fault? Had I pushed too hard? Had I rushed things? Had I imagined something between us that wasn't there? Was I crazy to be this upset over someone I'd known for a week? Had the amazing sex clouded my judgment?

Then there were the maybe's. Maybe I'd romanticized the whole hot farmer thing. Maybe I was only attracted to him because he was the anti-Tripp. Maybe the affair was just one big rebellion against rules for Thurber women. Maybe I'd get home and realize he'd never have fit into my life, I'd never have fit into his, and thank God he'd broken things off when he had.

But there were what if's too.

What if I'd come here for a reason? What if he was the something missing from my life? What if I wasn't supposed to give up on him? What if he needed me to help him heal? What if I never met anyone who made me feel the way he did? What if we were supposed to be together?

The mental and emotional anguish was too much. I craved

the familiarity of home, the feeling that I belonged somewhere. At six the next morning, I packed my bags, left a message for the property manager and the key on the counter, and drove home.

On the two-hour drive, I chugged crummy gas station coffee and cringed repeatedly at the memory of his rejection. It was like reliving the breakup with Tripp all over again! What was the matter with me? Why didn't anyone want me? Was I fundamentally unloveable? Was the prospect of a future with me so terrible? Did I smell? I sniffed my armpits.

Since it seemed like my deodorant worked, it had to be something else, and by the time I got home, I was convinced of my general worthlessness and repugnance.

Dumping my bags at the door, I went straight to my room, traded my shorts and blouse for pajamas, and flopped into bed. But I'd had so much coffee on the drive that sleep was impossible. I lay there, getting more despondent by the minute, until I finally gave up and called Jaime.

"Howdy," she said when she answered. "How's life on the farm? You get your four orgasms already today?"

"Not even close. I'm not even at the farm anymore." I pictured the sun coming up over the lake, shining on the horses in the pasture, creating shadows behind the barn perfect for kissing in. Was Jack awake? Had he even slept? Was he doing chores and remembering when I'd helped him?

"What happened? You sound miserable."

"I am." I closed my eyes. "Maybe I shouldn't be, but I am."

"Want to talk about it?"

"Yes. Where's Claire? Can you have lunch?"

"Crap, I can't. And Claire's looking at houses this afternoon. How about drinks right after work? Around six?"

"Where?"

"Bar at Marais? You probably missed your fancypants martinis."

"Not really," I said glumly.

"Damn, you *are* depressed. I'll text Claire."

"OK. Hey, can you do me a favor?"

"Of course!"

"Can you call Georgia Valentini and tell her I had to come home suddenly but I'll be in touch tomorrow? I'll forward her contact information." I couldn't bear to talk to her.

"Consider it done. Now go get a massage or something. A mani-pedi. Or a blowout! Those always perk you up."

"I'll be fine. Maybe I'm just tired." It wasn't exactly a lie. "I'll take a nap and see you after work."

We hung up, and I messaged her Georgia's number before tossing my phone aside. I didn't want a massage or a manicure or a blowout. None of those things would make me feel better, and in fact it kind of made me feel shallow and vain that I was the sort of person who regularly enjoyed those luxuries. Why didn't I use my resources for more meaningful things? What was I even doing with my life? How was I contributing to the greater good? Millions of people lived in poverty and I did nothing to help them! No wonder no one loved me!

I curled into a ball, knees tucked under my chest, butt in the air. "I'm a terrible, useless person," I moaned into my pillow. "My life has no purpose."

Eventually I got hungry, so I went downstairs to find something to eat, but even the contents of my fridge depressed me—suspicious cheese, expired milk, a jar of pickles, rotting lemons, mysterious takeout containers—and the freezer contained only ice cubes, a bottle of gin, and some frozen meals for one that spoke of my sad single status and inability to cook. "This is my life," I said as clouds of cold air billowed out. "Gin, loneliness, and Lean Cuisine." Sorta sounded like a country song.

In the pantry I managed to find a box of crackers that had probably been left over from a cocktail party in 2014, and I ate them while sitting on the kitchen floor. They were stale and tasteless. I sniffed at the cheese and decided I wasn't that desperate, so I ate the entire jar of pickles instead. After that, I went back to bed and hid under the covers, where I eventually fell asleep.

I woke to the ring of my phone around five. *Georgia Valentini calling.* Chewing on my lower lip, I debated taking it. Could I fake cheerful well enough to fool her? Old Margot wouldn't have thought twice. Was she still inside me somewhere?

I did my best to summon her. "Hello?"

"Oh, Margot, hi. I thought I'd get your voicemail. Your business partner called a bit ago and said you had a family emergency. I hope everything is OK." Georgia sounded concerned, and I felt guilty about the lie.

"Yes, everything's fine. It turned out to be no big deal." *Just my own existential crisis.*

"Glad to hear it. I just wanted to tell you how grateful we

are that you took the time to come here and jumpstart our efforts at marketing more effectively. You did your research, came prepared, got to know us, and really delivered."

"Thanks."

"And you inspired us to get moving on our restaurant dream, too. Even if the Oliver place doesn't work out for us, we're motivated to keep pushing toward it."

"I'm glad to hear it. Any news on the house?"

"Nothing too encouraging," she said. "But we're getting some estimates on what it would take to renovate the place, and Brad's helping us come up with a plan to apply for a business loan."

"I'm keeping my fingers crossed for you."

"I appreciate that, thanks." She paused for a minute. "Margot, I hope it's not out of line to ask if you're OK? You sound different."

I sighed. "I'm OK. I mean, I'll *be* OK. I guess."

She laughed sympathetically. "That does not sound good."

"I just…got my hopes up about something I shouldn't have."

"I understand." A few seconds went by. "Margot, he's sad too."

"I doubt that."

"Why?" Georgia sounded genuinely surprised.

"Because he's the one who broke things off. He doesn't want me. Not enough, anyway."

She sighed exasperatedly. "He *does*, though. I can see it. He's just so damn stubborn."

"Anyway," I said, "it's done. And it's what he wanted."

"I'm sorry, Margot. I really wish things were different."

"Me too." I needed to hang up before I started bawling again. "Bye."

She said goodbye and we hung up. Flinging an arm over my eyes, I wondered how she knew Jack was sad. Was he moping over coffee this morning? Had he been short with her? Lashed out? The thought made me angry. How dare he take it out on other people! He did this to himself!

Grumpy and depressed, I wandered into the bathroom, and looked at myself in the mirror. Yeesh. My hair was matted and tangled, my face was puffy, and my eyes were red-rimmed with circles underneath. "You know what?" I said to my reflection. "This is the real me, and if people don't like it, they can fuck off." I snapped a pony tail holder around my hair, threw on some old jeans with my Vassar T-shirt, tugged on some socks, and shoved my feet into sneakers. I didn't feel like the old me, so why should I look like her?

The Mercedes was a bit of a problem with my new image, but I'd think about that tomorrow.

"Wow." Jaime blinked at me. "That's a different look for you."

I'd gotten to the bar first and was sitting on one of the velvet sofas along the wall. My friends had just slid in across from me. "I feel different," I snapped. "Why shouldn't I look it?"

"No reason," she said with false brightness and a glance at Claire. "Want to tell us what's going on?"

"What's going on is that I've come to the conclusion that my life is meaningless."

"Margot, what on earth?" Claire asked, brows furrowed. "Your life isn't meaningless. Why would you say such a thing?"

"Because it's true," I said, lifting my expensive gin martini to my lips. After struggling with it for a few minutes, I'd decided a life without purpose was no excuse to drink cheap booze. "I don't contribute to society in any meaningful way. The world is full of terrible things like poverty and hunger and disease and abuse, and I don't do anything about it. I will live and die, and humanity will not be any better off."

"Wow," Jaime said again as the waitress approached. "Hold on, I'm going to need a drink for this." She and Claire gave their orders and sat back again. "OK. What happened?"

I didn't even know where to start.

"Is this about the farmer?" Claire's expression was quizzical. "Jaime told me about him, but last I heard, things were going well."

"They were." I took another drink. "But then he must have realized I'm a spoiled rotten city girl who doesn't care about anyone but herself."

"Oh, Jesus." Jaime rolled her eyes and sat forward. "Do I need to remind you of the work you do *for free* while I am trying to keep the lights on at our office? You're the most generous person I know, Margot!"

Claire nodded in agreement. "You're constantly attending charity lunches and volunteering at things. I don't know how you find the time!"

"OK, so your family has bags of money," Jaime allowed, "but there's a reason the hospital has a Lewiston wing and the art museum has a Thurber gallery. It's because they give so much."

"And remember last year when I mentioned the fundraiser at my school for that family who lost everything in a fire?" Claire said. "You were the first in line to write a check, and I happen to know it was the biggest one."

"But it's all so impersonal," I complained. "I don't feel like I'm really doing anything worthwhile except writing checks. And I've led this completely sheltered life. I don't know how to mow a lawn, change a tire, or grill a burger!"

"What the hell difference does that that have to do with anything? You're a good person, Margot." Jaime reached across the table and touched my wrist. "You're loving and smart and funny and successful and beautiful."

I arched one brow at her.

"Well, yes, you're looking a little ragged at the edges right now," she conceded, "but any other day, you're what every woman aspires to be."

"Then why didn't he want me?" I closed my eyes and felt tears on my lashes. "Why doesn't anyone want me?"

"I hope you're not talking about Tripp," Jaime said. "You wasted enough time on him. And as for Jack, I don't know, honey." Her voice got softer. "Maybe he just wasn't ready to want you. Maybe he's not over his wife yet."

"I guess that could be it. But I don't get that feeling." I chewed my lip for a moment. "He talked about loving her, and I have no doubt that losing her broke his heart. But he never said anything like 'I'll never get over her.' Although," I went on, the corners of my mouth turning down, "he did say he'd never get married again."

"Why not?" Claire asked.

I sighed. "He said he knew what he had, and it doesn't happen twice."

"Maybe he's crazy." Claire reached out and patted my arm. "Because I cannot imagine why any man wouldn't jump at the chance to be with you."

"Well, he didn't." Sighing, I lifted my glass to my lips again. "And it's got me messed up in the head. I really felt something for him, you guys."

"So soon?" Jaime asked as the server set their drinks on the table between us.

"Yes. At first I thought it was just a really intense physical thing, but…" I shivered, remembering the night he'd bared his troubled soul. "It was emotional, too. And it felt good, at least to me."

"So why did he break it off?" Claire wondered.

"Honestly, he didn't really give me a reason. We had a great day yesterday, and then…" I lowered my voice. "Last night we had sex on the living room floor of his house, where he'd lived with his wife, and it was really intense. Right after that, he suddenly ended things. Said we never should have gotten involved in the first place."

"Aha. You scared him." Jaime sounded confident as she sat back. "That's what I used to do, before Quinn. As long as it was just sex with a guy, I was fine, but if there was any chance of an emotional attachment, I was out of there."

"You even tried to do it with Quinn," Claire reminded us.

Jaime nodded. "Totally. And I didn't have the baggage

Jack has. Maybe he just needs some time and distance. Gain a little perspective. That's what I needed."

"Maybe," I said. "But we exchanged some pretty harsh words last night. And I flat out asked him to give me a chance, and he said no."

"Well, don't give up. He might surprise you." Jaime sipped her drink. "And if he doesn't, it's his fucking loss, because you're amazing."

"And strong." Claire patted my arm again. "You're one of the strongest women I know."

"I'm not," I said, feeling like a fraud. "I've spent my entire life just doing what I'm told Thurber women do, playing the role of dutiful daughter and society debutante. I can't think of one decision I made for myself that I'm proud of or one risk I took."

"I can," Jaime said loyally. "You quit your job and came to work with me. That was a risk."

"Not really." I wasn't going to let them talk me into liking myself. "I was never going to be poor."

"When Tripp said he didn't want to get married last year, you broke things off. *And* you said no to him when he proposed, even though part of you wanted to say yes," Claire added. "That was not easy."

"I didn't want to marry that jerk," I said. "I just liked the ring, which makes me shallow."

"Well, you should be proud as hell that you threw those scones. *I'm* proud of you." Jaime shook her head. "God, I wish I'd been there."

I allowed a tiny smile to work its way onto my lips. "I

guess I'm proud of that."

"See? And you can still make changes to your life. You don't have to play any role you don't want to," she went on. "If you don't want to work at Shine anymore, tell me. We can figure things out."

"No, I do. I like the work. I like helping people grow their dreams." I sighed, swirling the last sips of gin in my glass. "It's not that I don't like my life. I love my family, my friends, my work. And I'd be lying if I said being Margot Thurber Lewiston is really that tough. It's not. I mean, what do I actually lack? It's selfish to want more than I have, isn't it?"

"Margot, it's OK to want to share your life with someone," Claire said. "No one thinks you're selfish just because you want someone to love, and someone to love you back."

The lump was back in my throat. "I do want that. And crazy as it sounds, I had this gut feeling Jack could have been that someone. I'm just so frustrated and sad he doesn't see it."

My friends looked at me sympathetically. "I wish I had more advice," Jaime said. "But love is strange. When you're looking for it, it knows just where to hide. When you're not, it jumps out and clobbers you on the head."

"Don't I know it," said Claire, tipping back her drink. "Maybe that's what we're doing wrong, Gogo. We're looking."

I shook my head. "I'm sorry, you guys. I'm being a complete downer and I'm totally monopolizing the conversation. I had a disappointment, but I'll survive." A shaky smile made its way to my lips. "I actually started making this list of things I want to do while I was up there."

"Like a bucket list?" Jaime ate one of the olives from the

stick in her martini.

"No, more like Margot Thurber Lewiston's To-Do List for Having a Funner, More Fulfilling Life."

Claire grinned. "What's on it?"

"Stop fearing 30. Ride horses. Learn to Cook. Get involved with the food justice movement. Get a tattoo." It came out of nowhere, but as soon as I said it, I realized it was true.

"Wow," Jaime said for the third time today. "It's like a whole new Margot. What happened to you up there?"

"It wasn't just up there," I said. "I mean, it was definitely an intense week, but looking back over the last year or so, maybe even longer, I think this awakening has been a long time coming."

Jaime nodded and held up her drink. "To Funner and More Fulfilling Lives."

Claire and I lifted our glasses to hers and clinked. I felt better, and grateful for my friends, but a little piece of my heart still ached for Jack.

Maybe it always would.

CHAPTER THIRTY-ONE
JACK

The morning after I broke things off with Margot dawned sunny and warm. It aggravated me, since I wanted the weather to match my glowering mood. I did the morning chores sluggishly, my bones weary, my muscles lax. No pride in my work. No feeling of contentment or accomplishment. No hope that I might find something about today to enjoy.

Just emptiness.

I'd spent the entire night hating myself for what I'd done. But I'd had no choice—I'd known all along I couldn't have her. It didn't matter that she was willing to give me a chance…I couldn't take it. And she deserved someone whole, someone perfect, someone like her. She shouldn't waste that chance on me. I was too broken, too flawed.

But God, I could have loved her. Easily. Deeply.

If I were someone else, if my life had gone differently, if I'd met her sooner. What would that alternate life look like? Would we be married? Would we have children? For a moment I let myself picture them, a little boy with curls like Cooper, a little girl with blond hair and blue eyes.

I swallowed hard, imagining tucking them in at night, reading them a story, giving in to their pleas for one more song, one more kiss, one more hug. Then I'd share the rest of my night with Margot, share my thoughts, share my body, share my soul.

I could have taken care of her in all the ways she needed. We were different, but maybe our differences would have complemented each other. We could have fit together like two jigsaw pieces. She had book smarts and business savvy; I had physical strength and common sense. She had a gift with people; I had a gift with nature. I knew how to grow; she knew how to sell. She was smooth where I was rough, articulate where I was tongue-tied, social where I was aloof.

I could have loved her.

Sheltered her. Cherished her. I could have done the things for her she didn't know how to do, taught her things she didn't know, shown her things she'd never seen. And she could have been my link to the outside world, offering me refuge when I needed it. She could have taught me things too —she knew about art and literature and history. Things I'd never paid attention to, but didn't want to leave the world without learning.

I could have loved her.

I could have let her love me. I could have been a father. I could have been happy.

Instead, I was alone. But at least it had been my choice.

I didn't want to go to Pete and Georgia's that morning since they'd likely ask about Margot, but I'd run out of coffee, and

I needed the caffeine badly enough to risk it. From the moment I walked in, I made it clear I wasn't in the mood for talking.

"Morning, Jack," Georgia called as I entered the kitchen. She was feeding Cooper at the table.

With barely a harrumph in greeting, I crossed the room to the coffee pot and poured a cup. Even this damn kitchen reminded me of Margot. I could still see her sitting at the counter last night with her wine, eating at the table, laughing over cards. *Maybe this would have been our house.*

"What's going on today?" she asked.

"Nothing." *She'd be feeding our baby at the kitchen table.*

"Have you and Margot gone riding yet?"

"No." *We'd go riding together all the time.*

"Might be a nice day for it."

"I don't have time," I snapped. But she was right—it would have been a nice day for it. *I was going to take her camping tonight.*

She glanced back at me, her brows arched. "OK. Just a thought."

I swallowed mouthfuls of coffee, letting it scald my throat, glad for the pain. I wondered if Margot was still sleeping, if she'd go home today or stick around. Hopefully, she'd leave...I didn't think I could stay away if I knew she was here, and I had to. I had to.

"Do you and Margot want to do the market tomorrow? She seemed to really enjoy it the other day."

"No."

Georgia looked at me again, a little longer this time. “Everything OK?”

“Fine,” I said. But I wasn’t fine.

I couldn’t stop thinking about her. No matter where I went on the farm, something reminded me of her—the chicken coop, the barn, the pasture. The woods, the lake, the cabin. I went to the hardware store, and I swear to Christ, the cab of my truck even *smelled* like her. On a whim, I drove by the cottage, telling myself I wouldn’t knock on her door, I’d just see if her car was there.

It wasn’t, but a minivan was, and as I idled past, a woman came out of the front door carrying what looked like a bucket of cleaning supplies. *She’s gone.*

I was angry at myself for being disappointed. Annoyed at the way my chest caved. Alarmed at the ache in my heart.

What the hell? This was better, wasn’t it? I didn’t want her hanging around, tempting me at every opportunity. I wanted her out of town, out of reach, out of my life.

Later I took Cooper to the park, hoping that would boost my mood, but even that reminded me of Margot. Christ, would she never get out of my head? I’d done the right thing! When would I be rewarded with a little peace of mind?

That night I was so exhausted I fell asleep early, but I woke at two in the morning from a nightmare, yelling and shaking, the sheets soaked with sweat. I sat up, my heart beating furiously, my chest tight. Frantically, I looked around the room for danger, but it wasn’t there.

When my heart rate slowed, I swung my legs over the

side of the bed, and sat still for a moment to catch my breath, cursing my fucking subconscious for its unrelenting assault.

Minutes later, I stripped the bedding and tugged new sheets over the mattress. I thought about Margot's hands clutching at them. Leaving them twisted and shoved aside. Holding her beneath them. I got back into bed and lay awake, blinking at the ceiling. I wondered if I'd ever see her again. I wondered if I'd ever be able to forget her. I wondered if she missed me as much as I missed her.

I wondered if I'd ever stop asking myself *what if*?

A few miserable days later, I broke down and called her.

It was after midnight, which made me an even bigger asshole, but I couldn't go another minute without at least hearing her voice. I'd gotten into the habit of pulling up her picture on the Shine PR website, and the image was driving me crazy—I wanted those blue eyes looking at me. I wanted that smile to be flashed in my direction. I wanted that long blond hair slipping through my fingers. I wanted her light, her laughter, her lips on mine.

More than that, I wanted the feeling she gave me—that heart-pounding, gut-clenching, blood-rushing feeling that made me feel alive and vital and virile. I wanted to feel *wanted* again. I craved it.

But that was impossible, wasn't it? She'd never agree to see me. Not unless I apologized and admitted I'd made a mistake, and there was no way I could. It didn't matter that I wished things were different—they weren't. This wasn't a fairy tale. This beast wasn't going to turn into a prince, and she deserved a prince.

But I was starving for her. I needed a taste.

I paced next to my bed as I listened to the ring. *Please, please answer, Margot*, I begged silently. Voicemail would be OK, because at least I'd still get to hear her, but a conversation would be better. I wanted to feel close to her again.

She didn't pick up right away, and my hopes started to dwindle. *Why should she answer your call, asshole?* But then it stopping ringing, and I heard her breathing. Goosebumps blanketed my arms and legs.

"Hi," I said quietly.

"Hello."

"I wasn't sure you'd answer."

"I almost didn't." Her voice was hushed, and I wondered if she'd been asleep. My blood ran warmer as I thought of her under the covers.

"Did I wake you?"

"No."

"Good. I'm…" Shit. Now that I had her on the line, I couldn't think of anything to say. "I'm sorry to call so late."

"It's fine."

"So…how are you?" *Fuck. So stupid.*

"OK. You?"

She wasn't OK. I could hear it. And neither was I. "OK."

An uncomfortable silence followed, during which I thought of nothing I could say and ten things I couldn't, starting with *I miss you. I miss you so much I can't breathe.*

"Are you really OK?" she asked.

"No," I admitted.

"Me either."

"I want to see you so badly," I blurted. "I miss you."

"I miss you, too." She paused. "Does this...does this mean you changed your mind?"

I wanted to say yes so badly, I felt strangled by it. "No," I choked out.

"Then I can't see you, Jack. It wouldn't do either of us any good."

"Please," I whispered before I could stop myself. "I need you."

"No. I'm hanging up. This hurts too much."

"No, wait!" Panicked, I held out one hand as if she could see me. "Please don't go, Margot. I miss you so fucking much. All I do is think about you."

She said nothing at first, and then I heard soft, quiet sobs. "Why are you doing this to me? I'm trying to forget you."

My heart broke for both of us. "I'm sorry, Margot. I know I shouldn't have called. I'm just..." I closed a fist in my hair. "...so fucked up about this. I don't know what to do."

"What do you *want* to do?"

I exhaled, lowering myself to the bed. What I wanted was so simple. "I want to feel alive again." My throat thickened. "The way I felt with you."

She was openly crying now, and it was torture knowing I could make her stop. But the words wouldn't come—something inside me held them captive. Fear? Guilt? Shame? All of the above?

"Jack," wept Margot, "I can't do this. I want to be with you, but not unless you're ready to move on. I don't know what that would take, but it's something *you* have to figure out."

She was right, of course. It was on me to find a way out of the cold, lonely dark and into her light. But I felt immobile, chained to the past and unable to break free, even for her.

A moment later, she whispered goodbye.

Cursing, I set my phone aside and dropped forward, elbows on my knees, head in my hands. Instead of feeling better, I felt worse. Sad and angry.

What I *wanted* was one thing; what I was capable of was another.

Why the hell couldn't she see that?

CHAPTER THIRTY-TWO
MARGOT

If I'd made any progress getting over Jack in the last few days, the phone call set me back that much and then some.

What was he trying to do to me? To himself?

The tone of his voice, tender and sorrowful, told me how miserable he was. The things he'd said tore me to shreds—*I miss you, I want to see you, I want to feel alive again.* It was agony knowing we both wanted to be together and it was just his stubborn head getting in the way. Never in my life had I simultaneously wanted to hug someone and hit him with a scone at the same time. Did he just need more time?

But how much? How long would I be willing to wait? At some point, it would be pathetic rather than patient to keep holding out for someone who was never going to want me that way.

I had to get over it. Pick myself up, dust myself off, and try again with someone who wasn't so hell-bent on being alone forever. Someone who wanted everything I had to offer. Someone who recognized that the kind of chemistry we had didn't come along that often in life.

I started to get angry.

Damn him for not seeing what we could be. Sitting up in bed, I reached for a tissue from the box on my nightstand. *Damn him for being a coward when I need him to be brave. Damn him for being stubborn when all he wants is to give in.* I blew my nose, threw the tissue on the floor, and grabbed another.

I hope you're even more miserable than I am, Jack Valentini. Because this is your fault. I never rushed you. I never pushed. The only thing I did was care, and fuck you for being too scared to care back. I deserve better.

By the time I fell asleep that night, my nose was raw, my eyes were puffy, and my head ached, but I made up my mind not to waste any more time crying over Jack. Yes, it was sad that he didn't think he deserved to be loved because of his past, but that was his choice.

Plenty of people don't get to even make that choice, Jack. They never experience what we have.

Damn you for giving it up so easily.

My anger simmered throughout the day Sunday. I felt like I needed to keep busy so I wouldn't think about Jack, and I spent the day doing things like laundry, cleaning out the fridge, reorganizing kitchen and bathroom cupboards, and grocery shopping. It kept me occupied, but it didn't necessarily take my mind off Jack. Clothing I'd worn at the farm reminded me of him. Food and drinks reminded me of him. My bubble bath and shampoo reminded me of him. The damn produce section at Kroger reminded me of him.

Later in the afternoon I went to the bookstore and bought

some beginner cookbooks, and for dinner that night I attempted lemon chicken. It turned out pretty well and gave me a dose of confidence, even if I did feel a little lonely celebrating my first culinary triumph by myself.

Later that night, I was in bed reading a new romance I'd picked up at the bookstore (which I'd chosen for its premise and *not* because the guy on the cover looked like Jack, I swear) when my phone rang.

Jack Valentini calling.

I refused to answer it. It refused to stop ringing.

"Fuck you," I said. But my heart throbbed. I wanted to hear his voice so badly.

What if he'd changed his mind? What if he was calling to apologize? What if he'd realized we deserved a chance?

I grabbed the phone. *Whoa. Stay calm.* Summoning Old Margot, I took a breath and accepted the call.

"Hello."

"Hey." His voice cracked, and so did some of my composure. "How are you?"

Be strong. No tears tonight. "Fine," I said coolly.

"That's good."

Silence. My patience wore thin. "What do you want, Jack?"

"Just to hear you."

I closed my eyes and swallowed. So this wasn't an apology call. *Damn him!* "Why? To torture yourself?"

"I guess."

"I'm not playing these games, Jack." My voice wavered. "If you want to wallow in your own pain, you go right ahead, but I will not contribute to it. It hurts me too much."

"I'm sorry, Margot. I never meant to hurt you. I want so fucking badly to be someone else right now."

I bit my lip so hard I expected to taste blood. "I wouldn't want anyone else! How can you not see that?"

"You say that now, but you don't know what it's like to be with me." His voice was stronger. Angry, even.

"Because you won't *show* me! You're a coward! I don't even know what it is you're so afraid of! All I know is that you're throwing away the chance to be happy, and you're *taking* it away from me."

"I'm sparing you!" he blurted.

"You're sparing yourself! It's going to take work to move on, Jack. I know that. And I know it wouldn't be easy." I softened my voice. "But I'd be there for you. Don't you want to try?"

Silence. "You'd never be happy with me."

I took a breath and put my heart out there one more time, praying he didn't crush it. "Give me the chance to prove you wrong, Jack. I won't ask again."

"I can't," he whispered. "I want to, but I fucking can't."

I lost the battle not to cry, and hot tears spilled down my cheeks. "Then say goodbye, because this is all we will ever be."

"Margot, please—"

"Hang up!" I yelled. "I want it very clear that it's you who's walking away, Jack. It's *you* who thinks you couldn't love me."

"I know I could love you," he said without hesitation, his

voice full of anguish. “I just don’t deserve to.”

I steadied myself. Willed myself to stay calm. “Then say goodbye, and hang up.”

I held my breath, hanging on to one tiny thread of hope that he’d say something—anything—other than goodbye.

But he didn’t.

CHAPTER THIRTY-THREE
JACK

Margot's words cut deep. The truth always does.

You're a coward.

You're sparing yourself.

You're throwing away the chance to be happy.

I was a coward. And a fool. And an asshole. I knew calling her a second time was the wrong thing to do, but I was so damn lonely and depressed, I couldn't think straight. I hurt, and I wanted to feel better—she was the only one who could make it better, so I called her.

The logic of a fucking child.

I didn't blame her for getting angry or calling me names. Some part of my brain probably hoped that she would, I was so fucked up. And I was mad as hell at myself. What right did I have to call her, say those things to her, hurt her all over again? I'd only thought about *my* pain. But hers was real, too. I could hear it in her voice. I'd told myself a thousand times over the last few days that my agony was the price I had to pay for letting her get close, but what about the price she was paying? It killed me to think that she was half as miserable as I was. Did she really think I was walking away because I couldn't love her? It was exactly the opposite!

I lay back on my bed and covered my face with my hands. What the hell was I going to do? I couldn't live like this, torn between the past and the future, between two lives, between two selves.

It was like standing at a fork in the road—one path went nowhere, simply circled back upon itself in a never-ending spiral of solitude and sameness. The other went forward, and while I couldn't see what was at the end of that road, I knew it offered the possibility of being happy again.

But what would it take for me to feel I deserved a second chance?

A few nights later, Georgia invited me to dinner at the house. I accepted, grateful to escape the lonely silence of the cabin. Brad and Olivia were there too, and after dinner we went out to the front yard, where my brothers got on the trampoline with their kids.

Georgia and I sat on the porch rockers, drinking whiskey on the rocks and watching Pete try to do a flip. "He's going to break his neck," I said, chuckling a little.

"Oh God, don't even think it." She glanced over at me. "It's good to hear you laugh. Been kinda down this week."

I tipped back some whiskey. "Yeah."

"Probably no point in my asking this, but I will anyway. Want to talk about it?"

On the trampoline, my brothers bounced and laughed and took pictures of their grinning kids in mid-air. *I want that—I want it so fucking badly.* "I envy you guys," I said.

From the corner of my eye, I saw her nod slowly. "I get that."

"I thought I'd live in this house eventually, raise a family, all that."

"It's not too late, you know."

"You don't think so?"

"Not at all."

I thought for a moment, willed myself to be brave. "Georgia, can I tell you something?"

"Of course."

"I've been thinking lately, I served with guys who didn't make it back. Guys who were stronger than me. Braver. Smarter. Sometimes I wonder why I survived and they didn't. What was it for?"

She looked at me but didn't say anything.

"I used to think it was for Steph. For the family we'd have. But once she was gone, it seemed pointless again."

"You don't think you could fall in love again? Have a family?"

I hesitated. "I never used to."

"And now?"

"Now…" I inhaled and exhaled slowly, met her eyes. "Now there's Margot."

She smiled, her eyes lighting up. "So what's holding you back?"

"A lot of things." I stared at the ice cubes in my glass. "I fucked things up really badly, Georgia."

"I know."

Something hitched in my chest. “You’ve talked to her?”

Georgia paused, and I sensed she didn’t want to betray Margot’s confidence. “Yes.”

“I mean it when I say I fucked up. I hurt her.”

“Ask forgiveness.”

She made it sound so easy. “What if she says no?”

“What if she says yes?” Georgia countered.

“She could have so much better. Someone with money and cars and—”

“She wants you. Trust me.”

I looked her in the eye and spoke the truth. “I’m scared.”

“I know you are. And it’s gonna take some hard work, but I bet it’ll be worth it. I *know* it’ll be worth it, Jack. Even if Margot isn’t the one, you have to do this for you. It’s time.”

Nodding, I let her words sink in. “It’s three years tomorrow.”

“I know,” she said softly, her eyes tearing up. “But Jack, Steph would be the first one to tell you that you’re not honoring her by refusing to move on.” She reached out and touched my arm. “You’ve been using her to punish yourself. It’s time to let her go. I know it hurts, but it’s time.”

My throat closed, and I had to look away from Georgia’s tears before my own started to fall.

The following day, I went to the cemetery. Sitting in front of the stone the way I always did, I imagined Steph beside me and concentrated on the memory of her voice.

“Hey. I need to talk to you.”

What's up?

My throat tightened. "This is hard."

Talk to me.

I swallowed hard. "I met someone."

Good.

"Is it?"

Why wouldn't it be?

"Because she's making me doubt myself. She's making me reconsider things I'd already decided."

Like what?

"Like getting involved with someone again. Letting myself fall in love again. Spending my life with someone instead of being alone."

Sounds serious. What's she like?

"She's impossible. Spoiled rotten. A know-it-all city girl."

Laughter bounced off the stones. *Someone to put you in your place, huh?*

"She loves to try." I took a breath. "She's also kind and smart and beautiful. She makes me laugh."

You have feelings for her?

"I do, but…I don't know if I want them."

Why not?

"For one thing, it drives me crazy that she's nothing like you. I feel guilty—like I'm betraying your memory by falling for someone so opposite everything you were."

You're not betraying me, Jack. I want you to move on and be happy.

Tears sprang to my eyes and I touched my eyelids with

my thumb and forefinger. "I want to be happy too, I just can't seem to figure out how to get there and be OK with it."

Well, first, you need to go back to therapy. It's time to admit you stopped going because it was helping and you didn't want to get better.

I blinked. I'd never thought about it that way. In my mind, I'd stopped going because it was too painful to talk about my feelings anymore. Was Steph right? Had I let myself off the hook? Was quitting therapy just another way I'd sabotaged my recovery?

You know I'm right. Next, you need to clean out that cabin. Give my clothes away. Throw out my junk. Take my pictures off the damn wall. Better yet, move out. It's all just part of the prison you created for yourself, and you know what? It's imprisoning me, too.

It felt like a punch in the gut. "What?"

You heard me. You have to let me go, Jack.

Gooseflesh rippled down my arms. The back of my neck prickled. "But I—"

No backtalk, you. If you loved me—

"You know I did. More than anyone. You were the love of my life, Steph."

I was the love of the life you had then, Jack. I was your first love...but I'm not your last.

The breeze rustled through some nearby trees while I let her words sink in and dissolve the final doubts inside me. She was setting me free, and I had to do the same for her. A weight was lifted. "You're right."

Of course I am. Now I have one more request: Call that

woman and take her out for dinner. Poor thing is probably tied in knots wondering what the hell is going on in that thick skull of yours. You tell her I understand. You drove me crazy, too.

"I'm sorry, Steph. For everything."

I know you are, Jack. I forgive you. You ready to do this?

I nodded. "I think so. I can't say I'm not scared, but I think I know what I have to do."

Good. Go live the life you were meant to. You've got a lot of love to give, Jack Valentini. Don't you forget it.

"OK," I whispered, a shiver working its way through my body. "And Steph…thank you. You're an angel."

I listened for a response, but she was gone. I felt her absence as strongly as I'd felt her presence just moments ago. Somehow I knew she wouldn't be back.

I kissed my fingertips, touched the top of the stone, and said goodbye.

Later that night, I stood in my bedroom and looked around. It looked the same as it did every other night, but it felt different. For the first time, I recognized it as what Steph had called it—a prison. Steph was so *present* here—her clothing in the closet, her books on the shelves, her shampoo in the shower, our photos on the wall. But it wasn't entirely in memory of her; it was punishment. A lifetime sentence of solitary confinement.

Yet I'd brought Margot here. Kissed her. Touched her. And when she'd offered to stop, I'd been the one to press on.

I'd wanted her more than I'd wanted to preserve the sanctity of this space.

Would she forgive me? Would she still want the chance she'd asked for? I pictured her, and something in my stomach went weightless. I wanted to be happy again. For the first time in years, I felt like it was possible.

I glanced down at my left hand, where my wedding band still circled my finger. Slowly, I twisted it off, looked at it for a moment, then placed it in my nightstand drawer. I was slightly sick to my stomach for a moment, but after a few deep breaths, I was OK again.

It was time.

Over the next week, I made four important phone calls. One to my therapist, who was glad to hear from me, and scheduled an appointment for me within days. The second call was to Georgia, who said she would be happy to help me sort through and remove Steph's things from the cabin. The third call went to Suzanne Reischling's voicemail. I left a message saying I was finally cleaning out the cabin and told her to call me if she wanted to come by one night this week and see if there was anything she wanted. And the fourth call was to Brad—I wanted to sit down with him and see if there was anything I could do to help Pete and Georgia buy that house.

It made the most sense for me to buy them out and live there, especially since I was planning on moving out of the cabin anyway—too many memories there, and I was serious about moving on—and I wanted to have a place I was comfortable inviting Margot to.

Brad said he'd be glad to meet with me, and he'd be thrilled if I could buy him out. "Let me talk to the bank," he said. "I'll explain the situation, get the numbers, and we can sit down sometime this week."

"Sounds good," I agreed. "But don't say anything to Pete and Georgia yet. I don't want to get their hopes up."

My first therapy session was painful, but I'd promised myself I was going to be honest. For the first time, I told him how I really felt about Steph's death, the way it was connected to the incident in Iraq in my mind, and how that guilt had prevented me from moving on. While he couldn't ease my conscience completely, he did give me some strategies for coping with my feelings and dealing with the guilt, and urged me to use the meds to get more sleep.

He also told me about a weekly group therapy session for Veterans that he'd organized within the last year, and I began attending them. Hearing others talk about their feelings, tell their stories, admit to struggling with guilt and anxiety just like I did made me feel like I wasn't alone. Sometimes I didn't even talk at those sessions, and that was OK too.

Cleaning out the cabin was tougher. I got through it with Pete and Georgia's help, by remembering Steph's wish to be set free, and by watching Cooper play with Bridget Jones while we worked. But it wasn't easy or quick. We worked Wednesday evening and throughout the day Thursday. There were moments I choked up, moments I teared up, moments I had to walk outside and take a few deep breaths. Even so, there was no uncertainty. I knew in my heart I was doing the right thing.

On Thursday night, Suzanne came by, and her eyes misted when she saw the bags and boxes in the front room. "You really did it," she said, putting a hand over her heart.

"I had to," I said quietly, but firmly.

Her eyes scanned the room. "You took down the pictures. Why?"

"Because they were making it too difficult to move on with my life, Suzanne." I met her eyes directly, and noticed she didn't appear to resemble Steph quite so closely tonight. It was a relief.

"Oh." She trailed the fingers of one hand along a box. "Are you moving on with that blond woman?"

"That's none of your business."

"Sorry," she said meekly. "It's just hard this week."

Sympathy softened my tone. "I know. But she wouldn't want us to sit around and grieve her again. She'd want us to celebrate her life by moving on with our own."

She nodded sadly. "My mother wants everything, but she was too upset to come."

"I'll help you load it. I've got a four wheeler here, and we can take it to your car."

"OK." Closing her eyes, she sighed. "I really am sorry about what I said. You're right. Steph would want us to move on. I just miss her, and it helps to think that you miss her like I do."

"Apology accepted. And it's OK to miss her, Suzanne. I miss her too. But it took me a long time to get where I am now, and I like thinking she'd be proud of me for that."

"She would be. I'm sure of it." Suzanne sniffed, and then laughed a little through her tears. "She was a much nicer person than me."

Three weeks after she'd gone home, I was ready to apologize to Margot and ask for another chance, but I wasn't sure how to do it. An apology over the phone wasn't the same as coming face to face with someone and asking their forgiveness. Admitting you'd been wrong. Putting yourself out there. If I was going to ask for a second chance, I needed to do it in person.

But how? What could I say that would convince her to see me again without giving myself away? All day Friday I thought about it, trying to come up with something romantic and clever—but romantic and clever had never been my thing. I needed help.

Swallowing my pride, I went to Georgia.

She grinned. "I'm not sure what you should do, but I know someone we can ask." Scooping up her phone from the counter, she tapped the screen a few times. My own phone buzzed in my pocket, and I took it out.

She'd shared a contact with me. "Jaime Owen?" I asked. "Who's that?"

"It's Margot's close friend and business partner. Call her."

I frowned. Involve another woman in this? "I'm not sure."

"*Call her.*" Georgia squeezed my arm. "I'm positive

she'll know exactly what you should do."

I told her I'd think about it, stuck around to play with Cooper a little bit, then went home to brood about making the call. Georgia was probably right, but this was fucking embarrassing…it was one thing to call Margot and explain myself. She *knew* me. Calling this Jaime woman was another thing entirely. God only knows what kind of stories Margot had told her, what she thought about me.

That's your own fault. Make the call, asshole.

Groaning childishly, I dialed the number.

"Hello?"

"Hello, is this Jaime Owen?"

"Yes, it is. Can I help you?"

"My name is Jack Valentini. I'm—"

"Oh."

'Oh?' What does that mean? "I'm a friend of—"

"I know who you are." Her tone wasn't rude, just a bit aloof, but I'd expected that. She probably had a whole head-ful of things she'd like to scream at me, but I was technically still a client.

I wasn't sure how to proceed. "Georgia gave me your number."

"Did you have a question about your account?"

"No, it's not that. It's…" I took a breath. "I need to see Margot."

"Why?"

"To apologize."

"Why aren't you calling her?"

"Because I need to do more than apologize—I need to

make up for the way I treated her, for the things I said."

"You hurt her, you know."

I closed my eyes. "I know. I'm sure she told you I was a total dick to her. But it was the only way I could get her to leave."

"And you needed her to leave because you didn't care about her anymore?"

"No, because I cared too much," I blurted, wondering how I was going to explain that. But she surprised me.

"I knew it!"

"What?"

"I knew that's what it was." She sounded happy all of a sudden. "You started falling for her so you had to back off—or in your case, you had to scare Margot off so she wouldn't get too close. But you didn't really mean the things you said."

"Yeah," I said, mystified. I held the phone away from my face and stared at it a second. Was this woman psychic?

"You were scared," she went on. "Because letting her in meant you had to let go of yourself in a way. And you didn't think you were capable."

"Jesus," I said. "Who are you?"

She laughed. "Someone who understands. So now what?"

"I need to see her. I'd like to surprise her somehow, but I'm not sure how to do it."

"Surprise her, huh? Hmmmm."

"Yes. And I think I should go to her. Prove to her that —"

"Oh my God!" she burst out suddenly. "What are you doing tomorrow night?"

Other than work, I had nothing planned. "Nothing," I admitted, feeling a little pathetic.

"Good. Margot is attending a cocktail reception at the DIA. It's a fundraiser for the opening of a new exhibit in the Lewiston Gallery."

"DIA?" I wasn't sure what that was.

"Detroit Institute of Arts. Her family donates a lot of money every year."

"Ah." Of course they did. I braced myself for where this was going. "And?"

"And what better way to show her that you want to be part of her life than to introduce yourself to it? I have a ticket but I'll give it to you. I won't say anything to her."

"Isn't there a less…socially awkward way for me to see her? I'm not good with crowds, and I don't own the right clothes or anything."

"Do you own a suit?"

I cringed. "No. I guess I could buy one tomorrow, but… would it even fit right? What if I have to have it altered?" The last thing I wanted to do was show up at a fancy cocktail reception in a suit that didn't fit. I'd be uncomfortable enough in one that did.

"Listen, I know some people," she said. "Leave it to me. Can you meet me downtown tomorrow morning?"

This was clearly going to be an all-day thing, probably a two-day thing, and I'd definitely need Pete and Georgia's help with things around here. But I was pretty sure they'd pick up my slack for this cause. "I think so."

"Good. I'll text you time and place in a bit. Do you need a haircut or anything? I could book you an appointment."

I ran a hand through my hair and frowned. "Probably. Thanks."

"No problem. I'm really glad you called me, Jack. You're doing the right thing."

I thanked her again and told her I'd see her tomorrow. After we hung up, I called Pete and Georgia's and asked if they could cover the farm work for two days. Georgia was scheduled to work this weekend, but Pete said not to worry, that Brad could always pitch in. "You're doing the right thing," he said, echoing Jaime's words. "Good luck."

"Thanks," I said. "I'll need it."

CHAPTER THIRTY-FOUR
MARGOT

Having a funner, more fulfilling life was easier said than done, especially with a broken heart.

After Jack rejected me a second time, I vowed to do exactly what I wanted *him* to do—move on. He had feelings for me, but clearly he wasn't willing to let go of his past, and I wasn't sure he ever would. Every time I thought about it, I felt like crying, but I couldn't save him from himself. I could only work on me.

I focused on my list.

I signed up for cooking classes. Watched online tutorials. Read my cookbooks. Made lists of things I needed in the kitchen and filled my cupboards and drawers with cookware and gadgets. I grocery shopped with a critical eye, choosing local and organic whenever I could. Stopped eating out so much. Invited my friends over to try my pesto, my piccata, my potatoes au gratin. A hundred times, I stopped myself from taking pictures of my culinary triumphs and sending them to Jack so he could see my progress and be proud of me.

I went riding three times and made up my mind to buy

my own horse. There was something about that relationship I truly missed. Again I fought the urge to call Jack and share my excitement—there was no one in my life who understood the bond between a horse and human like he did.

Through a friend, I got involved with the Fair Food Network, a nonprofit dedicated to supporting farmers, strengthening local economies, and increasing healthy food access. One of their goals was to increase funding to Double Up Food Bucks, which helps low-income families make healthy food choices and purchase from local farmers. I used my family's connections to secure funds and support, and I also volunteered to create marketing materials to help spread the word about the program, teach people about the economic and health benefits of eating and shopping local, and advertising the days, locations, and hours of local markets that accept benefits. Was I single-handedly abolishing poverty? No, but the work was rewarding and I felt like I was contributing to the greater good.

And…I got my tattoo. It was mainly inspired by one of my favorite stories, *The Awakening*, by Kate Chopin. At first I was only going to get a little bird somewhere on my back—a tiny symbol of my own awakening. But then I realized I'd never be able to see it. I decided on my inner arm instead, and I also decided to go with words instead of a symbol. It made the tattoo bigger and more noticeable, but wasn't that the point? Now when I looked down, I saw these words inked on my fair skin:

The bird that
would soar
above the plane
of tradition
and prejudice
must have
strong wings.

Seven lines of elegant script that reminded me not to let myself be caged by the fear of what people thought or expected. I was my own person, and I could make my own choices. Strength was a beautiful thing.

Of course, it was inspired by Jack too, and I wanted nothing more than for him to see it. Night after night, I went over everything in my mind, trying to find the place where we'd gone wrong, but I could never find it. We were different, but that's what had given us our spark. I still felt that kick whenever I thought about him. Still craved his skin on mine. Still missed the way he'd talked and laughed and teased me. Still cried sometimes when I thought about his past.

Once, when I was talking with Georgia about new family photos for the website, she made a vague reference to Jack "working on himself." Though she offered no specifics, my hopes bloomed fresh.

But as the days turned into weeks and I still hadn't heard from him, they started to wither.

Muffy, as expected, nearly fainted when she saw my tattoo. "What on earth have you done to yourself? Will that come off?"

"I don't want it to come off, Mother. I like it." We were having cocktails in the Rivera Court at the DIA, and she looked around frantically, trying to shield me as if I were naked. The cavernous room was full of wealthy, well-dressed people sipping drinks and listening to a string quartet, but only one of them appeared scandalized by my ink.

"I just don't understand you these days, Margot. First the scone thing, then this volunteer business at a homeless shelter, and now a tattoo?" She shook her head. "Whose daughter are you?"

"Calm down, Mom." I patted her taffeta shoulder. "You should be happy about the tattoo. You wanted me to major in English, didn't you? *The Awakening* is a classic."

"Margot Thurber Lewiston, that is not the point. Your erratic behavior *is*."

"I've explained and apologized for the scone thing a hundred times. And I started volunteering at the shelter because I like helping people. And it only costs my time."

Muffy looked at me like I was nuts. "We donate money to those places so we don't *have* to spend time there."

I sighed. There was no use trying to explain it to her. "Well, I don't mind the time. What else have I got to do?"

"I'd rather hoped you might start dating again."

I took another sip. "It's not that easy."

"It is. You're simply too picky."

"What's wrong with picky?"

"Nothing, when it comes to hiring a cook, gardener, or maid. But finding the right husband shouldn't be that difficult."

I clenched my teeth. "I'm not going to settle, Mom. I want to fall in love."

"Don't be ridiculous. *Everyone* settles in marriage, Margot," she said, rolling her eyes like I'd said something childish.

"Even Thurber women?"

"*Especially* Thurber women." Again she looked at me as if I were crazy. "Every Thurber woman I've ever known has settled. Marriage isn't about being in love. It's about merging two families to create a better one. It's about preservation and lineage. It's about tradition." She sniffed. "Love is for children and poor people."

If I hadn't grown up listening to such ridiculous bits of Muffy's "wisdom," I might have been horrified. But she couldn't help the way she was. In her mind, falling in love was probably akin to Causing a Scene. Loud, messy, and indiscreet. But I didn't have to perpetuate her strange notions, and I'd teach my daughter differently.

"I'm sorry you feel that way, Mother. But *this* Thurber woman isn't settling." It was a small thing, maybe, talking back to Muffy like that, but for me it was huge. It had taken me years to find the voice to do it. "I'm holding out for what I want."

"And what is it you want?" Muffy sounded miffed. "The Prince of Wales?"

"Not even close. I don't need a prince, Mother. Just a good man. Someone who—" Over Muffy's shoulder, I noticed someone moving toward me. Someone tall, dark, and handsome. Someone dressed in a black suit. Someone who took away my ability to speak, think, or breathe.

My skin prickled with heat. My mouth fell open. I blinked. It couldn't be. Could it? What was he *doing* here?

Dizzy, I swayed on my feet, and my mother grabbed my arm. "Margot, are you all right?"

"I'm not sure," I said, still watching in disbelief as Jack drew nearer. Our eyes locked. "I feel a little dizzy."

"Dizzy? You never felt dizzy before you got that tattoo," she said, studying it suspiciously. "Maybe it's poisoning you."

"It's not the tattoo," I said. "Excuse me for a moment." I started to walk toward him, and my heart clamored faster with every step. Jesus Christ, he was gorgeous. The cut of the suit emphasized his slim torso and broad chest. His shoulders looked even wider. He'd gotten his hair cut, and it had been styled with some kind of product, slicked away from his face. His scruff was trimmed way back too. He looked polished and sophisticated.

And nervous as hell.

I felt a rush of protectiveness. *He hates crowds. He hates dressing up. He's doing this for me.*

But I also nursed some lingering anger and doubt. Was this just another 'I need to see you' thing? Was he here just to get a fix? Or punish himself? I wasn't going to play that game.

We met in the middle of the room and stood nearly chest to chest. My emotions were all over the place, my breath coming fast. Someone behind me dropped a glass, and at the sound of the crash, he glanced around sharply. My heart ached at his anxious expression, the tension in his neck, the sheen on his brow.

"Hey." Compassion moved me to slip my hand into his, lock our fingers. I was angry with him, but I also recognized how difficult this was. "Look at me."

His facial muscles relaxed slightly as he refocused on me. "Sorry."

"What are you doing here, Jack?"

"I came to apologize."

"For what?" I held my breath.

"For lying to you. For breaking things off. For being a coward." He grimaced. "You were right. I was afraid of what I was starting to feel. Of what it meant."

Hope was exploding like fireworks inside me. "What did it mean?"

"It meant letting go of things—my past, my guilt, my pain—and giving myself permission to move on. I wasn't ready to feel that way about myself. And I probably still wouldn't if I hadn't met you." His eyes skittered across the room again, and he swallowed. "Margot, I have so many things I want to say to you, but I'm not very good in a crowd."

"Then let's get out of here."

He frowned. "I promised myself I wouldn't do that—if this is important to you, then it's important to me."

"Jack, there is nothing more important to me right now than hearing what you have to say."

Relief eased his features. "OK."

"I have some things to say too."

He looked tense again.

"Follow me. We'll find a quiet place to sit down." My heart thumped wildly as I led him out of the room.

We held hands as we walked down the promenade and through galleries, searching for the right spot. Finally we found an empty room with a bench in the center, and I let Jack lead me to it. It was dimly lit to protect the art, and the deep red walls made it seem warm and romantic. The butterflies in my stomach were out of control, and I had to remind myself to stay calm. He was saying the right things, but was he really ready to be with me?

Jack kept my hand in his as we sat, and he looked down at our fingers laced together on his lap. "You got a tattoo?" He held my arm up and angled it so he could read the words. "It's beautiful. I love it."

"Thank you. I do too."

"What prompted that?"

"I decided you were right. It was time to stop worrying about what other people think. I was tired of being afraid of what people would say if I did something different."

He nodded slowly and he lowered my arm and took my hand again. "What did Muffy say?"

"She thinks I'm crazy."

He met my eyes and we both smiled. Some of my doubt dissipated. *This feels so good. Please let it be real.*

"You know, it's funny you decided *I* was right about something," he said. "I've been wrong about most everything." He looked down at our hands for a moment, stroked the back of mine with his thumb. "*You* were right. That night in the cabin." His eyes met mine. "I did feel something for you."

I couldn't breathe.

"I'd started to feel so much for you that it scared me. I felt like I was losing control, like I was losing myself. I panicked. Retreated. Tried to put up walls. But…" He lifted his shoulders. "It was too late."

"It was?"

"Yes. What I felt didn't go away just because I tried to shut you out. I didn't feel stronger or more in control after you left. Hurting myself was one thing, but hurting you made me feel cruel and weak. I felt like I'd crushed something frail and young and beautiful that couldn't fight back."

"That's exactly what you did." He needed to know how I felt too. "And all I could do was watch. I *felt* something for you. I felt something between us. But what could I do? I asked you to take a chance on me, and you said no. Twice!" My nose tingled and I fought against tears.

Jack shook his head, his eyes full of pain. "I'm sorry, Margot. I hated myself for saying no. I wanted to say yes so badly. I missed you constantly. I kept thinking about the way I felt when I was with you. I imagined what my life would be like with you in it, and I agonized over the choice I'd made to be alone." He closed his eyes briefly. "Finally, I realized how stupid I was being. How wrong I'd been to walk away from you. How much I wanted to give you that chance you asked for." He took both my hands in his and squeezed tight. "I came here hoping you'd still be willing to give me one."

My fears were unraveling, but I had to ask. "How do I know you're serious now? How do I know you're not going to panic and put up walls again?"

He squeezed my hand. "You don't. That's a chance you'll have to take on me. But I'm begging you to take it."

I swallowed against the lump in my throat. "You're ready? To move on, I mean?"

He nodded, looked me right in the eye. "Yes. In the last few weeks, I've made some really good progress."

"Like what?"

"I went back to therapy. I cleaned out the cabin. And I said goodbye," he finished quietly.

I knew what he meant, and it made me smile through tears.

He smiled too. "I want a new start, Margot. And I want you there with me. Say you'll give me a chance."

"Oh, Jack," I said softly. "That's all I ever wanted. I know I can't be your first love, but—"

"Shh." He put a finger over my lips. "I'm not looking for my first love. I'm looking for my last."

He leaned over and put his lips on mine. It was a sweet, soft, still kiss—but it was more than that. It was an apology, a promise, a new start. It spoke of letting go, of moving on, of falling in love. I shivered, and Jack put an arm around me. "You cold?"

"Not at all," I said, feeling warmth flow throughout my body. "Now I want to know how you found me."

Jack grinned sheepishly. "Your friend Jaime."

"Jaime!" I yelped. "She said she was too sick to come tonight!"

"She gave me her ticket."

I shook my head, trying to piece it together. "So you called her?"

"Yes. Last night. I was trying to think of a way to surprise you, and Georgia gave me her number."

I giggled, my whole body tingling. "Oh my God, this happened in one night? It worked. I'm surprised."

He just smiled at me for a moment, almost a little sadly. "I missed that laugh. I was scared I'd never hear it again."

"Now you can hear it as much as you want."

"I wanted to tell you." He cleared his throat. "I'm moving into the house. I decided to buy out Pete and Georgia so they can afford the Oliver place."

Squealing, I threw both my arms around his neck. He smelled delicious, and I breathed him in deeply. "Oh my God, that's amazing! I'm so proud of you."

His arms closed around me. "Thanks. I wouldn't have done any of it if it wasn't for you."

Unwilling to let go, I kept my chest pressed to his. "I feel like we have so much to catch up on."

"It's all good stuff."

"Pete and Georgia must be so happy."

"They are. And it's only possible because of Brad. He said he'd wait a little longer for me to buy him out so that I could afford to make this happen."

Reluctantly, I stopped strangling him and sat back. "I'm so happy for you. And for them. That's wonderful about

Brad, too."

Jack nodded. "For the first time in years, I feel like I can breathe. Like I have something to look forward to."

I couldn't stop smiling. "You don't know how happy this makes me."

He hauled me across his lap, and I looped my arms around his neck. "You don't know how beautiful you are when you're happy. I want to put that smile on your face every day." His brow furrowed. "But I'm hoping I don't have to wear this suit to do it."

Laughter bubbled out of me. "You can do it in nothing, believe me—and you're going to."

"Hell yes I am," he drawled. "The sooner the better."

"Not so fast, cowboy. You're wearing the hell out of that suit, and I need to get my fill before I take it off you, one piece at a time." I leaned back and admired him, my belly fluttering. "I didn't even think you owned one."

"I didn't."

My eyebrows shot up. "Jaime?"

"And Quinn. Nice guy. Knows a lot about clothes." He shook his head. "Mostly I just stood still and let them dress me."

"They did it well. When I saw you walking across the room toward me, I swooned. Nearly fell right over."

"I'd have caught you." His arms tightened around me. "I'll always catch you."

I'll always catch you, too, I thought as our lips met again. *Now let yourself fall.*

CHAPTER THIRTY-FIVE
MARGOT

I didn't want to stay at the event very long, but I did want to introduce Jack to my family. We found my father schmoozing a few voters in the Great Hall, and he shook Jack's hand enthusiastically when he heard Jack owned a farm. Dad probably thought I was helping him "shore up the base" with the introduction, but that was OK. Eventually I'd explain to him that Jack wasn't Big Ag and probably didn't have the same views on farming policy he did, but for now it was enough that they'd met.

My brother Buck raised an eyebrow at me when I introduced Jack as my date, maybe because I hadn't brought a date to a function like this since Tripp. But ever the charmer, he gave Jack his hand and a slap on the back like he was an old prep school buddy. When my brother learned Jack lived near Lake Huron, they talked for a few minutes about fishing on the Great Lakes, something they both enjoyed. Never mind that as kids Jack had *worked* on the boats while Buck had chartered them—it was something they had in common, and I was glad for it. Flashing Buck a grateful smile, we moved on to my mother.

Muffy was still in the Rivera Court. Near the bar, of course. "Mother, this is my friend Jack Valentini. Jack this is my mother, Muffy Lewiston."

"Nice to meet you." Muffy extended a hand, and Jack took it as she scrutinized him. "Valentini, did you say? Good heavens, what a lot of syllables."

I rolled my eyes. Muffy had a thing about syllables in a last name. One or two was ideal, three was fine as long as it didn't end in a vowel, but four—plus the vowel at the end—was just too much.

"Uh, yes." Jack looked at me for help.

"Jack owns and runs Valentini Brothers Farm in Lexington. That's where I was earlier this month."

Muffy reacted as if I'd said something absurd. "You were on a farm?"

"Yes. Doing some work for Shine. I told you that, Mother."

She studied him again. "He doesn't look like a farmer."

"I thought the same thing when I met him." I gave him a quick smile. "Would you excuse us? I think we're going to head out."

"Of course." Muffy dismissed us with a nod.

"Nice to meet you," offered Jack. "Wow," he said when we'd left the room. "For a small woman, she looks like she's got bones of steel."

I laughed as we headed for the museum valet. "She might."

"How'd I do?"

"Fantastic. Were you nervous?"

"I'm sweating bullets. I kept feeling like everyone was looking at me."

"Aww." Hooking my arm through his, I hugged it to me. "You have nothing to worry about. They were dazzled by your looks, and by the fact that there was a new face here. These things are always attended by the same people."

"Yeah?"

"Yeah." After we handed our tickets to the valet, we went outside to wait for them to pull our cars around. I turned to Jack and smoothed his lapels. "Thank you for coming tonight. I know it wasn't easy in there."

"It's a different world for me, that's for sure."

"Like me in the chicken coop."

He laughed and dropped a quick kiss on my lips. "Right. And you know what this means, don't you?"

"What?"

"Camping."

I wrinkled my nose. "Oh yeah. But not tonight, right?"

He laughed again, and I knew I'd never get tired of that sound as long as I lived. "Not tonight. Tonight I have a Luxury King room at the MGM Grand," he teased. "Would you like to stay with me?"

"Did you say luxury? That's like my favorite word." I fanned myself and whispered, "I'm so turned on right now."

"Good." He pulled me close. "Because I've got plans for you."

I shivered. "What kind of plans?"

"The kind where I make you come all night long, scream my name and beg for more."

I swooned.

This time he caught me.

The elevator at the MGM was crowded, and Jack pulled me back against him. "So many people," he said low in my ear. I thought he meant that there were too many people for him to be comfortable, but then he said, "Do you think they know what I'm going to do to you?"

I froze, my face growing hot.

"Do they know how soon I'm going to have my tongue between your legs?"

My mouth fell open.

"Do they know how loud I want to make you scream?"

I couldn't breathe.

"Do they know how deep you're going to take me?"

My legs started to shake.

"Do they know I'm getting hard right now, thinking about all the ways I want to fuck you tonight?"

Sweet Jesus. I spun around and whispered in his ear, "If I was wearing panties, they'd be soaked."

He inhaled sharply.

Ten seconds later, the doors opened and he grabbed my arm roughly, yanking me out behind him. He moved down the hall so fast I could barely keep up in my heels, and the moment the hotel room door shut behind us, he pushed me back against it. My evening bag hit the floor.

His mouth covered mine, his tongue driving between my lips as his fingers hitched my dress up to my hips. He groaned when he realized I'd told the truth, running his palms down over my bare ass and up the sides of my thighs. I pushed at his jacket, forgetting about taking my time to undress him and thinking only about what was beneath the layers of dress clothes. I needed to feel his bare skin on mine, needed those hard muscles flexing above me, needed his power and strength and size to overwhelm me.

He let his jacket fall to the ground and my fingers fumbled with the knot in his tie. But it was hard to concentrate because he moved one hand between my legs and his touch paralyzed me—he slid his fingers back and forth along the slick seam at my center and circled them gently over my clit. I finally got the damn knot to come loose just as he slipped two fingers inside me, and I clutched his shoulders, melting against him.

"I want to be right here." His voice was low and raw and intense. He pushed his fingers deep.

"Yes," I whimpered, riding his hand. "I want you there." I ran my palm over the bulge in his pants, wishing I could rip that gorgeous suit to shreds with my teeth like a wolf. God, I'd missed this feeling, this side of myself. Letting it take over was a relief and a pleasure and a high better than any I could imagine.

Jack dropped down and buried his face between my thighs, his tongue swirling over my clit. My legs trembled, and he slung one then the other over his broad shoulders. Then *he stood up*, my back sliding up the door, my hands flattening on the ceiling. Holy fuck, he was strong! Holding me there on his shoulders, his hands gripping my waist, he sucked my clit, flicking it with his tongue until I was writhing and gasping and making so much noise, I was positive the people in the elevator could hear us, no matter what floor they were on. Probably the people in the lobby too, and maybe even the people still at the DIA.

And yes—I screamed his name and begged for more.

He set me on the floor and I went at him like a cyclone, yanking off his tie and shirt and shoving down his pants. After wriggling out of my shoes and dress, I pushed him backward into the room and onto the bed, where I dragged off the rest of his clothes. Climbing onto his body, I straddled his hips, took his dick in my hand, and rubbed the tip between my legs. "You don't know how much I missed this."

"You're fucking crazy if you think that," he said, groaning as I slid onto him. His hands moved to my breasts, his thumbs flicking my nipples.

I bit my lip as I took him in deep and rocked my hips over his. He sat up, his mouth closing over one tight, hard peak, his fingers pinching the other. He sucked and bit and teased, lifting his hips to match my rhythm, both of us moving faster and faster. When he said my name, I knew he was close.

"Jack," I whispered. "I want you on top."

In two seconds, he'd flipped me onto my back and covered my body with his. *Yes, yes, yes*, I thought as his weight pinned my hips to the bed, as his cock drove deep and hard, as the muscles of his arms and chest and back and ass worked beneath my roving hands. I loved the gravity of him, the power he wielded, the punishing thrust of his hips. I loved the growl in his voice, the sweat on his skin, the roughness of his hands in my hair. I loved that he'd come here for me, that he wanted me in his life, that he was willing to make such drastic changes to have me.

And as all the coiled-up tension in our bodies released in powerful, rippling contractions that stopped our breath and stole our sight and splintered every last wall between us, somehow I knew in my heart and soul that I would love this man forever.

I would heal him, cherish him, adore him. I would believe in him, support him, work with him. He would be a lover, a husband, a father. And I would stay with him for the rest of my life.

But for now, I'd enjoy the fall.

EPILOGUE
JACK

I woke up even earlier than usual, but I wasn't surprised.

Today was a big day.

After checking to make sure that Margot was still asleep, I slipped out of our bed without even kissing her cheek like I wanted to. I couldn't risk waking her up.

Quickly and quietly, I hurried down the hall. When I passed the room that used to be Cooper's, I smiled. It was empty right now, and Cooper was asleep in his new "big boy" room across the street, but I hoped it would contain a crib and rocker again soon. Maybe even within a year.

My heart tripped with excitement as I took the stairs down a few at a time, careful not to hit any of the ones that creaked. I knew this house so well—its familiarity was a comfort to me. When I'd first moved out of the cabin, I'd been worried it would feel too big for me. I'd thought living there alone might make me sad, remind me I had no family of my own to fill it with.

But I hadn't been alone for long.

For a few months, Margot and I had dated long distance, but by Thanksgiving, I'd asked her to move in with me. She already spent several days a week up here, had clothes in the closet, a toothbrush in the bathroom, a table she used as a desk in a spare bedroom.

Hell, she had a horse in my barn.

I loved when she was here and hated when she left. My days were always better when I kissed her good morning, and my nights were always better when I held her close. I still battled anxiety and nightmares sometimes, but Margot took it all in stride. She was my calm, my rock, my haven. She pushed back when I needed it and let me breathe when I didn't. She understood me. She loved me.

And I loved her.

Silently closing the kitchen door behind me, I remembered when we first said the words, not too long after we began dating seriously. She'd come up to help me move into the house, and after a long day of cleaning and hauling and unpacking and organizing, she said she had a surprise for me.

It was a bubble bath.

I had to laugh as she undressed me and told me to get in the tub. But the scent of those bubbles and the feel of her wet skin beneath my palms took me back to a night months before, when I'd felt close enough to her to tell her everything.

Something in me must have known even then.

And as she rested her body on mine, her head on my chest, I wrapped my arms around her and felt an overwhelming sense of peace and warmth and gratitude that I was alive and well and here with her.

"I love you," I said out of nowhere.

She went completely still and then picked up her head. Her eyes searched mine and saw I was serious. "Jack," she whispered.

"Those are words that have never come easy to me, and I probably won't say them nearly as often as I should, but I want you to know that I do."

Her eyes filled. "I know. And I love you, too."

Margot didn't seem to mind that I didn't say the words much, even though I thought them—felt them—all the time. In fact, she told me she liked that it wasn't something I threw out there casually. It meant more to her when she heard them, she said, knowing that they didn't come easy.

And maybe the words didn't, but the feeling sure as hell did. I'd only loved one other woman, and I'd known her so long I couldn't remember falling for her this way—fast and hard and head over heels. I'd loved Steph deeply, but I loved Margot with a kind of intensity that shocked me. I hadn't known I was capable of it.

It made me want things—a ring on her finger, my last name on her driver's license, a house full of kids.

I'd never be rich, never be able to give her all the things she'd grown up with, never own a vacation home in L'Arbre Croche or a Mercedes Benz. But I knew Margot well enough by now to know that she didn't care about those things as much as she cared about me. About us. Oh, she was still a city girl, even when she wore her jeans and boots, but dammit, she was my city girl, and I loved her beyond words.

I smiled as I let myself into the chicken coop and slipped

my hand into my pocket.

I didn't like surprises, but Margot did.

I wanted to give her the surprise of her life.

MARGOT

I woke up and reached for Jack. He'd promised me he'd stay in bed a little longer this morning, since it was kind of a special day—the anniversary of the day we met.

Sometimes we looked back on that day and laughed at the way we'd stood there staring at each other across the kitchen, him broody and mean, me trying to be charming. "Was it love at first sight?" people sometimes asked us.

"Hell, no," Jack would tease. "I didn't want any rich city girl hanging around."

"And I couldn't stand him," I'd say. "He was dirty, sweaty, and rude."

But we belonged together, and it hadn't taken us that long to figure it out, all things considered. I'd gone back and forth for a while, but I'd been thrilled when he'd asked me to move in. Farm life was a bit of an adjustment at first—the smells, the early mornings, the never-ending list of chores to be done—but I grew to appreciate things about living in the country. I loved the quiet mornings, the lack of traffic, the charm of the small town, the sun rising over the lake and setting over the trees, the skies full of stars at night. When I missed the shops or bars or salons or restaurants, I'd zip down and meet my friends for an afternoon or evening. But I found I didn't miss city life too much, and I loved being around horses again.

The hardest thing had been leaving Jaime and Claire and our weekly Girls Night Out, but I saw them at least once a month, and they were happy for me. At first, I kept my job at Shine but cut back my hours, spending a lot of time helping Georgia with the new house, preparing to open the Valentini Farms Bed & Breakfast, and making sure the new marketing push went as planned. Once the B & B opened in May, I left Shine and dedicated myself completely to marketing duties at the farm and inn. I also volunteered for the Fair Food Network, reaching out to farmers and families in the region and continuing to help spread the word.

I'd never been happier, which befuddled my parents a little bit, but they seemed content to focus on my father's political career—he'd won his election—and give me a break.

Jack seemed happy too, and we'd grown infinitely closer since I'd moved in. His moods and silences grew easier to understand, his anxiety easier to manage. His nightmares were infrequent but terrifying, and I always wished there was more I could do for him, but he swore just having me there was enough. He loved me—I felt it, even if he didn't say it too often.

I sat up in bed and looked around. He'd left the blinds down, so it was still pretty dark in the room, but sun peeked around them. I glanced at the clock, which told me it was just after eight. "Jack?" I called.

Nothing.

There was no way he'd forgotten, because we'd talked about it before going to sleep. It wasn't like Jack to break a promise. I lay back again and gave it about ten minutes, then I sighed and threw back the covers. Maybe there was an emergency across the street?

I pulled on some jeans and a t-shirt and went downstairs. The front door was open, so I looked out on the porch. No one was there, although I noticed his truck was gone.

What the hell? It's like he forgot all about me.

Grumpy that a morning in bed was not on the horizon, I went into the kitchen. He hadn't even made coffee!

Angrily I poured the water and scooped the grounds, then crossed my arms and pouted while it dripped. The dumb old thing took forever, but Jack was funny about letting me replace things around here. Not because he was attached to them, but because he had a hard time letting me buy things for his house. "I live here," I kept telling him. "Isn't it my house too?"

He always said yes, of course it was, and hugged me in apology. Recently we'd had a long talk about redoing the kitchen, and when he balked at the cost of stone counters and tile floors, I'd put my foot down. "Listen. I am not trying to buy your love. I am trying to add a little bit of luxury to our lives because I like it and I can afford it and I'm spoiled, OK? You won't let me buy Brad out, so at least let me buy the damn countertops."

He'd grumbled about it but eventually caved, and a man was coming to take measurements this week. I was excited about it—I loved living up here with Jack, but I did miss a *few* things from my old life. And some high-end finishes in this beautiful old farmhouse could only make it better. I'd sweet talk him into things. I was good at that.

The smell of fresh coffee perked me up, and I turned around to reach for a mug. That's when I noticed the note on the counter.

Had to run out. Back later. Can you collect the eggs?

I groaned. Not only had he forgotten about his promise, he'd asked me to do my *least* favorite farm chore. For some reason, I could not get comfortable with it. Those hens hated me, I could tell.

But I dutifully put on my boots, grabbed a basket, and trudged over to the coop.

The hens clucked at me as I entered. "Yeah, I know. Good morning to you, too."

I checked the first box, and there was only one egg in there. I reached for it, scooped it up, and put it in the basket. The second box only had one as well, and when I went to place it next to the first, I noticed it had something written on it.

You're beautiful.

It made me smile. I turned the first one over, and the smile widened.

Good morning.

The writing was undeniably Jack's, and I looked around, expecting to see him standing there. He wasn't.

I went to the third box and pulled out the egg.

Did you think I forgot?

I started giggling, my pulse picking up. He did remember! And look at him being clever and romantic!

Grinning, I reached into the next box and took out the egg.

I love you.

And the next…

I will always love you.

My hands were shaking as I reached into the last box in the row.

Turn around.

Gasping, I spun around.

And there he was—going down on one knee.

My heart stopped.

He opened a ring box and held it out, his expression surprisingly calm, his dark eyes glinting. "I'm not saying I deserve you, Margot Thurber Lewiston, only that I'll keep trying as long as you'll let me. I've never loved anyone or anything the way I love you. You brought everything good back to my life—you brought *me* back to life, and I want to spend it with you. Will you marry me?"

I stood there, literally shaking in my boots, while I tried to find the wherewithal to move, talk, breathe, anything. A few tears slipped down my cheeks. "Yes," I squeaked, still clutching the basket.

"Want to put the eggs down, baby?" he asked, a smile tugging at his lips.

Nodding, I set the last egg carefully in the basket and put it on the ground. Then I moved closer to Jack and held out my hand, sobs working their way free from my chest. The ring winked at me from a black velvet Tiffany cushion, a gorgeous round solitaire set in a platinum band. My hand trembled as he slipped it on my finger.

I'd thought the ring that Tripp had chosen was perfect, but this one—this one—was *my* ring. Simple yet exquisite. Modern yet classic. Perfection.

"I love it," I sobbed, unable to stop myself.

He rose to his feet, laughing a little. "I'm glad. The way you're crying, I might have wondered."

I threw my arms around him and he held me tight, lifting me right off my feet. "I love you," he said in my ear. "I want this forever."

"Me too," I said, burying my face in his neck. My heart was so full it spilled over. "Forever."

THE END

ACKNOWLEGMENTS

I am so grateful to the following people: Jaime and Charles Collins, for talking so openly and honestly about PTSD and military matters; Amanda Williams Brown, for answering my "city girl" questions about life on a small farm; Lindsay Way, for an abundance of information on the Fair Food Network; Cheryl Guernsey, for being Jack's biggest champion day to day; Melissa Gaston, for everything she does to keep me organized, sane, and productive; Kayti, Laurelin, and Sierra, for being the best squad of snakes ever; Jenn Watson, for being superhuman publicist, reader, and friend; Candi, Nina, Hilary, and the entire Social Butterfly PR team for all you do; Rebecca Friedman, agent and friend, for honest advice and encouragement; Tamara Mataya, for fantastic edits that always make me smile; Laura Foster Franks, Amanda Maria at AM to PM Book Services, and Angie Owens for proofreading with eagle eyes; Letitia Hasser, for a gorgeous cover; Joseph Cannata, for the excellent visual inspiration; Laurelin Paige, Lauren Blakely and Corinne Michaels, for sage advice; Staci Hart for amazing feedback and long talks; Helena Hunting, for good times and colorful play money; the Peen Queens for feedback, laughs, and inspiration; the Harlots, for all your love and support; the bloggers who share my work and invite me to signings and review my books simply for the love of reading—THANK YOU; all my readers, for your support and enthusiasm—this is only possible because of you.

Finally, thank you to my husband and children, for your love, patience, and understanding.

ALSO BY MELANIE HARLOW

The Speak Easy Duet

Frenched (Mia and Lucas)
Yanked (Mia and Lucas)
Frenched: The Wedding Night (Mia and Lucas)
Forked (Coco and Nick)
Floored (Erin and Charlie)

Some Sort of Happy (Skylar and Sebastian)
Some Sort of Crazy (Natalie and Miles)
Some Sort of Love (Jillian and Levi)

Man Candy (Jaime and Quinn)

The Tango Lesson

ABOUT THE AUTHOR

Melanie Harlow likes her heels high, her martini dry, and her history with the naughty bits left in. In addition to AFTER WE FALL, she's the author of MAN CANDY, the HAPPY CRAZY LOVE series (contemporary romance), the FRENCHED series (contemporary romance) and the SPEAK EASY duet (historical romance). She writes from her home outside of Detroit, where she lives with her husband, two daughters, and one insane rabbit.

Find her on the web at www.melanieharlow.com or on Facebook at www.facebook.com/AuthorMelanieHarlow.

Printed in Great Britain
by Amazon